TEAM JOSHUA

A Novel by Frank G. Davis

AW
AUTHORS WILD

DEDICATION

I finished reviewing the edited version of *Team Joshua* on Veteran's Day of 2022. Many of the members of Team Joshua served in the military; Joshua, his twin brother Caleb, Pham and Mark all served in the Marines Corps. In all of the books in the Joshua series, I tried to capture their dedication to protect our country and the sacrifices they made.

This book is dedicated to all the men and women who served in all the branches of our military.

Thank you for your service. Semper Fi.

The second amendment to the United
States Constitution states:

*"A well-regulated Militia, being
necessary to the security of a free State,
the right of the people to keep and bear
Arms, shall not be infringed."*

March 4, 1789

INTRODUCTION

"Ladies and gentlemen, the governor of the great state of Oregon, the honorable Mark Johnson."

The audience in the legislature's auditorium rose from their seats as the governor made his way to the rostrum. It was a packed house, standing room only. Many of those present were grieving over the recent loss of loved ones. Reporters from national news agencies as well as local reporters were present to capture the governor's comments regarding the most recent mass murders. TV cameras were strategically placed around the auditorium to capture not only the governor's image but also the expressions of those in the audience. A dozen microphones were set up on the rostrum as well. A large number of the Oregon House and Senate members were also present, sitting close to the stage.

A large contingency of security staff was present. Every entrance to the auditorium had at least two uniformed and well-armed National Guard troops who checked every persons' brief cases and purses for weapons. Then each underwent body scans before they were allowed into the auditorium. The Guard leader, Colonel Peter Legleu, who was responsible for the governor's security, gave all his troops orders no one would be carrying any type of firearm into the auditorium. If anyone was caught with a firearm, even those claiming to be police or federal agents, they were to be detained. If they resisted, the troops were authorized to use whatever force necessary. Many, perhaps most, of those in attendance were angry, they wanted these atrocities to end. It was way past the time for action.

The governor walked slowly to the stage, his dark grey suit rumpled, his unshaven face was puffy and pale, his eyes swollen and red. It was obvious he'd been sobbing over the recent senseless murders at Woodlawn Elementary School.

He placed several pages of speaking notes on the rostrum, then gripped both sides to steady himself. He checked something on his notes, then raised his head to look directly at his audience and several video cameras as he tried to compose himself.

He waited until the murmuring of the audience subsided and began, "This has been a tragic day for all of us." His voice was sad and low as he continued, "As painful as it has been, I want to summarize what happened earlier this morning. At 10:00 am three young men and one young woman stormed Woodlawn Elementary School located in northeast Portland. They were all carrying automatic assault weapons and several magazines of bullets. Security cameras at the school showed them splitting up, shooting both of the security guards, one on the north side and the other on the south. They wounded both guards who returned fire but the killers were wearing flack vests and weren't injured. The killers then approached the wounded guards and shot them in the head several times with semiautomatic pistols.

"They entered the school through four separate exterior doors, all locked and chained shut. It is assumed they used some type of explosive device to blow the doors open. The school alarms went off when the doors were breached and calls were made to local police. The first police responders were at the school within ten minutes, six officers armed with side arms and vests approached the school and were shot by the assailants. Four were killed immediately, the other two were wounded and are currently hospitalized in critical condition.

"SWAT teams arrived fifteen minutes later. During that fifteen minutes, the principal, vice principal and all of the other staff members were executed in their offices. It appeared they were killed first then the killers methodically went from classroom to classroom, killing the teachers and as many students as possible.

"Two empty magazines were found at each classroom doorway. All of the classroom doors were locked from the inside when school began. The assailants carried battering rams which breached the doors. It looks like the killers stood in the doorway and sprayed each classroom with sixty bullets. Each of the empty magazines could hold up to thirty rounds. Once they emptied two magazines they moved on to the next class and so on until they ran out of ammunition.

"When SWAT arrived there was a gun battle. Two SWAT personnel were wounded, none were killed. Three of the assailants were shot and killed by SWAT, one was critically wounded and died shortly after they arrived at the hospital."

The governor stopped and took a sip of water from a glass on a side table. He was having a very difficult time composing himself. He turned his back on the audience for a moment to wipe the tears from his eyes with a tissue, then turned back to the audience. Before he continued, a news reporter raised her hand. The governor nodded at her to ask her question.

"Governor, I'm Sharon Emery from Live News 11. Has anyone been able to identify the terrorists?"

The governor shook his head. "No, Sharon, not as yet. We know there were three men and one woman. All were thought to be under the age of twenty-five. I've been told they were all members of the same gang. Our Portland PD detectives are working to identify the bodies and to see if they were members of a specific gang."

Other hands went up but the governor waved them off. "I have a lot more to say. I'll take questions when I'm finished."

He took another sip of water and his expression hardened. "Counting the teachers, staff and children, over a hundred were shot.

"Counting the dead, there were four law enforcement personnel, four assailants and sixty-seven school people, fifty-one of them were students…" he paused gathering himself. It took him several moments before he spoke again. When he did everyone could hear the pain in his voice, "Two of them were my grandchildren."

For a moment, the audience was completely silent, stunned by the news the governor's grandchildren were victims.

He quickly turned away as he began to sob loudly. One of his aides put an arm around him and guided him off the stage as another aide approached the rostrum and said, "The Governor needs a short break. He will resume his message in about half an hour. I assure you, you will not want to miss the rest of his message."

A half hour later, there was an announcement over the PA system to return to their seats for the remainder of the governor's message. When most of the audience was seated the governor returned to the rostrum.

He wore the same rumpled, dark grey suit with the wrinkled white shirt but the tie was missing and the collar unbuttoned. His expression changed. He still had a touch of sadness but it was overpowered by a look of determination.

Behind him, a large screen displayed the second amendment of the United States of America's Constitution which was approved by Congress on March 4, 1789. He turned back toward the screen and read it in a firm, strong voice, *"A well-regulated Militia, being necessary to the security of a free State, the right of the people to keep and bear Arms, shall not be infringed.*

"I want everyone here to stand up and read it aloud with me. I want to make sure everyone knows exactly what it says. If you don't read it aloud, you will be asked to leave this meeting. Please stand."

In surprisingly strong voices, the entire audience read the second amendment.

"Thank you," said the governor. "Please be seated."

Once everyone sat back down, he looked across the audience and began, "When the second amendment was made to our Constitution, it was to ensure the protection of the nation and to permit a man to provide food for his family. The guns at that time could fire only one shot, then required the shooter to stop and reload his weapon. The weapons of those days were called flintlocks and it could take several minutes to reload.

"Fast forward to today where the average person has access to as many weapons as they can afford or steal. Some of these weapons can fire as many as 15 rounds *per second* and have magazines that can hold up to 45 bullets before the shooter is required to reload. That would mean the shooter could fire all 45 rounds in three seconds.

"Initially, these types of weapons were developed for our military to be used in time of war. Unfortunately, they are now available to drug cartels, street gangs, those who promote ethnic cleansing and the mentally deranged as well as anyone who feels they need these weapons for protection.

"Their targets from the groups mentioned above can be rival gangs or cartels but during the last decade it can be anyone for any reason or no reason at all. The number of gun related deaths in the United States, excluding suicides, has increased steadily, especially after Covid-19. In 2021 they exceeded 20,000 deaths. In addition, the number of persons injured by shooters was 80,000.

"The people who track shooting deaths have created a new category. They call it mass shootings. They define a mass shooting as an event when four or more people are shot in one location within a short period of time. In 2021 there were six hundred and ninety-three mass shootings in America. Those numbers continue to climb, year after year after year. The increase is not linear, it's exponential. Last year the number of deaths caused by shootings in America increased fifty percent from the year before.

"What is even sadder is our federal government has done nothing to reduce these murders, except in some incidents where the police shoot and kill the assailant after he or she has already slaughtered the innocent. By that time, it's too little too late.

"This has to change. While the federal government dithers around and accomplishes almost nothing, we can wait no longer. After the shooting deaths of two hundred fifty-seven Oregonians in eight days, we can wait no longer. After the mass murder of men, women and children at five locations around our state, WE CAN WAIT NO LONGER. After the death of fifty-one school children in their classrooms… **WE WILL NOT WAIT ANY LONGER!**

"As the governor of the great state of Oregon, I will present a plan of action to take assault weapons off the streets. But let me tell you this. I have been a member of the NRA for most of my life and I have no intention of taking away hunters' rifles or shotguns or guns used for target shooting.

"My ultimate goal is this: One Person, One Gun, One Bullet. That means we revert back to the original spirit of the second amendment. Hunting rifles will not have magazines. You fire one shot and then you have to manually reload. The same applies to shotguns. No pump action or magazines, nor semiautomatic pistols."

Before the governor could continue, a man standing in the back of the auditorium began screaming, "No way!!! No way I'm giving up my weapons. You can't do that. The second amendment guarantees I can have all the guns I want. It's against the law to…"

Before the man could continue, the governor shouted back, "NO! What I'm suggesting isn't against the law. The law in Oregon is going change and you need to be prepared to live with it. If you don't like it, take your arsenal of weapons and move to California. They have more than twice as many shooting deaths per capita than we do."

The man began to yell again but people close to him started yelling back, "Shut up, jerk face. Let the Governor have his say," said a man standing close to him. Then more people started yelling at him to be quiet. But the man tried to out scream them.

The governor signaled to Colonel Legleu and gestured to have the man removed from the auditorium. He went kicking and screaming into the lobby area where he was charged with disturbing the peace, handcuffed and taken to jail.

When the audience settled down, the governor began as if nothing happened. "Starting immediately, it will be against the law for gun stores to display or sell any and all semiautomatic weapons of any type. Of course, ownership of automatic weapons, also known as machine guns, are already against both state and federal laws. All stores or licensed gun dealers will be required to return their inventory to the manufacturers within thirty days. Any store or individual who buys or sells semiautomatic weapons after tomorrow will be arrested on felony charges and may spend up to two years in an Oregon state prison when convicted. The same goes for anyone who buys or sells mail order guns."

When the governor paused to look at his notes, another man stood up and asked, "Governor, may I ask a clarification question?"

The governor looked up from his notes, spotted the man with the question, then nodded. "Make it a quick question," he said.

"I'm the owner of several gun stores in Oregon as well as Washington and California. Will I be allowed to transfer my inventory of semiautomatic weapons out of Oregon to my stores in the other states?" The governor seemed to be considering the question when the store owner added, "Most of my suppliers of the weapons you mentioned will not give me or other store owners a refund for returning their products."

After another brief pause, the governor answered, "If you wish to transfer your inventory to any other states, feel free to do so. As governor, the new laws I will be setting in place will be limited to Oregon. However, other states may not welcome an influx of your weapons. It's up to them to decide.

"Let me get back on track but let me thank you for your question." He took a quick sip of water before continuing, "Current owners of automatic or semiautomatic weapons who wish to keep them will be required to have them converted to single shot configurations. You have thirty days to make that conversion. Those who don't comply will have their weapons confiscated and will be fined. All owners of any type of firearms will be required to file for a permit within the next thirty days. All concealed carry permits are canceled. The purchase of ammunition for all firearms will be restricted to one hundred rounds per week per person. For the next six months, all Oregon gun shows will be canceled.

"Border checks for firearms coming into Oregon will begin immediately. Any unauthorized weapons brought into our state by car, truck, boat, aircraft or donkey will have them confiscated and destroyed. Those who attempt to sneak the forbidden weapons on foot across the Oregon border will be arrested, tried and convicted of arms trafficking. They will spend a minimum of two years in our state prison system.

"At the appropriate time, our police officers and detectives will no longer carry lethal weapons, only nonlethal weapons like Tasers, stun guns, pepper spray, batons and weapons with rubber bullets will be used. This also applies to private security company personnel and private detectives. Only SWAT teams, and of course our National Guard, will be allowed to carry semiautomatic weapons."

A reporter inserted a quick question. "How soon is 'an appropriate time?' Weeks, months, a year?"

The governor frowned at the interruption. "I don't have a timeline but I will not send out our law enforcement people unprotected. When the number of killings by automatic and semiautomatic weapons has dropped significantly, when there are no more mass shootings, when children are no longer murdered in their schools, then and only then will we consider limiting weapons for our law enforcement people. Please, no more interruptions, I'm almost done."

He looked down at his notes then asked the question, "How do we get to these goals? It's not going to happen overnight but it will begin tomorrow. Tomorrow we will open several weapon donation centers. They will be open twenty-four hours a day for the next thirty days. No questions asked. I guarantee all donated weapons will be destroyed. After the donation centers are closed, anyone in possession of a semiautomatic weapon will be charged with a felony and sentenced to a minimum of two years in prison.

"I know many of you may think this isn't fair or insist it's a violation of our constitutional rights. But after the recent massacres during the last month, we have to put a stop to this insanity permanently. This isn't a subject for debate. It's an executive order. The Oregon legislature cannot veto these orders. This is the best way I know of for the majority of us to not have to live in fear for our lives and the lives of our loved ones.

"I believe the only alternative to this approach is to declare martial law and have it enforced by the Oregon National Guard. It would include curfews and it could potentially turn Oregon into a police state. Nobody wants that but one way or the other we will stop these insane murders.

"More details will follow during the next few days. Please pray for the survivors of the holocausts and their loved ones who died needless deaths. Those of you who think they can get around these changes, I pity what will happen to you."

As he turned to walk off the stage, many in the audience stood up and began applauding. After a few moments they also began chanting, "One Bullet, One Bullet, One Bullet…"

CHAPTER 1

"On the Road Again"—Joshua

The team decided to take a break from our missions and recuperate. I almost died completing our last mission in New Orleans. Thanks to the help of the DEA, FBI, US Marshals and local law enforcement, we were able to successfully shut down most of the major drug cartels in the western hemisphere with an exceptionally small loss of life. The mission had many twists and turns but, in the end, it was a win, a huge win. Even with all the assistance from governmental agencies we never would have been remotely successful if it weren't for the help of the spirit of my dead twin brother, Caleb.

Only I know of the role he played. Only I know that he even exists. I died three times due to an attack of rogue US Marshals in Washington DC. I only survived because of Caleb's supernatural abilities.

It turns out members of the DC elite wanted our team out of the picture. They wanted to take over the cartels, their main interest being to become trillionaires overnight. Caleb, after saving me, showed them the errors of their ways.

We decided to lease a huge motorhome with a trailer large enough to carry the War Wagon and take a leisurely road trip from DC to Portland, Oregon. Several of us had friends and family living there and I needed more time to convalesce before we took on any new missions.

With the death of the Apostle, the code name of our primary contact within the government, we weren't sure if there was ever going to be any additional missions. But that was an issue for another day.

Once things settled down to a dull roar, the four of us (five if you count Caleb, six when you include Mark's Marine dog, Sarge) went motorhome shopping. We settled on a Newmar Bay Star. It was rated top of the line and we were sold on it the moment we came aboard. This was the 2019 model and it had more bells and whistles than we could ever imagine. It was 34 feet long and powered by a Ford Triton V-10 gasoline engine. It had two slide outs that gave us more floor space than a small apartment and much more luxury. It had just barely enough head room to accommodate my six feet, seven-inch height. It could sleep up to six adults, plenty of room for our four adults and a dog. Caleb doesn't sleep. It also had a built-in trailer hitch which we would need to bring the War Wagon with us.

The four of us (Simone Cantrell, Mark Riley, Pham Bin Minh and myself) all went through a two-hour driver's training course to familiarize us with the quirks of handling a house on wheels. It was time and money well spent.

It took us the better part of the next day to load up the motorhome. As we began loading, Pham said, "This is one sweet home. I never lived in a house as nice as this."

The rest of us agreed and Mark added, "It's going to be one sweet ride all the way to Portland."

Not to be out done, Simone smiled broadly and added, "Henceforth, she shall be known as Sweet Ride, Sweetie for short."

The three men stared at her. "You're kidding, right?" asked Mark.

"Sweet Ride is fine but no way I'm calling her Sweetie," added Pham.

Simone looked hurt. "What's wrong with Sweetie?"

"It's too girly," replied Pham. Mark nodded his head in agreement.

"But she's a girl!" she whined.

They both stared at her, not sure what to say. It looked like she was going to burst into tears but then she started laughing hysterically. "Gotcha, boys. It's Sweet Ride and nothing else."

Caleb thought to me, *That girl can be vicious at times.*

Does that bother you?

No way, I thought it was funny as hell.

Our last night in our hotel room in the nation's capital we laid out our route to Portland. It wasn't direct. We planned to head to California with several side trips, then turn north to Portland.

Caleb checked the internet and found out Ole Miss had a football game next Saturday afternoon against Mississippi State in Oxford. I mentioned it to the others and they agreed that would be our first stop. Caleb ordered tickets online for the four of us. I looked forward to seeing Coach Trevor, his coaches and players one last time.

Early Friday morning we checked out of the hotel and took an Uber to the secure parking garage where Sweet Ride and the War Wagon trailer were waiting for us. We did a walk-around to make sure everything was shipshape and headed out to the I-40 onramp.

Mark volunteered to be our first driver and I road shotgun. Sweet Ride was so big, it seemed like I was sitting in the next room. Simone and Pham were strapped into the recliner seats behind us watching the news on one of our large flat panel TVs.

We left early enough to avoid most of the rush hour traffic. The view through the immense windshield was spectacular. As the pilots say, "It's a CAVU day," Ceiling And Visibility Unlimited. With the engine in the rear, there was hardly any noise. After a short drive on I-40 we connected to I-81 South. It was going to be about a 13-hour drive to Oxford. About an hour later, I reclined my seat and drifted off to sleep.

Every four hours we would take a break and change drivers. Pham was the second driver, followed by Simone, I drove the last hour into the home of the Landsharks just as the sun began to set.

I called ahead and told Coach Trevor we were coming. He was very excited when I spoke with him and cleared us with security to park in the secure area of the football stadium parking lot.

We took an Uber from the lot to Steak and Shake just in time for dinner. Coach Trevor, coach Blakely, the strength coach and my former boss, joined us along with a few of the players, who met us at the restaurant. It was almost three years since I'd seen them. Those who were freshmen and sophomores were now juniors and seniors. It was like coming home again.

Their stay with us was brief, they still had to prepare for tomorrow's game but I had to admit how good I felt seeing so many of them again. They helped me immensely to recover from the trauma of losing my brother and then to adapt to the presence of his spirit. I will be forever indebted to them.

On their way out, Coach Trevor gave us four passes to the West Sky Boxes, with all the food and drink we desired along with luxury seating.

We all attended the game, including Sarge dressed in his therapy vest. He was well behaved and only begged the occasional treat. He put up with all the petting and attention without any protest. Best of all, the Landsharks crushed the Bulldogs.

Coach Trevor invited me into the locker room at half-time for a brief pep-talk. Most of the juniors and seniors went crazy when I walked in. I was the surprise guest the coach promised. They were already ahead, winning 30 to 0. They were all pumped and I yelled to be heard, "You guys are monsters. Don't stop now. This is only a game but you need to show them just how bad you are. Keep it up! GO LANDSHARKS!"

We won 67 to 0. It was very impressive. They dominated every aspect of the game. I was sure they would win the SEC title. What a rush!!!

When the game was over, we thanked the coaches and players for their outstanding hospitality. We said our goodbyes, boarded our motor home and headed out to our next stop.

CHAPTER 2

The Governor's Office, Salem Oregon—Governor Mark Johnson

"Governor, do you realize you have just committed political suicide? The next election is two years away. In my opinion, you have no chance of being re-elected for a second term. I know you're upset about what happened at Woodlawn but this is way…"

I raised my hand to stop Geri Blake, my PR advisor, from continuing. "I don't care, Geri. At the present time I have no intention of running again. Depending on how things go, I may resign early and move out of state."

Geri's mouth dropped open, then she began to sputter, "You can't be serious! After all the hard work we went through to get you elected, you're going to throw it all away?"

My secretary interrupted, "I have the Speaker of the House on line one. He's not a happy camper."

I tapped the line one button. "Hello, Clifford. How…" before I could say anything more, the speaker began shouting at me.

"What in the hell are you doing, Mark? Have you lost your mind? You must know you're violating the Oregon constitution in so many ways? I took a quick survey of the representatives and you don't have enough votes to push these changes through. We have a mid-term election coming up in a couple of weeks and our people are scrambling to get re-elected. This isn't going to help them or you."

I waited for him to run down. When he paused for a breath I said, "I'm declaring a state of emergency. I don't need the support of the legislature. This is the most important thing I can do and I intend to implement those changes in our gun laws, as quickly as I can. I can no longer turn my back on these killings as if it was business as usual. If it means I won't get elected for another term, so be it."

I stopped talking, waiting for Cliff to answer. After a few seconds pause, he said in a more controlled voice, "They're considering having you impeached, Mark. If they get enough votes, you could be out before any of these changes take effect." He paused again, then added, "If that happens you'll take a lot of us with you."

"This will sound insensitive, Clifford but I don't care. I'm not a career politician. I can't in all good consciousness do nothing and let these killings, these murders, continue. There is a point when we have to stand up and say, 'enough.' For me that point was yesterday. I believe the majority of Oregonians will support me on these measures. If they don't, they don't but I have to try."

"You're being unreasonable, Mark. Don't you realize the Supreme Court will shut you down before you even get started?"

"So be it, Clifford. Thank you for your call and your concern but my mind is made up."

Oxford to Roswell, New Mexico—UFOs Here We Come—Pham

While the parking lot at the stadium was clearing out, we did a quick inspection of Sweet Ride, followed by opening up the trailer and doing a once over of the War Wagon. When we were satisfied everything was in ship shape, we buttoned up the trailer and headed to the closest gas station to fill up.

It took a while to fill up the 80-gallon tanks. While we waited I went online to check the latest news. I was stunned by the news out of Oregon. I waited while Mark took care of refueling and paying the tab, then Joshua moved us out of the gas station into a nearby Walmart parking lot to discuss how the Oregon's governor Emergency Declaration could affect us.

Joshua asked the first question, "Since you're a certified Oregon attorney, does the governor have the authority to unilaterally make these laws?"

I shrugged my shoulders. "I'm not sure but there is a precedence. In March 2020 the governor declared Emergency Declaration 20-03 giving her the authority to make unilateral decisions regarding the Covid-19 pandemic. This allowed her to bypass the legislative process which could take months of debate before each new law would go into effect. Under the Emergency Declaration, also referred to as an Executive Action, it allowed the governor to make new laws regarding treatment of the disease in a day. So, the answer to your question is a qualified probably to yes."

Simone frowned, then asked, "What type of qualifications are you concerned about?"

"The Oregon legislature and the vast majority of the Oregonians were in favor of the governor making fast decisions regarding Covid-19 treatment," I answered. "It may not be the same for gun control. My opinion is that there will be considerable push back from the population at large. If that's true, the legislature can vote to impeach the governor and reverse any new laws he mandated while the Emergency Declaration was in effect. It's really too soon to tell how the public will react."

Joshua considered what I said then asked, "What do you recommend we do?"

"I think we should closely monitor the news to see how the public is responding to the new laws." I replied. "We should also watch how other states react to the new Oregon laws."

Joshua asked a follow up question, "Do the feds have to follow the new laws? If the answer is yes, we need to rethink taking the War Wagon and personal weapons into Oregon."

"It shouldn't affect us. Federal laws trump state laws as a general rule. However, each agency will have to decide if they are going to comply with state laws."

"Okay, let me summarize," Joshua said as Mark climbed into Sweet Ride. "Pham, you're responsible for updating us on the situation in Oregon. In the meantime we continue the next leg of our trip west. It's a 15-hour trip to Roswell. Dallas is half way there. How about we lay over in Dallas in the evening and continue on to Roswell in the morning?"

They all agreed. "I'll take the first leg and Mark can take us into Dallas," said Joshua as he moved to the driver's seat.

Marked looked around and asked, "What did I miss?"

"Nothing important," answered Simone.

Two hours from Dallas, Pham gave us our first update, "It looks like the Governor used his Executive Order to acquire several abandoned waterfront warehouses next to the Willamette River close to where it meets up with the Columbia River. They've already begun accepting donated semiautomatic weapons for destruction. They've brought in equipment needed to reconfigure rifles and pistols to single shot capability and have staffed up to reregister all weapons to the owners after the modifications are made.

"On the first day over a thousand rifles were donated. Inspectors from ATF were in charge of categorizing the weapons and to determine if each weapon was salvageable or should be destroyed. None of the local gangs in the Portland area donated any of their weapons. It looked more like they were window shopping for additional firearms. ATF kept a close watch to make sure none of the weapons grew legs and walked away. Weapon sales by the gangs is a huge source of revenue for all of them. I'm sure they'll try to squelch the new laws."

Joshua listened intently on my comments, then said, "Perhaps we can be of service to get the gangs to be more…cooperative?

Caleb thought to Joshua, *Perhaps I could do a little reconnoitering and help take their assault weapons and other nefarious hardware off their hands. I could zoom up there tonight while y'all are sleeping, check it out and be back before anyone wakes up.*

Sounds like a plan to me, thought Joshua. *But I want to see some of those little green men before I leave Roswell.*

I'm Your Midnight Man—Caleb

We pulled into a large, well-lit parking lot on the outskirts of Dallas. The lot had a noticeable incline but we used the hydraulic jacks to level the floor. Next step was to activate the two slide outs to give us maximum floor space.

Sarge was patiently sitting in front of the side door and was the first one out. He bolted to the first light pole support to do his business and waited for Mark to clean up after him. He licked Mark's hand to show his appreciation as they walked toward the Super Walmart to drop off his poop bag in a trash can.

The rest of the crew also decided to stretch their legs and did a couple of laps around the Texas size parking lot. I estimated they could have dropped three football fields into the lot with room to spare.

Joshua was the last out and he started a slow trek around the edge of the lot, checking the location of the other vehicles as possible threats. Of course, I used my special spirit abilities to do a much more thorough search.

We chatted as we made the first trip around the lot. Our 'chatting' was really telepathic communication between human brother and the spirit of his dead twin. That would be me.

Joshua 'asked' me, *What's your plan for this evening?*

I 'replied,' *I thought I'd cuddle up with a glass of chardonnay and a good book. How about you?*

He glared at me or where he thought my spirit might be.

Oh, you want to know my plan to discover gangland assault weapons in the greater Portland area?

He gave a curt nod and I continued, *I thought while you and the crew are sleeping all snug in your beds, I'd drop by your Portland PD friends, hack into their Gangland Task Force database to find the locations of the worst of the gangs, then pay them a visit to determine where they keep their weapons. I'll probably make a detailed inventory of their multiple weapon sites and send the data to Sweet Ride's computer (your eyes only, of course). When you wake from your beauty rest, I'll be there to answer any questions you might have.*

By the time I was done, Joshua was smiling widely. *You are such a tool, bro,* he thought back to me. *Anything else you want to share?*

As a matter of fact, yes, I thought back. *Since we are technically on vacation and have several planned stops before getting to Portland, maybe you would want to share this information with your two Portland PD detective friends so they can get a head start on rounding up the gangs' weapons.*

Excellent idea, he responded. *When do you plan to leave?*

I'm already gone, bro. Catch you on the flip side.

I transported to the Portland PD at midnight their time. I need to explain something here to those not familiar with spirits. When we transport from one location to another we can choose the time to arrive and depart from various locations. It's kind of like time travel but not really and there are limits.

Case in point. I left Dallas at around 2000 hours or for you civilians 8:00 pm. Dallas is on Central Time which would be 6:00 pm in Portland which is on Pacific time. I wanted to get to Portland late at night and when I transported I arrived at midnight, which would be 2:00 am the next day in Dallas.

When I returned to Dallas after spending a couple of hours hacking into the Portland Gangland Task Force data base and downloading the information I needed, I chose to arrive at 6:00 am. I wanted to get there when Joshua and the crew were getting up so I didn't have to wait to debrief Joshua on what I found out.

Are you confused yet? I know I was when I first started transporting but I got used to it. Since spirits don't sleep, I didn't have any jet lag problems. Sorry for the interruption in the flow of the story. Where was I?

Oh yeah, Mark was the first one up to let Sarge outside to do his business. He did his business so often, I wondered if he should get a business license. The rest of the team rolled out of bed a few minutes after Mark and Sarge finished their morning jog.

An hour later, Pham and Simone made breakfast for everyone, kind of a Creole/Vietnamese combo that all agreed was delicious, including Sarge. Unfortunately, spirits don't eat but being bonded to Joshua allows me to enjoy the meal as much as Joshua. If he enjoyed the aroma of the food, it's taste and the sense of feeling full when the meal was over, so did I.

Mark volunteered to clean up while Joshua and I took a stroll around the parking lot so I could give him a private data dump. Actually, Joshua strolled and I floated along beside him. It wasn't like we weren't going to share the intel with everyone, we just wanted to be careful not to reveal a ghost was the source. Hopefully, in the not too distant future there would be the big reveal but not just yet.

It turns out Joshua had previous encounters with detectives Joey Hong and Bill Cody from the Portland PD. Since then, they'd been assigned to the Gang Task Force. Everything we needed to know about the Portland area gangs was available in the Task Force database. It was easy for me to access the data base and I felt like shouting 'Eureka!' (Greek for I have found it!). Apparently, most of the gangs set up along ethnic lines.

At the top of the list were the Chinese Tongs, kind of a conglomeration of several families, each with their own leader. They seemed to have a ruling council who set the standards for their behavior. The families go back generations beginning in the 1800s. Joshua had some contact with one of the Tongs over a year ago regarding human trafficking. It ended badly for nine of their soldiers and the demise of that entire Tong family in the Portland area. Most of the remaining Tongs limit their crimes to the China Town area of Portland.

The Tongs were followed by a Neo Nazi group who called themselves The Skin Heads. Not very original but apparently innovative thought was beyond them. They were known as white supremacists who wanted everyone who wasn't white to go back to the country of their origin and they didn't mind killing those who refused to leave.

The black gangs were a loose consortium of smaller groups with specific interests such as drugs, prostitution, human trafficking, murder for hire and anything else that would turn a buck.

Mi Casa was the name used by a Hispanic gang. In Portland, it was ruled by one man and his family. It was very much a family operation. In turn, the local leader reported to an unidentified cartel leader somewhere in Mexico. They were also involved in anything that would bring in the money.

The last gang on the PD list was the Lords of Chaos. Their membership seemed to be open to all races as long as they loved Satan and hated everybody else. Membership was opened to all sexes. Rumor had it, to become a member in good standing required the newbie to kill at least one person. This last gang was considered the prime suspect for the murders at Woodlawn Elementary School.

I visited all of the gangs supposedly secret hangouts. It turns out they weren't too secret.

It took very little searching to find where each gang stashed their weapons. All of them had huge caches of all types of weapons and explosives.

All the gangs were smart enough not to store their explosives where they resided. They stored the majority of their firearms in their hideouts which was also where they slept.

As I silently wandered through each hideout I wasn't surprised to notice most of them slept with their firearms, which is probably the reason they didn't sleep with another gang member.

Almost all of the gangs stored their explosives underground in basements or cellars a mile or two away from their sleep houses. That meant if I detonated the explosives most of the energy would be directed upward, focusing the damage to the above structure, such as a house, garage or shed. After I checked to make sure there weren't any people in the buildings, I decided to have a little fun. I used my secret Spirit Powers and detonated all of the underground explosives at the same time. Each of the explosive caches were located several miles apart and the explosions certainly got lots of attention. What a RUSH!!! It was better than any July 4th fireworks show I'd ever seen, louder too.

I have to admit there was some collateral window damage to the nearby abandoned homes but hey, nobody got hurt, just a lot of debris scattered everywhere for miles.

I left a message for Joey Hong on his computer, giving the location of the firearms for all of the gangs mentioned above and signed Joshua's name. I emphasized he was only to share the locations of the gangs' firearms and that he got that information from a confidential informant. I suggested he may drop a hint more information might be forthcoming. I asked him to text Joshua if there was any interest from his bosses.

"You WHAT?!!!" screamed Joshua. He said it out loud but we were so far away from Sweet Ride, I was sure nobody heard him. *You left him a message without my approval?* he thought back to me.

Chill, bro. Look at it as a jump start of the Governor's program. By now the Portland PD, along with ATF, have confiscated a huge number of firearms from the gangs and probably made a number of arrests for possession of said weapons. They are also probably sweating the leaders of the Lords of Chaos on accessory to murder charges.

Joshua still looked stunned but at least he wasn't screaming.

I hesitated for a moment, trying to read my brother's emotions. I detected high adrenaline levels but they were dropping. His panic was dropping as well and I waited a couple of beats then thought to him, *This could be a real opportunity for us. If detective Hong is smart, he'll share that Team Joshua may be the CI behind this bust and could be invaluable in reducing other types of murders. In the meantime, let's enjoy the rest of our trip and wait to see if anyone contacts us.*

CHAPTER 3

Hello Aliens—Mark

When Joshua returned from his morning walk he looked different, stunned might be the best way to describe it. Sarge noticed it too and jumped down from his favorite recliner to meet Joshua as he opened Sweet Ride's middle door and climbed the two steps into the lounge area. Sarge sat down directly in front of Josh and looked up at him with an expression of concern, making kind of a whining sound.

Joshua reached down and petted Sarge gently on the head. "I'm fine Sarge, just need to rest from the walk."

The sound of his voice made Simone and Pham turn to look at him. Clearly, the tone of his voice said things weren't fine but he didn't want to talk about it. He turned to me and said, "Let's hit the road, Mark. We're burning daylight. I'll relieve you in four hours."

He walked to the back of the bus into the master bedroom and closed the door behind him. I fired up Sweet Ride, checked the GPS input and headed out to I-81 S. Simone waited a few minutes then headed back to the bedroom to join the boss.

True to his word, he relieved me four hours later. He looked and acted normal again (whatever that means) as he drove us into Roswell about three hours later. Ah, the power of a woman's touch.

It was the first time any of us had been to Roswell. The best way I could describe it was weird. Pham said it was a small town capitalizing on a legend from the distant past. I'll stick with weird but in a good way.

I found a large parking lot with a lot of spots occupied by motorhomes from all over North America. Many of them had bumper stickers exhorting alien life with catchy phrases. My favorites were associated with alien abductions. The best one, in my humble opinion, was a cartoon of a man bent over a table with a little green alien standing behind him with one of its appendages deep in the human's backside. The text read: "I Love Alien Anal Probes. None of the team shared my opinion. Their comments varied from dumb to sick.

Another strange pastime seemed to be to trick out your ride to resemble a UFO. Some people must have spent a small fortune making their vehicles resemble what they assumed a real UFO looked like, although I doubt any respectable alien would have been caught dead in a motorhome decorated to resemble a mothership with colorful flashing strobe lights and punk rock blaring from monstrous speakers. Ah well, to each his own.

I seemed to be the only one of our group to find the campiness of all this entertaining. Pham thought it was an insult to all alien life forms throughout the universe. However, they were amused at the alien costume I bought for Sarge, especially the voice synthesizer which made his bark sound unearthly.

Everyone enjoyed visiting one of the museums dedicated to showing numerous details about the crash of a UFO on July 7, 1947. There was very little hype, just news reports with photographs of the crash debris and all the conflicting views of the reports from the Air Force. It presented the evidence and let you decide for yourself if aliens really crashed near Roswell or if it was debris from a weather balloon or possibly it was all just a hoax.

We spent the night in our non-UFO'd but very classy, motorhome. We turned on the exterior lights and activated the security system to ward off any crackpots who could be wandering around at all hours of the night. That included any alien life forms that might have taken a fancy to our Sweet Ride.

Bright and early the next morning, we left Roswell and headed to the Grand Canyon. So far no one from Oregon contacted us but reports about the explosions in the Portland area were all over the news. That was followed by numerous reports of raids by ATF and local police uncovering thousands of illegal firearms. That included a surprising number of automatic weapons in addition to semiautomatic.

A final note was the arrest of five members of the Lords of Chaos. They were charged with accessory to murder and a speedy trial was anticipated. The Oregon governor suggested they all receive the death penalty… by a National Guard firing squad. He was quoted as saying, "Let the penalty fit the crime." Several members of the Guard who lost loved ones in the attack on Woodlawn Elementary volunteered for the firing squad. The volunteers suggested weapons recovered from the Lords of Chaos be used to carry out the execution.

CHAPTER 4

What a Grand Canyon!—Simone

I loaded the GPS, fired up the engine and headed out of Roswell on US Highway 285 North to I-40 which would take us through Albuquerque in a little over three hours. Joshua would take over just west of Albuquerque. It would take us another six hours to make it to the Canyon. Mark was going to drive the last two hours to get us to the South Rim, ETA to the canyon was 1600 hours (or 4:00 pm MST). Sarge would be riding shotgun when Mark drove.

Driving in the western part of the US was very different from driving in the East. There were very long stretches between populated areas and most of the populated areas were still considered low density. Albuquerque was the last major city we would see for the remainder of this leg of the trip. Most of the drive was through wide open spaces. We saw several sign posts along the way reminding us 'Next Gas Station 100 Miles.' In the east you only had to drive a couple of miles in any direction to take your pick of places to fuel up.

I'm not complaining, the view was beautiful and it was great to get away from city traffic. My part of the drive was very relaxing. I tuned on an easy listening channel on Sirius and enjoyed my drive time, commercial free.

When Joshua relieved me, Mark and I made lunch while Sarge sampled the food to make sure it wasn't tainted. We stopped at a rest stop outside of Gallup, New Mexico, to eat and listened to a local radio station that broadcasted in one of the Native American languages. You don't get that type of entertainment back east. When lunch was over, Pham gave us an update on the situation in Oregon.

"It looks like the Oregon Governor's popularity rating is off the chart," announced Pham. "There is still considerable push back from both liberals and conservatives but Governor Johnson's program is gaining a lot of momentum with the majority of the Oregonians.

"I was particularly interested in an interview he did on a local Portland talk show. When asked how he felt about the success of the new laws against semiautomatic firearms were going, he said the following."

Pham turned and punched the play button on the recorder and the TV lit up with the image of the governor. "We've only seen the tip of the iceberg. Don't get me wrong, I'm very pleased about the success our program is having in reducing the number of dangerous weapons in our state. Between the voluntary surrender of semiautomatic weapons and the raids on several criminal gangs in the city of Portland by our local police and federal ATF people, we have taken over 10,000 weapons off the street. And that's just during the first week after the new gun laws were put into effect. If you add in the number of guns returned from gun stores to the manufactures or sent to other out of state stores, it's up to over 13,000."

"What's the next step?" asked the talking head.

"I'm not sure about the next step but I have some very serious concerns about a particular type of killer. How do you stop the average person on the street who's having a bad day and decides to take out his anger by shooting his family or his neighbors or a bunch of people he doesn't know in a shopping mall or church? It seems to me since the Covid-19 pandemic, there has been a dramatic change in the way some people think. They seem to believe, at least on a subconscious level, they have the right to extract vengeance on anyone they feel has wronged them. Even worse, they get so angry it doesn't matter who they kill. It was just a way of releasing their anger. A substantial percentage of these killers commit suicide when they realize what they've done. Others just don't care and will continue to kill whenever they get pissed off… until somebody puts them down.

"Actually, now that I think about it, we could probably trace this trend back even earlier than Covid-19 when postal workers were getting let go from their jobs. Some of them showed up for work and shot and killed their bosses and co-workers. It became so prevalent, it even coined a name. They called these killings as going postal.

"I've got my people compiling some figures regarding this trend in killing but I strongly believe limiting the availability of firearms could reduce this number of murders substantially. I really want to know if there is any way to avoid these types of killings."

Pham pushed the End button on the recorder and we all sat quietly, considering the question the governor posed.

"Does anyone think it's even possible to have any effect on this category of murders? How do you keep people from being angry?" I asked the team.

"Good questions, Simone," replied Joshua. "Let's all think about possible answers to those questions as we continue our drive to the South Rim. Who's driving the last leg?"

"I am, Josh," answered Mark. "We should be there in a couple of hours. Where's my co-pilot?"

Sarge barked twice and jumped into the front passenger seat. I strapped his harness to the seat belt and whispered into the dog's ear, "Keep a lookout for wild animals, Sarge."

Sarge barked twice, licked my hand and began intently scanning the horizon.

I looked at Joshua. He smiled at me and said, "I want to do some research for about thirty minutes." Then he turned and headed back to the bedroom and closed the door behind him.

"Research, my ass," I said to no one in particular. "He just wants to take a nap."

Private Meeting with Caleb—Joshua

I turned on my laptop and logged on to my email to see if I'd any messages from detective Hong. Nothing yet but I just wanted to be prepared if anyone, especially Simone, interrupted our private meeting.

What do you think, Caleb? Do you think you can use your spirit powers to get answers to the Governor's questions?

Maybe, he thought back to me. *I know I can track what a person is thinking about at the moment but I never tried to read a bunch of people all at once and pick out potential murderers. I can give it a try when we get to the canyon. There ought to be a lot of people to scan but I'm not sure how well this will work.*

Why not?

Every human brain is unique. Twins or triplets are exceptions. They're close to being identical but even they have slight differences.

I'm nothing like you, I interrupted.

How so?

Well for starters, I have a brain and you don't, I replied.

Oh, I'm sorry. I thought this was going to be a serious discussion…pecker head.

Sorry, Caleb. I couldn't resist. All business now.

I hope so, he thought back to me. *The differences become greater as the twins and other multiple birth siblings are exposed to different life experiences. By the time they reach adulthood, there are very few similarities.*

The differences between average humans is a magnitude greater. However, I think they can be lumped into categories and we can try to identify which brain types can lead to violent behavior. Once we know that, I can decide what I can do, if anything, to prevent a person from committing a murder.

A question occurred to me, *When you say all brains are different, do you mean physically different which causes them to process information differently? Maybe structurally different would be a better way to describe it. If so, would that physical difference cause them to process incoming stimulus differently?*

Wow! Look at Mr. Wizard. Excellent question, bro. The answer is a qualified yes.

How is it qualified?

I have no idea but I think I know how to get an answer to your questions and my own questions as well.

He paused to see if I had any other comments. I didn't, so he continued, *I'm going to contact my spirit teacher and see if he can offer any suggestions. I'll be back soon to fill you in on what he said.*

There was a knock on the door. "Joshua, can I join you? I won't make a sound. I'm tired from driving; I want to take a nap."

I mumbled something and dove into bed and started fake snoring. Simone opened the door and laid down next to me.

I could 'hear' Caleb in my head, *Ain't love grand!*

<u>Once More Into The Breach, Dear Friend—Caleb</u>

Every time I consult with my spirit guide, I find it kind of creepy. Why does he insist on creating the Hollywood setting for our meetings? It's always this great summer day with puffy white clouds in an azure blue sky with beautiful landscaping. It's just too pretty.

And why do we have to appear as avatars instead of just communicating spirit-to-spirit? It seems really weird to have a body again and to hear and speak out loud. At least our avatars always looked like we did when we were alive. He was the spitting image of my last Marine Company Commander, Captain Collins. But our clothes changed from visit to visit.

Instead of being dressed in a Marine uniform his outfit looked like he was dressed for a round of croquet. I have to admit he always looked good in white linen pants, a white long sleeve shirt covered by a powder blue sweater vest.

I didn't have a choice of attire; this time he dressed me in light green Bermuda shorts, knee high stockings in matching color with white shoes and a darker green polo shirt. I looked like a black version of a six foot, seven-inches tall Jolly Green Giant. Only I didn't feel jolly, not one bit.

"Good day to you, Master Sergeant Caleb Brown. How may I help you?"

I began to lay out my questions for him when he raised his hand to interrupt me, "Do I have to remind you I have no advice to offer when it comes to humans?"

I rephrased my approach, "How about human-spirit interaction?"

"Perhaps, continue and I will decide if I can offer you any advice."

"Thank you, sir. Can a spirit read a human's mind and determine if he or she wants to kill someone?"

"Absolutely," he answered immediately.

I was encouraged and expanded my question, "How about if a spirit is in a crowd of humans can the spirit determine all the people who want to kill other humans?"

"It's a little more complicated but yes. With practice, the spirit in question would be able to determine which humans are considering murder."

"One last question, would the spirit be able to keep the humans from attempting to murder others?"

"Absolutely not! Spirits aren't permitted to interfere directly with any human actions."

That wasn't the answer I was hoping for. I began to thank him for his judgement when he interrupted me again.

"You're a very mature spirit and as such you have advanced abilities. Do you remember when you were informed you could see into the future for a very short period of time?"

"Yes sir but I've never attempted to use that ability."

He shook his head in mild annoyance. "Why do we grant you these abilities if you aren't going to use them. I leave you to think how you might apply this ability to your problem."

Before I could thank him, he looked at his watch (why would a spirit even have a watch?). Then he said, "Time for me to go. Hope this helps you, goodbye." And he was gone. So was the luxurious setting. I was back in Sweet Ride as we pulled into the parking lot at the South Rim of the Grand Canyon.

CHAPTER 5

Down the Bright Angel Trail—Joshua

The parking lots were jammed. They had several lots dedicated to motorhomes, fifth wheelers and trucks pulling trailers and campers. We managed to find a spot about a mile from the trailhead for Bright Angel Trail. It was longer then the South Kaibab Trail but it was a more gradual change in elevation. Indian Garden was located about four and a half miles down from the trailhead. It had drinking water, porta potties and mules. If you were too feeble to walk down to Indian Garden you could rent a mule along with a guide to tell you about the surroundings as you made your way to the bottom.

It was about a ten mile hike to the bottom and the descent was approximately 2,000 feet. The air temperature at the bottom could be 15 to 20 degrees warmer than the top. When you reach the bottom, a bridge takes you across the Colorado River and leads to a campground on the other side.

It was a beautiful day and the trail was crowded. We planned on going to Indian Garden, resting for a bit, then climbing back up. It would take roughly four to five hours to hike to the bottom if you were in decent shape. If you're not in decent shape you have no business going past Indian Garden. The trip to the bottom is doable but getting back to the top is a very different story; the trip up can be a killer, literally. For those who can't make the climb out, you have two options: you can fly out in a rescue helicopter which can cost as much as $15,000, or you can rent a mule for the ride back up. The latter will cost you about $200.

Caleb remained at the lookout point next to the trail head and read the thoughts of those starting the hike and those returning. He would be joining us at Indian Garden for a while and then transport to the campground at the bottom. He would join us back at the trailhead after we finished our hike back to the top.

It was a great day for a hike. The temperature was in the cool 70s and the view as we started down the trail was breathtaking. It was more like a stroll than a hike. Of course, Mark brought Sarge along in his therapy vest and he was well behaved as usual. Even when some small children ran to him squealing with joy, he didn't panic as they petted him vigorously. He just stood there and took it. He even licked one little girl on the arm who was pulling on one of his ears. She screamed with delight and of course he had to lick all the rest of the children. The only thing that seemed to bother him were the mules.

The mules had the right of way when they were on the move down the trail. Sarge seemed unsure if he should let them pass. A very large man on top of one of the mules inadvertently pulled on the reins and his mule turned towards Sarge who now considered the mule a threat. He began to growl and bared his fangs which the mule didn't like and he kicked out at Sarge. The dog nimbly moved away from the kick and looked back at Mark for instructions. Marked used a subtle hand sign to signal Sarge to back off and heel. He quickly lay down next to Mark as the mule team walked by but his body was tense, probably hoping Mark would turn him loose. I could almost read his mind, *Let me take him, boss. He's no big deal.*

It took us a little less than two hours to get to Indian Garden. There were a lot of picnic tables available for the hikers on a patio area with fabric sails providing shade. A row of porta potties were available some distance from the tables. We all moved to a table close to the trail and watched as a steady stream of people walked by in opposite directions. There were so many people walking by, it reminded me of the rush hour pedestrian traffic on sidewalks in many American cities.

Simone slung the backpack off her shoulder onto the table and pulled out several water bottles. "Everyone needs to drink a full bottle before we head up." She also removed a collapsible bowl from her backpack and poured in a bottle of water for Sarge who wasted no time in slurping it all up.

The way the tables were positioned gave us a great view of the canyon. You could follow the winding trail as it meandered through the twists and turns through the canyon walls. You couldn't see the Colorado from here but the trail seemed to get smaller and smaller and the people looked more like two lines of ants moving up and down a narrow path.

Pham looked at his watch and said, "I think we should be heading back soon. The later it gets, the heavier the traffic returning to the top."

I looked at Simone and Mark. They nodded in agreement and we headed back up the trail. We were halfway there when Caleb contacted me. *Josh, we got some action at the lookout point. I think I figured out how we can deal with this type of killer.*

It took us a little more than two hours to return to the top of the canyon. The sun set but there was enough twilight for me to take a quick scan of the area. I didn't see the action Caleb mentioned and I 'asked' him.

Chill, bro, he thought to me in reply. *I was able to handle it. No one was killed or even mussed up. I'm very proud of myself. Let's wait until we're alone and I'll lay it all out.*

We walked another mile and climbed aboard Sweet Ride. Twilight had passed and except for the lights in the parking lot, it was dark. I had to admit, I was a little bit tired as well as hungry. Simone suggested I rest for a bit while Mark and her made dinner for us. Of course, Sarge volunteered to get rid of any tidbits which fell on the floor of the kitchen area.

I wanted to rest but I didn't want it to look like I couldn't handle a little hike (or maybe a medium hike). I went to the fridge and got a bottle of water for everyone. Mark poured a bottle in Sarge's bowl as Pham took his bottle with him to the computer station in the lounge area and logged on. The rest of us also moved to the lounge area to drink our water and chat.

After a sip from my water bottle I asked Mark, "Do you still have your apartment in the Woodlawn District in Portland?"

"Not anymore," he answered. "When I left for the New Orleans mission, I moved out. I put all my stuff in a secure storage unit which wasn't much. I rented the apartment furnished. By the way, the kitchen in Sweet Ride is twice as big and ten times higher tech than what I had in my apartment."

Caleb knew what I was doing and gave me about fifteen minutes to relax before the debrief.

"Do you plan to rent another apartment in Woodlawn?" Simone asked as she petted Sarge who sat between her and Mark.

"I like Portland but I don't want to go back to Woodlawn, too much pain there." He smiled and said to the group, "Besides, I'm a member of Team Joshua now. Wherever the team goes, Sarge and I go. Isn't that right big guy?" Sarge barked once at the sound of his name.

I finished my water and stood up. "I think I'll take a shower while dinner's being prepared."

"About time," Pham said from behind the computer. "You really smell ripe."

I ignored him while the other team members chuckled. I walked into the bedroom suite and closed the door behind me.

Caleb made a sniffing sound (I wondered how he did that with no nose) and agreed. *You definitely need a shower. You be needin' one for a few days now.*

I took off my clothes, threw them in the hamper ignoring Caleb's jab. I turned on the shower, stepped into the rain of hot water and thought to him. *You can start your debrief now, bro.*

CHAPTER 6

Hopefully, A Breakthrough—Caleb

I'm really excited about what I found out while you and the team were sightseeing.

Are you pouting? asked Joshua.

Of course not, I answered, then paused. *Maybe a little bit.*

Didn't you take a few moments to look at the canyon while you were doing your investigation? Didn't you get a chance to see all of the canyon from top to bottom and we only saw a small portion of it? he asked.

Yes but I didn't get to do it with the team, I replied.

But didn't you get the chance to discover some new incredible information that none of us know anything about because you're wasting time pouting instead of briefing me?

He had me. *Okay, bro. Sorry for the attitude. Let the briefing commence. Do you want the full story or just the bottom line?*

I'm almost done with my shower, so just the bottom line for now.

Tough, you get the whole story but I will slow down time for you so you will eat in about five minutes your time, which would roughly be thirty minutes in our time.

Really? You can do that?

I did my best to synthesize a chuckle. *Stick with me and I will show you magic you've never dreamed of. As long as you are within the bubble of my existence, you can experience some of my abilities.*

Joshua finished his shower, put on clean clothes, and sat in a chair next to his king size bed.

This is what I told him. I scanned roughly 10,000 people who visited the canyon while we were there. I moved from group to group and stopped time while investigating the brains of each person in each group. I moved down Bright Angel Trail, the camp grounds at the bottom and then up the South Kaibab. I made sure I finished my investigation within a couple of hours. Actually, I finished in time to see them walking up the Bright Angel trailhead. From my perspective, I'd spent several days, almost a week, to make sure I checked them all.

What was I looking for when I investigated all those people? In my opinion there are two categories of individuals who commit murders. They are what I will call rage killers and psycho killers. Individuals from both categories kill as little as one person but also multiple people as well

Of the two category of killers, rage killers are the easiest to identify prior to them actually committing their murders. Examples of measurable pre-murder traits are body temperature, heart rate and testosterone level. There are also physical behaviors that lead up to the murder associated with rage killers such as screaming, shouting, cursing and preliminary violence which leads to the actual murder or murders. Rage killers believe they are justified in committing murders against those they feel have wronged them in some way.

Psycho killers have very little in the way of observable behavioral traits, however they may have a history of killings of insects and animals which can ultimately lead to killing human beings.

I focused mainly on rage killers. Ever since the Covid-19 pandemic, the number of rage killings have grown at an exponential rate worldwide. I blame this increase on the changes to peoples' lives caused by the disease. This resulted in both fear and anger which led to a greater tendency to violent behavior. However, it's been years since the pandemic ended but rage killings continued to increase. I asked myself, why wouldn't rage killings decrease once people were able to return to their pre Covid-19 lifestyles? Why would the number of rage killings continue to increase?

I spent the better part of my first day doing internet research on this topic (no time at all in the real world but it was well worth my time). Many so-called experts believed the reason for the continued increase in rage killings is because even though the pandemic ended several years ago, it will take decades for the world to return to normal. In other words their position is don't bother trying to fix it. It will return to 'normal' sometime in the distant future. I wasn't particularly enamored with this belief.

There were other theories but the one that intrigued me most was a detailed paper written by relatively unknown team of scientists and medical doctors. They suggested a side effect of Covid-19 was a permanent change to the brain of some people who'd been infected by the disease and survived. Just as the strains of the disease mutated, their brains were also permanently mutated. They hypothesized that the mutation resulted in more violent behavior in those who'd been hospitalized by one or more of the mutated strains.

They emphasized that this was only a hypothesis and a considerable amount of research would be needed to verify their position. They indicated they'd done a limited study of a dozen people from different parts of the US who'd been hospitalized with the disease and subsequently survived. Within less than a year after they'd been released from the hospital, each of the patients attempted to kill one or more individuals. Five of them were successful. Two of those were killed by police for failing to surrender following the murders.

Now for the most interesting part. The two who were killed by the police underwent autopsies which included examination of their brains. Both of these two killers had brain scans when they were admitted to their respective hospitals and both brains were considered normal (the scientists used a lot of technical jargon but the bottom line was the brains were normal). The examination of their brains after the autopsies revealed there were substantial changes to the structure of both brains. And here is the really interesting fact, the mutated brains were almost identical.

One of the scientists suggested the mutated brain looked very similar to the those of ancient prehistoric men (Cro-Magnon and/or Neanderthal). He used words like reverse evolution.

One last comment before I wrap up this part of the debriefing. The same scientist mentioned above also indicated he strongly believed the offspring who were conceived after one or more of their parents had mutated brains were very likely to also have some level of brain mutation. It was noted that this scientist was asked to leave the group. I wasn't surprised.

After I completed my research, I began scanning for indications of mutated brains. I knew this was a long shot but it gave me a starting point for my own research. I was gifted with the ability to scan the inside of peoples' bodies. That ability led me to help save Joshua's life when he was shot with a bullet that fragmented, leaving shards very close to his spine. I was able to remove the shards and accelerate his healing. This time I was acting like an MRI and was able to quickly determine if a person's brain was mutated. (During my internet research, I'd seen pictures of a mutated brain compared to a normal one.)

I'd lock on to each individual, freeze time and sneak a quick look at their brain. After the first thousand, I was getting discouraged. They were all normal. I thought maybe there was no such thing as a mutated brain. But during the next thousand I discovered three, two men and one woman. I spent some time with each one, checking out their behaviors and looking for signs of rage but finding none. When I accessed their thoughts they were normal human thoughts, they were enjoying their vacation with their families (by the way, none of their offspring had any brain mutation). Even with their mutated brains, their thought processes seemed very normal (no indication of Cro-Magnonism thought, whatever that was).

When I'd completed my scan of all 10,000 visitors to the canyon, I discovered a total of twelve mutated brains, none of whom had any violent thoughts. I transported back to the lookout area next to the

Bright Angel trailhead and watched as more people started down the trail. Then I heard a collision in the parking lot right in front of the lookout area.

A large motorhome (not ours, praise the Lord) was crashed into by a very expensive looking electric vehicle, I think it was a Lucid. It looked like the motorhome was driving down one of the parking lot aisles, when the Lucid backed into him causing extensive damage to both vehicles. What ensued was a prime example of road rage.

I transported to the scene and went to investigate. Obviously, the Lucid driver was at fault. With all the bells and whistles on the Lucid, how could the driver miss seeing the motorhome? The driver jumped out of the car when I froze the scene. He was a large man, not quite as big as Joshua (or me when I had a body) but still well built and very pissed off. I let the scene progress in slow motion. The first thing I noticed was the Lucid driver's brain: it was mutated. The next thing I noticed other than his anger was his build; he was well muscled and apparently liked to show it off wearing a tank top to best display his massive biceps, triceps, deltoids and pectorals'. It also showed that he had lots of body hair, a long dark beard, a mustache that covered his entire upper lip and long, unkempt dark brown hair. He looked like a prehistoric man (maybe the scientist was right). The last thing I noticed about the man was the 357 magnum revolver he was pulling out of a holster attached to his belt. I froze the scene and checked out the motorhome.

The Lucid hit the back of the motorhome hard causing a lot of damage. The engine was located in the rear and steam was venting from the louvered engine cover as it made strange unnatural sounds. The driver must have shut it off. I let the scene run at very slow speed and watched the passenger side door open and another large man stepped out of the side door holding what looked to be a pump action shot gun with a short barrel. I froze the scene while I scanned his brain. It was a two-for-one special, two mutant brains for one stop.

This was going to get interesting very quickly. Lucid driver was standing next to the motorhome's driver-side window which had a reflective film covering it making it impossible to see the driver. Lucid man was holding his magnum up and pointed at where he thought the driver would be sitting. He'd just cocked the hammer, when the motorhome driver stepped around the front of the vehicle. He pumped the shell into the chamber and pointed the shotgun at the head of Lucid driver. I quickly froze the scene before any shots were fired.

It took me as least four hours (my time) to find a solution to keep one or both of them from being blown into oblivion. With the scene frozen, I tried out one of my new abilities for the first time. It allowed me to see a moment or two into the most probable future. I wasn't seeing reality, I was seeing what was most likely to happen if I didn't change things. The most probable seen was messy and very deadly.

Lucid driver tried to turn his revolver towards Shotgun man. Shotgun man pulled the trigger and vaporized Lucid driver's head. It was loud and blood was everywhere. I also noticed a little boy standing with his family across from the shootout took a shotgun pellet into his leg and he began screaming while his parents tried to comfort him.

I tried everything I could think of to calm the beast that had taken over their recently mutated brains. I would try out ideas and run the into-the-future ability to see the effect. I lost count of how many murders I watched. Most of the time Shotgun man prevailed but Lucid driver managed to kill Shotgun man a couple of times. I was really getting sick of this trial and error approach when I came upon a solution. It wasn't very practical but it was a start.

I froze the scene and transported myself into a pharmacy and froze the pharmacy while I shopped for various drugs. I decided on injectable dopamine and something that would lower testosterone. The other injectable I got has a name I can't pronounce or even spell. It's similar to Narcan which can absorb heroin in an amazingly short period of time. The stuff I got absorbs testosterone. I unfroze the pharmacy as I transported back to the canyon.

The first thing I did was to make sure their firearms wouldn't fire. That was a chore in itself and I won't go into the details of how that was accomplished. Trust me, their weapons would be on safety when I unfroze the scene.

The next thing was to shoot them both up with dopamine and the stuff that absorbs testosterone. I then made sure both drugs diffused into their brains. When I could tell they were saturated, I ran another into-the-future look and saw them both look very puzzled, then they both collapsed onto the pavement. I hoped I hadn't overdosed them.

I unfroze the scene and saw essentially the same thing as the into-the-future probability had shown. Except they dropped their weapons when they collapsed, and a woman from the Lucid came running to Lucid driver's aid and the family of Shotgun man came barreling around the front of the motorhome to help the dad to his feet.

Both men looked confused but it wasn't long before the men were smiling and were positive everything was alright. I took the liberty of transporting both weapons out of sight under the motorhome.

A few minutes later, several police cars arrived with flashing lights and sirens. Both drivers were arrested on numerous charges, handcuffed and placed into different cruisers. Before the police closed the cruiser's rear door, I heard Lucid driver say, "What's all the fuss? Nobody was injured and I'm sure we both have insurance on our vehicles. As soon as I'm released, I want to enjoy my vacation."

The officer said to his partner as they got into cruiser, "I think he's on drugs. Nobody is that happy when they wreck their car, especially a Lucid."

To summarize, what happened at the canyon isn't something that could be realistically applied to solve the rage killing problem. However, it did give us some ideas on how to proceed. I feel we determined some, if not the majority of the rage killings can be attributed to brain mutation as an aftereffect from Covid-19. I think a goal for us should be to help in any way we can to return the mutated brains to normal again. It may never happen but we should give it some serious thought.

CHAPTER 7

California Dreaming—Simone

After we finished our dinner, Joshua turned on the large flat screen TV in the lounge and we watched the news coming out of Flagstaff. Most of us were surprised to hear about the big dust up in the Grand Canyon parking lot. Joshua seemed like he'd already heard about it. Thankfully, no one was injured but we decided to head out for a little night drive to California.

But first, Pham gave us some interesting news which would change our travel plans, "Detective Hong has replied back to Joshua's email. He said he reminded his boss how you were instrumental in shutting down human trafficking at Portland's Terminal 6 almost two years ago. Hong also told his boss you were coming to the Portland area in about a week and were interested in helping out with the reduction of killings in Oregon. Hong's boss went up his chain of command. The bottom line is Portland's police commissioner went to the Governor and the Governor would like to meet with you and the team as soon as possible."

The rest of the team was impressed but somewhat wary. They were planning on some R&R and calling on old friends in the Portland area. A few of us expressed our concern about Joshua's health. Was he ready to get back into action?

"Hell yes," he said. "It'll be at least two or three days to drive to California if we head to San Francisco and bypass San Diego and LA. By the time we get to Oregon, I'll be in fighting shape. Send an email reply to Detective Hong telling him we should be in Salem within four days, if the good Lord's willing and the creek don't rise."

His comment was met by a chorus of groans and shaking of heads.

"What's all this negativity?" Joshua asked with a tone of annoyance.

Pham answered, "Boss, nobody under the age of ninety says anything about a rising creek. It's kind of embarrassing to hear you say it."

Joshua scowled and replied, "If it was good enough for my papa, it's good enough for me." He stood and we could see a slight smile forming as he added, "I think I'll take a little nap. That hike plum tuckered me out."

There was more moaning as he walked to the bedroom and closed the door behind him. I was sure he could hear the laughter coming from the lounge.

Mark sat in the driver's seat and fired up Sweet Ride's V-10 engine. Sarge jumped into the passenger seat and waited for me to connect his harness to the seat belt. Pham was cleaning up the kitchen and putting plates into the dishwasher as Mark entered our destination into the GPS.

It was going to be a 12-hour drive to San Francisco. The three of us would drive four hour shifts while Joshua caught up on his beauty rest. While Pham cleaned up the kitchen and locked down all the loose stuff, Mark retracted the two slide outs and turned down the cabin lights to a low glow. While the two men were busy, I did a quick walk-around to make sure all the external storage bays were locked down, double checked the awnings were retracted and looked to make sure nothing crawled under our motorhome. I also checked to make sure all our external lights were working. That included headlights, taillights and running lights.

Before I climbed back inside, I noticed a wrecked Lucid being hauled onto a tow truck bed. The motorhome the Lucid rammed into was nowhere in sight.

"We're ready to roll, Mark," I said and Sarge barked in agreement. Pham was sitting at the computer station with a dim dome light shining down on him. I sat down in a recliner and strapped in as Sweet Ride began moving out of the parking lot.

"We're going to stop in Williams to top off the fuel tanks before jumping onto the westbound I-40," said Mark. "It's all freeways from there to San Francisco."

I watched the lights from the traffic leaving the canyon through the massive windshield. When we arrived at a Quik Trip in Williams, I got out and handled the refueling. It took a while and I restocked snacks and drinks from the adjacent store while the tanks were being filled. Once the tanks were topped off, I climbed back aboard, stored the goodies and headed back into the master bedroom. Joshua was sound asleep and I joined him, setting my watch alarm for four hours from now. I was going to be the next driver.

CHAPTER 8

I Left My Heart in San Francisco—Joshua

Pham was scheduled to drive the last leg to San Francisco but I was well rested and decided to let him sleep. Simone pulled into a truck stop to refuel and I was waiting for her as she finished, paid for the gas and climbed back aboard.

"Hello, sleeping beauty. What are you doing up?" she asked.

"I got enough sleep and feel wide awake now. I told Pham to go back to sleep," I answered as I sat in the driver's seat. Actually, I had to wait a few minutes as the seat repositioned to accommodate the difference in size between Simone and myself.

A really nice feature on Sweet Ride was each driver could program their favorite driver seat position then store it in the seat's memory. All I had to do was tap the Seat 1 button and the seat automatically shifted for the proper height, distance to the pedals and incline angle on the back of the seat. It also adjusted the position of the steering wheel and side mirrors. Each of us programmed their desired seat position before we ever left WDC. I was Seat 1, Simone was 2, Pham 3 and Mark 4. The features I really liked the most were the heated seat and the chair massager for the driver's back and bottom. What more could a driver ask for?

I waited for Simone to walk back to the bedroom and gave her time to get into bed before I drove out of the truck stop and back onto the freeway. I also did a quick check of Pham and Mark and saw they were sound asleep on their beds. Sarge liked to sleep in the recliner next to Mark's sofa bed. I heard a chorus of snores as I headed for the freeway. When we crossed into California, the speed limit dropped to 65 mph.

Caleb and I had been conversing as the others slept. He began as soon as I sat down in the driver's seat, waited until the seat/mirror adjustments were made and turned on the butt massager. (Every vehicle I buy from now on will have massage capabilities.)

You know bro, we're never going to eliminate rage killings. They've been around since Cain slew Able. Having mutated brains may increase the number of murders but getting rid of guns will not keep people from getting pissed off enough to kill each other. Sure, without guns the head count will decline significantly and I agree that guns are the preferred way of killing. However, angry people will find other ways to destroy each other. When they don't have a gun to kill with, they will revert to what is ever handy, a knife or sword, a hammer, an ax or even a frying pan will do. I think killing someone with only your bare hands is the last resort. But you and I have both seen men and women beating someone they hate or fear into a bloody piece of dead meat. Until the good Lord comes again, this is going to continue.

I nodded as Sweet Ride accelerated to the California speed limit of 65 mph on the I-5 North and thought to him, *You're right, Caleb. However, that doesn't mean we shouldn't do our best to minimize murders of all kinds. We shouldn't become callous to the pain and suffering these killings cause, not only to the murder victim but also to those who loved them.*

What you did at the Grand Canyon was incredible. You saved not only the two men from gruesome murders, you saved a small child from being wounded in front of his parents. And you probably kept the accident scene from turning into a bloodbath. Did you know the girl who jumped out of the Lucid was also packing heat?

What?!! No, I didn't know that.

Simone mentioned she saw it on one of the news channels while you were debriefing me in the bedroom. There was another man and two women in the motorhome. All were carrying guns and about to exit their motorhome when the police stopped them and confiscated their weapons. Can you imagine how much collateral damage would have happened in that crowed parking lot?

Damn, Josh. That makes me a hero!

Don't let it go to your head, I thought back at him.

I don't have a head, he replied.

Just as well. It would have swelled to twice normal size. But yes Caleb, you're a hero. Unfortunately there aren't a hundred or a thousand of you to stop more rage murders. You can't do it all by yourself. We have to find a better way.

The sun should have risen an hour before we got to San Francisco but it was hard to tell with all the rain. The cloud cover was so thick the sun was invisible, just a small area of lighter gray. The freeway was drenched and very slippery and I noticed several cars and one semi-truck and trailer rig that spun out and sitting off the shoulder of the highway. I had to slow down to maintain control of our ride. However, there were some drivers who thought they could weave in and out of traffic to maintain the speed limit of 65 mph. Of course that led to a number of accidents and even more near misses. It was a perfect setting for road rage.

A silver Mustang zoomed by us doing at least 75 mph, the driver acting like Richard Petty. It only took him a few minutes before he disappeared in the heavy rain. Ten minutes later all lanes of traffic were at a standstill.

Fifteen minutes later, two highway patrol cars went by us on the shoulder with flashing lights and screaming sirens. The sirens were loud enough to wake the rest of the team. Sarge jumped into the passenger side seat with his front paws on the dash as he looked out the windshield.

Simone came up behind me and looked over my shoulder at the stopped traffic. "What happened?" she asked.

"Not sure," I answered. "I think there was a traffic accident which has caused everyone to stop."

Mark joined Sarge on the passenger seat and they both tried to see what happened, the visibility was probably less than a 100 yards.

Pham stood looking out the windshield for a few seconds then went back to his computer to see if he could get any news update. "No news yet," he said.

A moment later, he heard the distinct whumping sound of a helicopter. It appeared out the bottom of the cloud layer. It was a rescue helicopter and it slowly moved up the median and we watched until the rain obscured it from view. We could still here the rotors whumping but it was fading and eventually we could no longer hear it.

It took another half hour before they opened one lane of the freeway. The helicopter lifted off fifteen minutes before that and we watched it disappear into the clouds. Traffic moved very slowly until we passed the scene of the wreck. It looked like at least three vehicles were involved. It was hard to tell because there was so much destruction. The only car I recognized was the back of the silver Mustang. There was no front end, just a merger of twisted metal, plastic and glass covered in blood. As hard as it was raining, I thought the rain would have washed it away.

After we passed the wreck, all the highway lanes were opened and traffic began to pick up speed. I moved to the slow lane and set the cruise control for 60 mph. There were a lot of other cars moving at a slower pace but before the rain stopped, a couple of cars and one pickup truck went by us doing at least 90 mph. What is wrong with those people? This wasn't road rage, it was just plain stupidity.

The rain stopped when we reach San Jose. It was early morning and the skies were bright blue dotted with puffy white clouds. We were a little behind schedule due to the traffic accident as we turned onto I-280 North, merged with the I-5 and headed up to San Francisco.

The rest of the team was up and about. It was about an hour's drive from San Jose to San Francisco and I decided to continue driving until we were on the north side of the Golden Gate Bridge.

We'd stop for a quick breakfast in Sweet Ride at a rest area near the bridge. Mark would be the next driver as we headed north to Oregon.

I exited I-5 North to Highway 101, also called the Pacific Coast Highway. It extends all the way from San Diego in the south to the northern most part of the state of Washington. It's a beautiful scenic drive, unfortunately we were only going to see a small portion of it as we crossed the Golden Gate.

Before we got to the bridge, Pham asked me, "Do you want the good news or the bad news, boss?"

"Give me the bad news first," I answered. "I like to hear the good news last. It gives me a better frame of mind."

"Okay," he said with a smile. "There's a hefty toll to cross the bridge."

I gave him a quick glare, then asked as I turned my attention to the approach to the bridge, "How hefty."

"Fifty dollars for the motorhome and trailer," he replied.

"Really?" asked Mark who sat down in the front passenger seat with Sarge. "That seems way too much."

"I agree but we're only going to make the crossing once and I hear there's a great view of the bay," said Simone as she walked up behind my seat.

"Not to worry," said Pham. "You only have to pay the toll when you cross the bridge going south."

Caleb thought to me, *About time we caught a break,* as we started up the ramp to the bridge.

Traffic on the bridge was heavy and slow during the morning rush hour. There were sidewalks on both sides of the bridge with fences that permitted pedestrians to walk across or to just go far enough to get a terrific view of San Francisco Bay. Caleb informed me it was also a fairly popular spot to commit suicide, until a metal netting was recently installed to catch the jumpers.

As we started our drive across the bridge our team gathered to take in the view. Mark had been to San Francisco several times and visited some of the tourist sites. He shared about his visit to the prison on Alcatraz which now was a tourist attraction. He'd also been to Treasure Island located half way across the bay from Oakland.

"Oh look!" said Simone. "A little boat is sailing under the bridge."

Mark looked at Pham and they both began to laugh.

"What's so funny?" asked Simone.

"That's not a little boat, Simone," said Pham. "It's an aircraft carrier. It just looks little because it's a long way down from the bridge to the water."

We crossed the bridge and pulled into the first rest stop to have our breakfast, stretch our legs and get another view of the bay. About an hour after our stop we refueled and continued our journey northward to Salem, the capitol of Oregon. It was going to take a little more than nine hours to reach Salem but according to both Mark and Pham, it was a pretty scenic ride; we'd be arriving in Salem around 6:00 pm.

Mark was driving with Sarge in the passenger seat. Pham was on the computer checking for updates from the governor's office. He was also going to contact Detective Hong to see what we could expect regarding bringing our weapons and War Wagon into the state. Simone was watching for news updates on the TV. Caleb decided to transport to the Oregon border to see firsthand what we could expect.

Noticing my expert team had everything covered, I decided to take a nap.

CHAPTER 9

Checking the Border Crossing—Caleb

The I-5 enters Oregon near Siskiyou Summit. The summit has an elevation of just over 4,300 feet and was usually snow-covered in winter. It was fall and there hadn't been any snow yet but the sky was lead gray from horizon to horizon with intermittent drizzle, typical for Oregon this time of year.

The Oregon Army National Guard set up a checkpoint at a rest stop just north of the Oregon border and three miles south of the summit. All vehicles entering Oregon were required to undergo an inspection before being allowed to continue northward. If any firearms were found, the drivers were allowed to choose from three options. First option: If their firearms met the requirements of the new law, they were allowed to continue into the state. Second option: If their firearms didn't meet the requirements of the new law and they didn't wish to surrender them, they were escorted to the southbound lanes of the I-5 and required to return to California. Third Option: If their firearms didn't meet the requirements of the new law and they chose to continue into Oregon, their firearms were confiscated and they were allowed to proceed.

If unlawful firearms were discovered and their owners refused to surrender them, the firearms were confiscated anyway and their owners were arrested. If they resisted arrest, the Oregon Army National Guard troops were authorized to use whatever force necessary to keep them from entering the state.

I stayed at the checkpoint for a couple of days (and nights) to observe the inspection procedure and was very impressed at the thoroughness of the guard member searches. I was mildly surprised at how many dogs were used to help speed up the inspections. Sarge would be proud of how quickly they could find the clandestine weapons.

The inspection procedure was as follows: The inspections were divided into three lanes. The first lane was for motorcycles and passenger cars, including SUVs. This lane went very fast. If any illegal firearms were found, the vehicles were sent to a holding area and the drivers and passengers were given their three options.

The second lane was for pickup trucks and vans. They took a little longer than the first lane but still went pretty fast; when no firearms were found they were on their way in five to ten minutes.

The last lane was for big trucks, semi-truck and trailer rigs, motorhomes, fifth wheelers and anyone towing a trailer. They could take up to half an hour to complete the inspection. Our Sweet Ride towing a trailer with the War Wagon inside was going to take longer.

There were at least six state police cruisers available to chase down any bolters who decided to see if they could outrun the law. While I was there I saw at least a dozen bolters. Their attempted escapes brought to mind the lyrics from an old song: *I fought the law and the law won.*

Bolters were transferred to prisoner transport busses along with those detained by the guard and driven to the a nearby building recently refurbished with holding cells.

The confiscated firearms were collected and stored in an armored truck. Once the car was full, it was escorted by one of the state police cruisers to a nearby firearms recycling facility for destruction. There were two armored trucks used for the firearms transport.

I was very impressed with the whole system. I found out they had similar checkpoints at every main highway with a border crossings not only with California but also all of them connecting Washington and Idaho. I also discovered they had inspections set up at every major port along the Oregon coast from Astoria to Coos Bay and up the Colombia River to the several ports in Portland. In addition, inspections were done at most of the state's major airports.

Of course it was impossible to cover every highway, seaport and airport all day, every day but there was a plan to randomly check the smaller ones every once in a while, using local police and sheriffs.

I wanted to see just how effective the inspection process was. Did it justify the expense? One metric I'm sure Pham would be interested in was the cost of inspection, confiscation and firearm destruction per firearm. As expected, it wasn't cheap. The number of firearms destroyed or modified to a single shot version was available and that final number was staggering. The first week it was over 10,000 and each week it declined. A month after the governor's laws were in place, approximately 25,000 firearms were off the streets.

Of course the two major metrics of interest to the governor and the public at large were how many people had been shot and how many people had died from those shootings. The first week, there were significant reductions in both categories and the trend continued for two more weeks but after that, it seemed to plateau. The governor was a realist. He knew they would never eliminate shooting deaths but he felt the current number of deaths-by-gun remained unacceptably high. He wanted to know why and how to get that number lower, as low as was humanly possible, especially the deaths of children.

I felt pretty sure that was the question the governor was going to ask Joshua.

CHAPTER 10

Run for the Border—Joshua

I woke from my nap well rested. Mark just finished driving his leg of the trip to Oregon and pulled into a gas station near a rest stop. The early autumn drizzle had stopped and a few holes in the stratus cloud cover let the blue sky peek through.

Sarge was the first one out the door looking for a place to do his business. The rest stop was surrounded by hundreds of large pine trees. To me any tree with needles instead of leaves is a pine tree, even if it's a fir, a spruce or some other breed of tree with pine cones.

We watched as Sarge ran from tree to tree, trying to decide which was the perfect business tree. He must have stopped to sniff at least ten of them before he found the perfect one. He circled the massive tree several times but stopped on the back side. His business completed, he bolted from behind the tree, ran to an adjacent giant pine and dove into piles of needles at the base of the tree. He rolled around on his back making a lot of grunting noises while we all watched his antics. After a few minutes he stood up, shook a few times to get rid of the pine needles stuck to his fur, picked up a pine cone in his mouth and ran towards us. He stopped in front of Simone and dropped the cone at her feet.

Simone said in a sing song voice, "For me, Sarge? What a good dog. Thank you so much for the present!"

Sarge licked her hand, barked twice, then bounded into our motorhome and waited for the rest of us.

Pham took care of refueling Sweet Ride while Simone carried her pine cone in one hand as we walked to the convenience store to get some snacks. When the tanks were topped off and all the snacks were purchased we got back aboard and headed out for the second leg.

Simone was driving and I took the passenger seat while Pham went back to the computer with a strawberry fruit juice bottle in one hand and a bag of nachos in the other. Mark and Sarge shared a recliner as they watched a replay of the Oregon State Beaver's football team play against the Ole Miss Landsharks. Since neither Mark nor I had seen the game, it was just like watching it live. I moved from the passenger seat to the other recliner to root for Old Miss. Mark, who'd played for OSU, and I really enjoyed trash talking each other. Ole Miss won by a healthy margin but truth be told, the Beavers played a very physical game. It was really great to step away from the real world and all its problems for a few hours and just enjoy a football game. Caleb timed his return from the Oregon border checkpoint to be with me for the game. It really brought back good memories for us both.

When it ended, Caleb gave me a debrief on the checkpoints. He also shared some of the metrics regarding the impact of the governor's new gun laws.

I'd put air buds in both ears with my smart phone on my lap then closed my eyes. Hopefully, I appeared to my team to be listening to music as I listened to Caleb's report. A few minutes after he finished, Pham touched me on the shoulder to get my attention.

"Boss, I got some news from Detective Hong," he said. "Is now a good time for me to tell you what he said?"

I appeared to be shutting off the non-existent music and pulled the air buds from my ears and answered him, "Sure, Pham. Now's good. Let's move up front and you can pass the intel on to all of us."

Simone switched on the autopilot as Pham updated us. I sat in the passenger seat while Mark and Sarge stood behind me. Pham stood in between Simone and I.

"It's pretty much all good," he said. "Hong informed us that we will not have to give up any of our weapons when we cross into Oregon. The Governor's office will send us a document that says we don't have to even go through the inspection process. He will be sending me a copy of the document and also to Colonel Pete Legleu, the commander of the Oregon Army National Guard and the head of the Governor's security team. He is supposed to meet us at the checkpoint and escort us to the Governor's office in Salem. We are asked not to carry any visible weapons while in the capitol building."

"That is good news!" I said and everyone agreed.

The rest of Simone's drive was uneventful. It was the first time we'd used the autopilot feature and it worked as advertised. Traffic had been light and during Pham's update the autopilot kept us right on track with no alerts. However, I noticed while Pham was speaking, everyone, especially Simone, kept glancing out the windshield checking to make sure we were on the right path. When Simone's drive time was over we made a brief pit stop to change drivers.

Ten minutes later, I climbed into the driver's seat, fired up the V-10 Triton engine and made sure the autopilot was in the standby position. I was old school. It wasn't that I didn't trust the technology, I just trusted myself more.

It was a little before 5:00 pm when we arrived at the Oregon border. We'd slowed down to barely a snail's pace at about 4:30 pm and crawled the next half hour until we arrived at the checkpoint. As advertised, traffic was divided into three lanes and we were diverted to lane three with the big trucks, vehicles pulling trailers and other motorhomes.

We crept along stop and go until finally a team of several National Guard members and one dog who could sniff out firearms approached us. Actually, the dog could smell the residue of the gun powder that remained in the cleanest of firearms.

When Sarge saw the dog through the side window he got all excited. One of the soldiers gestured for us to stop and open the passenger side door at mid cabin. Pham met her at the open door with the document from the governor's office. She read it quickly and waved for us to move out of the lane and head to the inspection area.

I shut down Sweet Ride and stepped outside to speak to the inspector. She reread the document and I could see her frown. "I'm sorry sir but we haven't received any notification that verifies this document."

I frowned back and said, "Colonel Pete Legleu is supposed to meet us here and accompany us to Salem for a private meeting with the governor."

She turned back to one of her inspection team members and yelled, "Corporal Kline, check with HQ and see if the Colonel is supposed to meet with these people."

"Roger that, Lieutenant," came the reply and the young man did a quick about face and jogged to a double-wide trailer they used for an office. Two minutes later he jogged back, "The Colonel is in route. ETA 10 minutes. No inspection required. The Colonel offered his apologies for the inconvenience."

The lieutenant raised an eyebrow in surprise. "That's the first time I've ever heard him apologize to anyone. Who are you people?"

I put my finger to my lips then said, "It's a secret."

She rolled her eyes as she shook her head in disbelief then turned to her team and said, "We're done here. Head to the next lane three vehicle. She turned back to me and said, "Enjoy your stay in Oregon, Secret Agent Man." Then she jogged after her team.

The rest of us climbed out of our motorhome and I began to say something to Mark when Sarge bolted by us and headed toward another inspection team. One of the team members was leading his dog around the vehicle. Sarge blew past them and ran around to the car's trunk and quickly sat down. He barked twice as he starred at the trunk. The soldier looked around trying to identify where Sarge had come from.

He looked at our team and yelled, "Is this your dog?"

Mark yelled back, "Yes he is. I think your dog may have missed a weapon in the trunk of that car."

The dog handler glared at Mark and yelled at him, "You need to control you dog."

Mark responded casually, "Why don't you check the trunk of that car first. Probably under a spare tire or maybe in one of the wheel wells."

The handler yanked hard on the dog's leash and almost drug the whining animal to the back of the car. He had the driver open the trunk and surprise, surprise. They discovered two Uzi machine guns in one of the wheel wells and a semiautomatic assault rifle in the other.

The handler totally lost his cool and began shouting angrily at his dog and yanking hard on his collar as the dog whined in pain.

Before I could stop Mark, he was running towards the handler to restrain him from hurting his dog any further. Sarge beat him to it. He lunged at the man and chomped down on his groin. Now it was his turn to whine and cry.

The man was screaming, "Get this wolf off of me. He attacked me. I want him put down."

Mark signaled Sarge to let go of the handler and he immediately released his grip on the man's private parts and moved to sit quietly beside Mark.

Another member of the inspection team checked out the handler and called for a medic. The team leader looked at his man's injuries and walked over to Mark. "I need to take control of your dog."

"Not happening," replied Mark. "Your man is at fault. He was injuring his own dog and my dog stopped him."

"He could have killed my man," responded the team leader.

"No way" answered Mark. "If Sarge wanted him dead, he would have killed him instantly. He was only restraining your man from further damaging his own dog. Your man isn't even injured. Sarge is a Marine trained dog and I'm his handler. Your man has no business working with a dog. He doesn't have the patience required to train a dog correctly."

By then the medic spoke up, "Your man is fine. No injuries at all but he may need to change his shorts."

The team leader turned to the rest of the team and asked, "Did anyone see Private Sharp mistreating his dog?"

Two of the team members nodded. One said, "We've told him several times not to treat his dog so roughly but he'd just blow us off. He'd always say he knew how to train a dog and we didn't."

The team leader turned to the handler and looked disgusted as he said, "As of now, you're on report, meet me in the trailer." He looked around at the rest of the team and asked, "Does anyone here know how to care for a dog? We need to have him checked out by a vet to see if he's okay. But there aren't any vets stationed out here."

When nobody volunteered, Mark looked at me and I nodded my approval. He stepped up and said, "I'll check him out if it's okay with you."

The team leader looked warily at Mark, then asked, "Are you sure you want to do this?"

"Absolutely," Mark replied with a smile. He gently picked up the dog and carried him to Sweet Ride with Sarge walking behind him with what looked like a dog grin to me.

CHAPTER 11

The Leader of the Pack—Caleb

Mark, with the help of Simone, checked out the dog while Sarge sat quietly watching every move they made. I also watched. I was curious to see how they treated the dog's injuries. I considered using my spirit skills if they needed them but after a few minutes it was obvious they were getting the job done without my help. I decided to split my time between watching the dog repair and what was happening with Josh and Pham.

The dog was panting heavily interspersed with whining caused by the pain. Mark gently restrained the dog as Simone very carefully removed the choke chain collar from the dog's neck. Simone examined the collar for some kind of ID tag, but quickly put the collar down on the table and said, "The tag says his name is Brute and his collar is covered in blood."

"His neck has multiple bleeding wounds," said Mark. "They're not deep but I'm sure they're painful. Simone, can you get the vet med kit? It's with Sarge's other stuff under the sink."

She found the kit and gave it to Mark who took out a packet of gauze pads. The pads were coated with a mixture of antiseptic and lidocaine. The antiseptic was to prevent infection and the lidocaine was to reduce the pain. He used a beard trimmer to remove the fur around wound sites then cleaned the wounds with the gauze pads. Next, he took out a sedative filled small syringe from the med kit and gave Brute a shot. Within minutes the panting stopped and the dog relaxed as he drifted off to sleep.

Simone used her smart phone to take multiple pictures of the dog's injuries to document the treatment Mark provided, just in case anyone had any doubt how badly the dog had been treated.

Mark took out a cushion from under the sink. Sarge rarely slept on it, but Mark asked Sarge if it was okay for Brute to rest on the cushion. Sarge barked twice to signal it was okay. Simone placed the cushion in the master bedroom next to one of the chairs. Mark carried the dog and gently laid him on the cushion. Sarge followed them in and immediately laid down next to the dog. He licked the injured dog on the top of his head once and curled up next to him. Mark didn't have to give Sarge any orders. He knew instinctively he was to watch and protect his newly found friend.

As Mark and Simone quietly closed the bedroom door behind them, Simone commented, "We should change the dog's name. He shouldn't be called Brute. That would be a better name for his handler."

Meeting with the Colonel—Joshua

While Mark and Simone took care of the injured search dog, Pham and I waited outside our motorhome to meet with Colonel Legleu. Caleb was bouncing back and forth between us. Apparently, he didn't want to miss anything.

I was the first to hear the *whump-whump* of the approaching helicopter. The rain temporarily subsided but the sky remained overcast as the bird came in over the landing pad, hovered briefly as it turned into the wind, then gently touched down.

One man jumped out of the open side door and ran slightly bent over to avoid the still moving rotor blades. When clear of the blades, he stood up and walked briskly towards us. He was wearing his Army National Guard uniform and I could see the silver eagles on his shoulder epaulets identifying him as a colonel. Two others, very large men also in National Guard uniforms, followed quickly behind the colonel. I assumed they were his body guards, both were well muscled and almost as tall as me but not as well muscled nor as good looking. As the colonel introduced himself, the two men continued to scan the area for potential threats. All three wore battle vests and carried side arms. I was surprised to see the colonel was Hispanic, not that it mattered but I was pretty sure Legleu was a French name so the unique mix was not something I ran into often.

I invited the three of them into Sweet Ride to continue our discussions but the colonel shook his head and said, "I'll join you inside your motorhome but my two men will stand guard outside. First, I need another ten minutes to handle a disciplinary issue."

He turned abruptly, and headed for the office trailer, his two security people on either side of him still scanning for potential trouble. As I watched them, Mark and Simone stepped out of Sweet Ride to join us.

"Is that the Colonel?" asked Mark.

"Yes," I answered. "I think he's going to visit the dog abuser before he meets with us."

Mark turned to Simone and said, "Let's join them. I want them to see the pictures you took of Brute's wounds."

As they hurried to catch up with the colonel and his bodyguards, Pham and I climbed aboard our motorhome to wait for all of them to return. Ten minutes later, Mark opened the door and he, Simone and Colonel Legleu entered.

"Welcome aboard, Colonel. Let me introduce you to my team. You've already met Mark. He's a highly decorated Marine. He was a dog handler during the war in Afghanistan. His dog, Sarge, is also a highly decorated Marine and member of our team. You'll meet him later. Simone is a former DEA agent and was the DEA lead for our last mission."

I paused and the colonel asked, "Would that be the mission in New Orleans where you took down five major drug cartels?"

I nodded and the colonel added, "That was some piece of work. I heard you almost died, shot several times by rogue US Marshalls. That wasn't too long ago. Are you fully recovered?"

I smiled and replied, "I'm almost good as new. I was fortunate to have a great medical team available."

Caleb thought to me, *That weren't no medical team, bro. Dat was all me. Tell this dude it was the spirit of your dead brother that saved your bacon.*

Maybe later, Caleb. I thought back.

I gestured to Pham and continued my introductions, "This is Pham Bin Minh, also a Marine and a sharp shooter during Afghanistan. He's an accredited lawyer in the state of Oregon and handles all of our legal issues. He is also our IT guru. Have a seat," I said.

Mark and Simone headed for the bedroom to check on the injured dog as Pham and I joined the colonel at our dining table.

"Let's get to it," began the colonel. "First, let me apologize again for all the delays. This last one is really disturbing. I need to find out how that private ever became a dog handler," he fumed. "Then he tried to deny he'd injured his dog. Even when your people showed me the pictures of the dog's injuries, he denied everything. What an asshole."

He paused for a moment to change gears, then said, "Well that's enough of that issue. Let me layout what Governor Johnson has in mind. First, logistics. My two assistants and I will be joining you and your team on the trip to Salem. That will take about an hour. Once we arrive at the capitol, Mr. Brown will do a meet-and-greet with the Governor."

I interrupted him and asked, "Will my team be joining us?"

He shook his head and answered, "Unfortunately no. For security reasons, we are limiting the number of people who visit with the Governor. He has received a number of death threats since his new firearm laws went into effect. Even though we screen all of the Governor's visitors, there have been two recent attempts to assassinate him."

"Really?" I looked at Pham.

"There were no reports of assassination attempts on any of the news channels," Pham replied.

"That's correct," said the colonel. "The attempts came in the Governor's office. One was with a knife, the other by strangulation. Neither attempt was released to the press. As a result of those attempts, every visitor has to undergo a body scan before entering the office and once inside, they must stay on the other side of the Governor's desk. All visitors must be escorted either my myself or one of my vetted security guards. We remain in the office with the Governor until the meeting is over."

"Strangulation doesn't seem like a very likely method to kill somebody," I said.

The colonel smiled and replied, "You're correct, it isn't. It was attempted by a former member of the Oregon senate. He lost his seat in the house in the recent primary election and he blamed it on

Governor Johnson. What started out as a calm discussion ended up in barroom brawl. The ex-senator asked for a private meeting with the Governor and he complied with the request. I was standing outside the office door but when I heard the yelling and screaming I entered the office and subdued the ex-senator. As a result of that attempt, there will not be any private meetings, at least not in the near future."

"Is there anyway the Governor can be introduced to my team?" I asked.

"Yes, of course," replied the colonel. "We have a small conference room adjacent to the Governor's office. Are you familiar with Zoom?"

"I am," answered Pham. "It's a way to conduct live meetings between people in different locations. With the right set up, those locations can be in adjacent rooms, locations in different states or locations across the world. Zoom meetings can have both video and audio so it's about as close to having the meeting in the same room as possible."

"That's correct, Pham," replied the colonel. "So when I introduce Mr. Brown to the Governor, he can also be introduced to the rest of the team in the adjacent conference room. After the introductions, the Governor has requested that the rest of the meeting will be limited to the three of us. Apparently, he wants to limit his comments to prevent them from leaking to the media."

I frowned and said, "Colonel, I can vouch for my team. They all have top secret clear…"

The colonel raised his hand to stop me. "This has nothing to do with your team members. Our concern is that Zoom might be hacked and comments intended for a limited audience could go viral. Feel free to share the details of the Governor's comments with your team."

Mark stepped out of the bedroom with Sarge in tow. I could sense the colonel was surprised at the size of Sarge. Sarge paused a step, then continued walking beside Mark. "Colonel, this is the last member of our team. His name is Sarge. Sarge this is Colonel Legleu. The Colonel is our friend."

Sarge continued to walk toward the colonel and sat down next to him. "Colonel, please pet Sarge on the head and say hello. After you've done this he will be your friend."

Without hesitation, the colonel reached out and placed his hand on Sarge's head and pet him as he said, "Hello Sarge. Am I your friend? I sure hope so. I would never want to be your enemy." Sarge barked once, wagged his tail and laid down next to the colonel.

The colonel looked up at Mark and said, "Thank you, Mark. Sarge is one remarkable friend."

Mark responded, "Thank you, Colonel. I agree." Then added, "We're burning daylight, anybody interested in getting to Salem?"

The colonel nodded and I said to Mark, "You've got the helm. Let's head out."

Mark sat down and touched the number 4 button and fired up the V-10 while his seat and mirrors repositioned themselves. He switched the video display to give him a rear view from the War Wagon trailer.

The colonel comm'd his security detail to come aboard and there was a knock on the door. I opened it and the two men entered and strapped into the recliners.

Simone came out of the bedroom and sat next to Mark in the passenger seat while Pham, the colonel and I remained at the dining table with Sarge still lying by the colonel's feet.

Mark turned his head and glanced back at the interior of the motorhome and asked, "Is the ship secured?"

I did a quick glance on the living area and answered, "The ship is secured."

He turned to Simone, "Are we clear aft?"

She checked the view behind the trailer and reported, "All clear aft."

Mark glanced at me and asked, "Is the word given, boss?"

I nodded and answered, "The word is given. You are cleared to launch."

Mark put the select lever into reverse and slowly backed Sweet Ride clear of all obstacles. He shifted to drive and moved forward, bypassing the checkpoint traffic and merging with 1-5 North. As we picked up speed, Simone began to sing in a low voice, "On the road again. I can't wait to get on the road again, making music with my friends. I can't wait to get on the road again."

The colonel smiled and said, "Thank you Willie Nelson."

CHAPTER 12

The Capitol Building, Salem, Oregon—Caleb

A few minutes before we arrived in Salem, I thought to Joshua, *Josh, we need a secure place to store Sweet Ride and the War Wagon trailer. Maybe the Colonel could help us with that.*

Glad you thought of that, Caleb.

"Colonel, we need a secure location for our motorhome and trailer. Is there anywhere close to the capitol complex we can use?"

"Good question, Joshua. There is an underground parking garage reserved for state government staff and visitors like yourselves. There are two general entrances and exits to the garage area and one secured parking area with separate entrance and exit. There is a security person on duty twenty-four/seven at the entrance and that part of the garage has routine security patrols who walk the area every twenty minutes."

Josh, don't forget to tell him about the built-in security features on the motorhome and War Wagon.

Give me a break, Caleb. It was next on my list.

"Colonel, we have a pretty sophisticated security system on our motorhome and the vehicle in the trailer." *Are you happy now?* my brother thought to me.

"Could you brief me on their features?" asked the colonel.

"If anyone comes within ten feet of either vehicle, a very loud alarm sounds. If they get within five feet a voice will give a verbal warning," answered Joshua.

"What does the verbal warning say?"

"Something to the effect that if they touch either vehicle they will receive an electric shock which could cause severe pain, unconsciousness and possibly death," replied Joshua.

The colonel sat quietly for a moment before asking, "Is that a bluff?"

Joshua replied, "No sir. It's not a bluff. So far nobody has died but most people who have ignored the warning were shocked unconscious, some had to be hospitalized."

The colonel paused for another moment, then said, "Duly noted. In addition to your security system, we will cordon off the area around both the motorhome and the trailer."

Colonel Legleu directed us to the entrance to the secure underground garage. He called ahead to make sure the capitol security people responsible for our parking space were there to guide us in. Mark and Sarge decided to stay onboard Sweet Ride with the injured dog. The rest of the team (minus me) headed to the elevator which would take them to Governor Johnson's office and his nearby conference room with a big screen Zoom set up. Pham set up the onboard computer so that Mark could also sit in on the Zoom session.

Mark had been directed to park the motorhome and trailer next to a concrete wall which prevented anyone getting near the starboard side or our boat. That left only the door on the port side next to the driver's seat.

The garage crew brought in heavy wooden barricades that completely blocked access to the motorhome and trailer. In my opinion the barricades were the perfect way to discourage anyone from approaching our ride and trailer. With Mark and Sarge inside we were doubly protected.

<u>Getting to Know You, Getting to Know All About You—Caleb</u>

Being totally satisfied with the setup, I transported just outside the governor's small conference room as the rest of the team, without Joshua, entered. I noticed Colonel Legleu's two bodyguards replaced the other guards as Joshua and Colonel Legleu entered the main office. I decided I should follow them.

My first reaction to the office was, it's good to be king. While Colonel Legleu introduced Governor Johnson to my brother, I snooped around the office. I saw the camera for the Zoom meeting and a large TV (maybe 85 inches) that served as the monitor.

I could see the rest of the team on the monitor and they sat quietly in the small conference room as Joshua and Governor Johnson exchanged small talk. There was a brief blip on the screen as the monitor added Mark and Sarge to the display. Joshua and the governor sat down in what appeared to be very comfortable chairs. The governor remained behind his enormous desk that had more bells and whistles than a circus calliope. As I peeked over the governor's shoulder, I must have seen half a dozen different display screens under the glass top covering the desk. They all went dark as the governor gave his full attention to the introduction of our team members.

Following the protocol established by Colonel Legleu, Joshua sat in a chair on the other side of the desk as he began the introductions. The colonel stood at the right side of the desk, closest to the governor. He never sat down and kept scanning the room for any indication of trouble.

I was moderately surprised the governor spent so much time with each team member. He must have had one of his people brief him on each of the team but he acted as if we were longtime friends. That would exclude me, of course. Only Joshua knew I existed. The governor had no idea how much I contributed to the team. But it didn't bother me, at least not too much.

When he came to Mark, the governor's whole demeanor changed. There was a touch of sadness in his voice, "Mark, I understand you were born and raised in Oregon, is that correct?"

"Yes sir. I lived most of my life in Portland except when I attended college at Oregon State in Corvallis."

"When did you move to the Woodlawn District?" he asked Mark.

"After our tour in Afghanistan with the Marines, Sarge and I decided to move closer to my parents. They lived about a mile from me on Dekum Street," Mark answered.

"What a splendid dog you have. I was told he also served in Afghanistan with you and both of you were highly decorated. Thank you both for your service," he replied and I could detect his voice was getting softer and sadder.

"Just doing our duty, Governor but thank you," replied Mark.

I thought he was going to move on to Pham but he surprised me, "Mark, I understand you graduated from OSU and before that you were at Benson Polytechnic High School but could you tell me where you attended elementary school?"

Mark paused before answering, realizing where this was going. He was looking down at Sarge who stood up and leaned against Mark's leg, sensing something was bothering him. Mark looked down as he reached out and rested a hand on the big dog's head and said, "It's okay, Sarge. I'm fine" Then he looked up at the governor and said, "I attended Woodlawn Elementary School. It was a short walk from my parent's house. Some of the best years of my childhood were at that school."

There was complete silence in both rooms and motorhome for what seemed like an eternity before the governor spoke again, his voice barely a whisper, "Have you visited the school since the...the incident?"

"Not yet, sir. But I plan to. I understand they're turning it into a memorial site," said Mark and I could see tears forming in the eyes of the governor as well as our team.

The governor tried to speak but he was so choked with emotion, nothing came out. He glance up at the colonel who took his cue and said, "I think it's time for a short break. We'll regroup in ten."

Joshua stood up and headed for the conference room. As he passed through the office lobby into the hall, I thought to Joshua, *Are you okay, bro?*

Without stopping he thought to me, *I've been better…a lot better.*

We regrouped and ended up with Josh introducing Pham, another life-long Oregonian. I thanked God he grew up nowhere near the Woodlawn District.

Let's Get Down to the Real Nitty Gritty—Joshua

With the introductions completed, those of the crew in the conference room headed back to our motorhome with one of Colonel Legleu's bodyguards providing escort. I called ahead to let Mark know they were coming and to deactivate the alarm system until they were aboard.

An IT tech removed all of the Zoom equipment and I secretly asked Caleb to scan the room for any bugs. He was happy to comply as the governor, the colonel and I sat down at a table in one corner of the office as Caleb reported the office was clean. Before we began, an orderly brought in a tray of snacks and drinks on a cart with crystal glasses, small China dishes and linen napkins. Like Caleb said, it's good to be king.

We each took something from the snack cart and sat down at the table with at least six feet of separation.

Governor Johnson finished his pastry, took a sip of coffee and opened a folder with what I presumed were his notes on what he wanted our team to accomplish. Before he could speak, Caleb thought to me, *There's bugs on the snack cart. Don't say anything. Activate your own scanner.*

I reached into my pocket and touched the button on my scanner; it began to beep immediately. The colonel looked at me as I put my finger to my lips, stood up and moved to the snack cart. I pulled my scanner from my pocket and swept the cart. I killed the audio alert and my scanner went into blinking light mode. The closer I got to the bug the more rapid the blinking. When the light stopped blinking red and went to a continuous green, it was within an inch of the bug. I discovered three bugs in a matter of seconds, one under the silver coffee pot, one under the snack tray and one attached to the cart. Caleb was looking over my shoulder and chatting non-stop.

Without touching the bugs, I pushed the cart out of the office and into the lobby. I told the security guard to find the person who'd brought in the cart and restrain him. I didn't want the orderly speaking to anyone until I got back.

When I went into the office, I could see the colonel was angry. "Joshua, thank you for your quick action but I'm in charge of the Governor's safety. Don't start giving my people orders. You need to work through me," he said with a glare.

I turned to him and glared back. "Colonel, I was nearly killed twice during last year because I didn't take charge of my own security. I'm not going to bet the third time's a charm. I would suggest you have the snack cart in the conference room searched for bugs. Don't let your people touch any bugs they find. They may have fingerprints that could lead to who placed the bugs on the carts. I would also recommend you have the Governor's office, lobby and conference room swept again before the Governor goes over any orders he has for me. I'll be waiting in my motorhome."

I turned back to the governor who looked stunned by what just happened in his office. "I look forward to hearing your plans for my team, Governor, just as soon we are reasonably sure your enemies aren't listening in."

Without further discussion, I walked to the elevator, escorted by the other bodyguard and sequestered myself and my team in Sweet Ride. An hour later, I was requested back at the governor's office. The same bodyguard escorted me into the office.

Before either the governor or the colonel could speak, I said, "Did you find any prints on the bugs?"

Colonel Legleu answered, "Yes, and we discovered at least two sets of prints. We haven't yet identified the owners of those prints but we're searching our database and expect to have the prints ID'd soon."

"Which database are you using?" I asked gruffly.

"Why do you ask?" he replied, just as gruffly.

"Because I have access to databases you don't have and faster search engines. By now, whoever placed the bugs on the cart or carts are aware we are looking for them. They will be looking to get out of town as quickly as possible."

Before he could rebut me, I asked, "Have you caught the orderly who delivered the carts?"

"No," he answered reluctantly. "The regular orderly didn't show up for work and a temp was brought in to replace him."

"Have you sent someone to detain the orderly who didn't show up for work? You should be questioning him right now. Did you check with the temp agency to ID the replacement for the regular orderly? If so, you need to bring that person in for questioning right now and see if their prints match the ones on the bugs."

I stopped talking and waited for the colonel to reply. "You can't talk to me like that!" he fumed, barely in control of his temper.

"I just did and I will continue to talk to you like that until I get answers to the questions I just asked you. I want these people caught. I want to find out who's behind the bugging. The bugs they used were very sophisticated which means they are very expensive which means powerful people are trying to get information to sabotage the Governor's plans. I believe the first mission for my team is to neutralize these people. They will turn out to be an important part of the reason the number of killings isn't declining."

I stopped talking and quit glaring at the colonel. Then I glanced at the governor who'd been staring at me as I dressed down his security chief. "What do you think, Governor? What are your orders for me and my team?"

He looked at me with an expression of determination. "You're in charge of bringing down the people behind the bugging of my offices."

He turned and stared at the colonel and said, "You 're to turn over any and all information he requests regarding his investigation. Your job is to make sure nobody kills me until my goals to reduce the killings, the firearm killings are met. Do you understand?"

I could tell he wasn't happy with the governor's decision but without hesitation he answered, "Yes Governor, I understand. Mr. Brown, I will provide all the information you requested."

He turned to the governor, came to attention, saluted briskly, did an about face and left the office.

The governor turned to me. "Good luck on your mission. Keep me directly informed of your progress. You may go anywhere you need and carry any weapons you deem necessary to carry out your orders." He paused as if a new thought occurred to him then continued, "I would recommend you consider Portland as the most likely place to hunt for these people but I have every confidence you will leave no stone unturned."

I said goodbye to the governor and left the office. As I walked through the lobby, Caleb thought to me, *What happened to your escort? Man, you must have really pissed off the Colonel. Either that or he trusts you completely and figures you're now one of the Governor's team…Nope, I vote for the first one.*

I walked across the garage and climbed into the motorhome driver's seat, moved the seat back, stood up and headed for the lounge area to brief the team on our new mission.

I'd just begun when I heard a phone ring. I didn't know whose phone it was. Everyone checked their own phone and shook their heads, it wasn't any of theirs. It wasn't my usual phone but it seemed to be coming from a locker where I stored my gear. I opened the locker and pulled out a duffel I hadn't looked into for months. I reached in and found a phone, then pushed the receive button. I placed the phone against my ear and said, "Hello, who's calling please?"

There was some brief static then a familiar voice answered, "Black Bond, this is the Apostle."

CHAPTER 13

And the Dead Shall Rise Again—Caleb

Jumping Jehoshaphat!!! An expression our dear papa was fond of saying when he was surprised. Joshua and I were surprised, really surprised, off the chart surprised to hear from Joshua's handler. We were led to believe he'd been murdered by a senator from Arizona almost a year ago.

Joshua nearly dropped the phone, but managed to recover it. The first thing he said was, "I thought you were dead!"

"I was, for a while at least. To use one of your favorite expressions, 'I was mostly dead, not completely dead.' This phone is no longer secure but you will be receiving a new burner phone soon. We've got a number of things to discuss. Tell your brother Caleb hello for me. Talk to you soon."

Double Jumping Jehoshaphat!!! He knows about me? How can he possibly know about me? Joshua looked as stunned as I felt and I noticed his knees buckled. He had to grab hold of the back of the chair to keep from falling.

The rest of the team were also stunned but more from Joshua's reaction to the short call. Simone grabbed his arm to steady him and guided him into the nearest recliner as Mark said, "Who was that? Are you okay?"

Pham handed him a bottle of water and waited for Joshua to recover from the shock.

Josh took a sip from the bottle and sat it down on a side table, "That was the Apostle. That was the code name of my government handler. He was supposed to have been killed, murdered by a rogue senator at the end of the last mission. I was his only field agent but I think I've mentioned his code name once or twice."

"So what does he want?" asked Mark.

"I don't know yet. He supposed to get back in touch soon," replied Joshua.

'Soon' turned out be less than an hour. There was a loud rap on the driver side door and Simone scanned the security monitor. "It's one of the Colonel's bodyguards. He's got a small package in his hand. Should I let him in?"

"No, just open the door," answered Joshua.

Simone opened the door and the bodyguard said, "I've got a package for Joshua Brown."

"I'll take it," said Simone.

"No you won't," responded the guard. "Mr. Brown is the only one I'm allowed to give it to and he has to sign for it."

Simone moved out of the driver's seat and Joshua stepped out of the motorhome. "Where do I sign?" asked Joshua.

"Not so fast," smirked the guard. "First, I need to see a picture ID."

"Really? Is this the SOP you put everyone through?" replied Joshua in an annoyed tone of voice.

"Nope, just you. Colonel's orders."

Without another word, Joshua produced his US Government driver's license with a picture of his face and handed it to the guard. The guard scrutinized it thoroughly then handed it back. Instead of handing Josh the package the guard said, "Please extend your right hand, palm up so I can scan your thumb print."

Slowly, Joshua stuck out his right arm and the guard scanned his thumb. There was a soft beep confirming he was who he said he was. Before the guard could say anything else, Joshua said in a very deep, threatening voice, "If you ask for a retina scan, go tell your boss he has to come down here to take it in person."

The guard did a poor job of concealing a smile as he said, "A retina scan isn't required, Mr. Brown. Please sign the receipt."

After he'd finished signing, the guard handed him his package. He also gave him a large manila envelope.

"What's this?" asked Joshua.

It's your written orders along with your pass card for entry and exit from the secured parking area. Please keep the card in your vehicle at all times. You all have a nice day."

Joshua watched as he walked away then climbed back into the motorhome. He handed the envelope to Pham and began opening the package. It was the burner phone from the Apostle. He was just about to power up the phone when he heard Pham begin to chuckle.

"What's so funny?" asked Mark.

"It's our orders. Guess who signed them?" asked Pham.

"Who?" asked Simone.

Without looking at the orders, Joshua pursed his lips and shook his head then said in a really angry voice, "That son-of-bitch Colonel Pete Legleu!"

He thought to me, *One of these days I'm going to have to hurt that man!*

Messages from the Apostle—Joshua

When I powered up the burner phone there was a text waiting for me. It read:

> As soon as you activate this phone, go to the app called APOS052$. Download the app. It will encrypt and decrypt all texts and voice messages between us. As soon as the download is complete, the app will self-destruct to prevent any further access. I will be communicating with only you and Caleb. As soon as the app is loaded text me at 'blKBnd700.' I will acknowledge your text. Five minutes later I will call you.

He knows about me., thought Caleb. *How can he possibly know about me? Did you tell him?*

Of course not, I thought back. *I never told anybody about you. They'd think I was crazy.*

Then how can he know?

I thought about that for a moment before I replied. *He's really smart, besides he has all the hospital records of how some of the doctors thought I'd multiple personality disorder. Maybe he thinks you're just a figment of my imagination I use to rationalize you aren't really dead.*

Oh damn, man. Tell me I'm not just something you conjured up because you didn't want to believe I was dead. Tell me you believe I'm still alive in spirit form.

Caleb, maybe the Apostle is just fishing. Maybe he's trying to determine if you're real or a figment. He could be testing me to see what I'll reveal.

That's crap, man. I ain't no damn figment. I know it and have proved it to myself many times over that my spirit still lives. No figment could every supply you with all the intel I discovered.

Okay, Caleb, calm down. I believe you're the real deal but when he starts asking me questions about you I need to be careful what I tell him. You understand?

Okay, I be calm now but I ain't no fig.

I decided to get away from the colonel and head to Portland as the governor suggested. At our request the security parking people removed the barriers from around our vehicles and helped us maneuver out of the underground garage. Mark was driving and on our way to I-5 North he pulled over at the closest park. I was headed to the bedroom to make my call to the Apostle when Sarge came trotting out with his new best buddy in tow. The team had made suggestions on the dog's new name. They finally decided on Sniffer. It was an okay name but not my first choice. Maybe it would grow on me.

As soon as we stopped Sarge and Sniffer were waiting at the portside door. Simone opened it and both dogs bolted for the trees. I grabbed a couple of poop bags and followed the frolicking fellows as they raced around the park. I was really happy to see Sniffer seemed to be in good health. Mark and Simone took turns tending to his injuries but he'd only been out of Sweet Ride to do his business. You'd never know he'd ever been hurt. After fifteen minutes of doggy frivolity, they jumped back aboard, begging for chow.

Once the dogs were fed and strapped into the passenger seat, Mark headed to the on-ramp to the I-5 and set the cruise control to 65 mph; that's the speed limit in Oregon for motorhomes and trucks. I walked back to the bedroom and closed the door. I sat down at the foot of the bed, powered up the burner phone and accessed the app as instructed. Five minutes after it was downloaded, the phone rang. I spent the next half hour talking to the Apostle. Of course, Caleb was listening in. However he never mentioned Caleb, much to my brother's disappointment. Instead he filled us in on what happened to him, his new responsibilities and how we were to relate during the mission in Oregon. He told me I could share with my team whatever information I considered pertinent.

My first question was, "How did you escape dying? The senator seemed pretty certain he'd killed you."

"It was a contract shooting. Did he tell you he was the one who pulled the trigger?"

"He gave me that impression but I don't remember how he phrased it," I answered.

"Actually it was one of the men on the senator's payroll. The senator loaned the shooter his cap and ball revolver from civil war days. He said there wouldn't be any way ballistics would be able to trace the weapon. Fortunately for me, those weapons aren't very dependable by today's standards and the shooter never fired the weapon before.

"I'd just finished my workout at one of the gyms I belong to. I was scheduled for an 8:00 am meeting with the senator so I went to the gym around 6:00 am. I prefer going early when they're only a few people training. The shower room was empty when I stepped into the shower at 7:00 am.

"I was all lathered up with soap when the shower curtain was ripped open and a man with a revolver thrust the gun at me and pulled the trigger. It misfired and he pulled back the hammer on the single action gun and tried to fire again. I reached out and grabbed the barrel of the gun and turned it away from me as he pulled the trigger for a second time. This time it fired. The ball missed me but the sound was deafening as he yanked the gun barrel from my soapy hand. I lost my balance on the wet tile shower floor and fell back against the shower wall as he cocked the gun again. It misfired again but before I could stand up and defend myself, he fired for the fourth time.

"There was another deafening explosion and the ball hit me in the chest, just below my heart. The impact drove me back down to the shower floor, hitting my head against the back wall. My memoires of what happened after that are very vague. I heard people yelling, I think there was a brief fight but have no idea who was involved. I heard one more gunshot then I passed out.

"When I regained consciousness, I was in a hospital room. Several days passed and I was told I died on the operating table several times. The odds of me surviving were very low. I'd been shot twice before, once in my arm and the other time in my butt. The latter had been the most uncomfortable but it was nowhere near as bad as being shot near the heart.

"In addition to my bullet wound, I had a severe concussion. I was told I might not regain part of my memory. During my recovery period, I died twice more. The last time they had to defibrillate me numerous times before my heart stabilized.

"It has taken several months of rehab to get well enough to make this call. I'm told by my doctors I'm on the road to full recovery but it's going to take several more months before they will turn me loose.

"But enough about me. How are you and your team doing?"

Caleb thought to me, *Tell the Apostle I got the senator to commit suicide with the same gun he used on him.*

Are you sure you want to reveal yourself, Caleb?

You said he already knows.

No I didn't. I said maybe he's fishing for clues.

Okay, okay. You're right. But someday I'm going to tell him.

"Hello? Joshua, are you still there?"

"Yes. Yes, I'm here. I'm just shocked to hear about all you went through. So glad to hear you're on the road to recovery. Are you sure you'll be able to take an active part in our mission?"

"Absolutely, I'll just have to support you from my rehab facility at least initially instead of in person. I have all types of computer equipment available to me and several of our old committee members have contacted me once they were informed I was still alive. Now that the Arizona senator is no longer with us, they're very anxious to see how the Oregon Governor's plan to reduce firearm deaths is working out. They're willing to help support your mission financially with no questions asked. I will be your go-between. You will contact me with any request for intel, funding or special equipment you need and I will make sure it happens. Just so you know, a Marine two-star has joined the committee."

He paused, then added, "I'm being told I can't have extended phone conversations. Where are you now?"

"We're on our way to Portland. We should be arriving within thirty minutes," I answered.

"I'll call you again in a couple of hours and we can go into more detail. Signing off."

CHAPTER 14

Pastor Boa and the Vietnamese Children—Joshua

Coming north on the I-5 through the Willamette Valley was truly a scenic ride. It was mile after mile of beautiful rich green trees towering over both sides of the freeway. We were about ten miles from where the Willamette River flowed into the Columbia River on the North side of Portland, also called the City of Roses. Wild roses grew everywhere along the road adding their perfumed scent to the ride.

"Hey, boss," said Pham. "Aren't we close to where Pastor Boa has his school? How about we contact him and make arrangements to visit with him and his wife Cam? I'd love to see how they're doing."

Sounds like an excellent idea, Caleb thought to me. *That was your second trial mission, one of the three where I wasn't allowed to help you. The Pastor and his wife are really great people. Wouldn't you like to see them again? Why don't you give them a call? See when they could take us on a tour of the school and meet with the Vietnamese children you rescued.*

Simone was driving and asked, "Can somebody fill me in on the second mission? Joshua never briefed me on his previous missions before New Orleans."

Mark spoke first, "That's when I first met Joshua. I was a security guard at Terminal 6, one of the ports for cargo ships to load and unload cargo on the Columbia River. He was there to rescue about a hundred Vietnamese children who'd been kidnapped in Vietnam. It was the worst case of human trafficking in Portland history. Boss, why don't you share the details with all of us?"

"Yeah, boss," said Pham, "Fill all of us in on the details. I didn't get involved in the mission until you'd rescued the children and taken them to Pastor Boa's church. I was only involved in getting all the children adopted. I'd like to hear about how you rescued them."

I nodded my head and began, "When I'd finished my extensive training, most of which was at the Marine training facility at Camp LeJeune, I was sent on three trial missions. All of them were set up by the Apostle. He briefed me on the mission details and objectives and provided logistic support to make sure I'd everything I needed for a successful mission."

I stopped for a moment to organize my thoughts. It seemed like it was a decade ago but the more I thought about it, I realized it had been almost two years ago. A lot happened since then but the memories of that mission came flooding back to me as I briefed the team on what happened.

"I was sent to Terminal 6, a huge cargo port on the Columbia River, a few miles downriver from Portland. A Japanese container ship off-loaded nearly a thousand containers at the terminal coming from various ports in Asia. I believe the last stop in Asia was Singapore before it sailed for Portland. Five of those containers held about a hundred Vietnamese children who'd been sold by their parents."

"That's terrible!" gasped Simone. "Why would anyone sell their children?"

"The parents were told there were rich Vietnamese in Ho Chi Minh City who wanted to adopt them. The parents who sold their children were dirt poor, barely able to feed themselves. Men came to villages all over Vietnam and gave the parents a few dollars promising them their children would be much better off living with rich Vietnamese adopted parents," I answered.

"The children were told one lie after another. The last lie was they were now being shipped to America to be adopted by rich Americans. At first the children were well treated during their three week trip to Portland but by the last week, they were horribly abused. Several died before they got to Portland, their bodies dumped into the ocean.

"When the ship arrived in Portland the five containers with the children inside were off-loaded and placed in a storage area. My mission was to rescue the children and take them to a safe place."

Mark added, "That's when I first met Joshua. He had some forged documents saying he was going to attend a top secret meeting at two in the morning and I wasn't supposed to tell anyone. At first, since his name wasn't on the list of approved visitors, I kept the barricade down and told him to leave but after he showed me his fake orders, I let him enter the container storage area. About half hour later he came driving out in one of the Terminal 6 tour busses. I couldn't see who was inside but I figured it was all part of this top secret meeting."

"And Mark was right," I said. "It was part of my mission to rescue the children and take them to safety."

"How did you get the children out of the containers," asked Pham. "You never told me about that part of the mission."

"At the time, that information was classified," I answered, "But I can share it with you now if you're interested."

"Of course we're interested!" shouted Mark. "We're hanging on your every word."

"Okay, let me continue. I drove my modified Humvee to the container site. As I'd been told, there were people already waiting outside of the five containers. It was very late and there was no one else around. There were nine men all dressed in black. My orders indicated I would probably encounter men from a local Chinese Tong. I got out of my ride dressed in Marine combat gear, including heavy duty body armor, body cam and my .44 caliber magnum semiautomatic pistols. This was before I'd upgraded to the .50 caliber Auto Mag.

"I spoke to them first in English. When they didn't reply, I switched to Mandarin then used Cantonese telling them they were all under arrest on charges of human trafficking and several other charges. I told them to place any weapons they might be carrying on the ground. Instead they attacked me and I was forced to kill them in self-defense, all nine of them."

"You shot all nine of them?" exclaimed Simone.

That's all me, Joshua. Tell them I'm the one who adjusted your shooting so you can't miss. Give me some credit, dude!

Instead of giving away Caleb's identity, I answered, "I had some excellent training before they turned me loose on my trial missions. Where was I? Oh yes, I drove my vehicle to where they kept the Terminal 6 tour buses, returned to the five containers, cut off the locks and took all the children and placed them on the bus. We drove out of Terminal 6, heading to the church in the West Hills of Portland which had a Vietnamese Ministry as part of a Christian church.

"Pastor Boa and his wife Cam contacted Pham at my suggestion and made arrangements for the adoption of most of the children by Vietnamese church members. As a bonus, the Apostle got funding approved to set up a boarding school for those who weren't adopted in the first round. Even those who were adopted also attended the school. Teachers were provided to teach the children English as well as normal class subjects.

"I have spoken briefly to Pastor Boa several times and things seem to be going well for the school. I haven't contacted him since the New Orleans mission began. Pham, would you please give the Pastor a call and see if we could visit him when we arrive in Portland?"

"Will do boss," replied Pham.

While Pham made the call, I was thinking back to how that mission went down. It was really satisfying to have been a part of rescuing those children. Then Pham interrupted my reverie, "Boss, we may have a problem. I called the Pastor's cell number but it was answered by someone who didn't speak Vietnamese but spoke very broken Chinese. Could you talk to him?"

I took the phone and said in Mandarin, "Hello, my name is Joshua, May I please speak to Pastor Boa?"

I waited for a few seconds but there was no reply. I tried again in Cantonese. This time a man answered, "What want for Pastor. No here. No call. Go way."

Before he could hang up, I repeated in English, "Could you please put either Pastor Boa or his wife Cam on the phone. I need to speak with them regarding visiting their boarding school for Vietnamese children."

There was another long wait with some muffled whispered voices in the background. A different voice came on the line, perhaps a women's voice. She spoke in English, "School has new management. You must pay to visit school. One hundred dollar per person."

"Where is Pastor Boa? Please put him on the phone."

"You must pay to talk to Pastor."

I was losing my patience and beginning to worry about what was happening at the school. "I don't have to pay anything to visit the school. I own the school and I will be there in a few minutes. If you have done anything to hurt the pastor, his wife or the children you will go to prison for a very long time. Do you understand?"

After another long pause with muffled whispers, the woman answered, "No Pastor Boa. No wife. New owner, must pay. Now one thousand dollars per person."

I hung up and said to Pham, "Give the school address to Simone. We're going to call on the new owners of the school, full battle gear and weapons."

Before we headed for the boarding school, we checked with the church to see if Pastor Boa and his wife might have been at the church instead of the school. The senior pastor informed me they hadn't seen the pastor or his wife since the Vietnamese service the previous Sunday, four days before. That wasn't unusual for them; they spent a lot of time assisting at the school.

Simone pulled the Sweet Ride into the parking lot of the boarding school and Pham, Mark, Sarge and I exited out of the starboard side door. Sniffer remained with Simone; he wasn't ready for combat.

Mark and Sarge went to the front of the motorhome and Pham and I to the rear. I could see a heavy metal chain was used to secure the main door and a series of wooden barricades made access to the door very difficult. There were no cars in the parking lot, just signs on the barricade with large red letters saying: **This School is Closed Until Further Notice**.

I called the Portland PD and asked for detective Hong. When he answered I said, "We have a situation that needs your immediate attention." I gave him a quick sitrep and the address of the school. I asked for police to assist in determining what happened at the school. He said they would be on site within 15 minutes.

While we waited for the police, I signaled to Mark to launch the drone. It climbed above the motorhome and began a slow circuit of the school. I watched on the iPad as it scanned for any indication of life or possible entry points we could use. There were a couple of broken windows on the second floor around the corner from the entrance. Unfortunately, none of the openings were large enough for the drone to enter but Mark maneuvered it close to the opening and took a look inside one of the two rooms. The room was empty but completely trashed as if someone had been searching for something. It was the same for the second room. The rest of the rooms had curtains or blinds preventing any further investigation.

Mark continued moving the drone around the school and discovered a possible entry point in the rear of the building. It looked like a door that led to the school's kitchen. It wasn't chained and there were no barricades.

I couldn't wait. I had Mark fire a flash bang grenade through one of first floor windows. When it went off, I used the explosion as a distraction and I ran behind the school to the kitchen door. It was locked but there were small glass window panes in the upper part of the door. I used the butt of my Auto Mag to break the window nearest the lock, reached inside and unlocked the door. Thinking it might be a trap, I had Mark fly the drone into the kitchen and then through all the first floor rooms where the doors remained open. I followed close behind the drone, opened some of the closed doors and did a quick search, no students, no staff and no perps. If there were still people in the school, my bet was they were in the basement.

Mark and Sarge joined us in the kitchen while Pham did a quick search of the second floor. Mark had Sarge do a very fast search of the basement area. He was wearing his own body cam on his armored vest and we could follow his search pattern on the iPad. It was a silent search and Sarge was so good at being stealthy the perps never heard or saw him.

All of the nearly 200 students and teachers were sitting on the floor in groups of ten. Each group had an armed perp guarding them. We saw Pastor Boa sitting in a chair next to his wife. They both had their hands cuffed behind them.

None of the perps were guarding the stairs which told me these were amateurs. Mark and I slowly made our way down the stairs and slipped into the shadows.

Three of the perps were questioning them in a language I couldn't understand. It sounded Asian but I'd no idea what they were saying. One of them, a large man with a short sword hanging from his belt, was obviously getting angry at the Pastor's response to his question. He slapped him hard across the face splitting his lip. Blood began to drip down from his lip to his chin. Cam shouted angrily at the man who struck her husband. The perp turned and looked as if he was going to strike her when Pastor Boa yelled at the man. Looking at the Pastor and his wife made me think this questioning had just begun. Neither Boa nor Cam had been roughed up.

Caleb, I thought to him, *what are they saying? I don't understand them at all.*

It's a Cambodian dialect, I think they're demanding money, lots of money. The Pastor said they didn't have any money. Everything at the school was paid for by the American government. The perp didn't believe him and struck him. The wife called the man a coward and used some very naughty words to describe him and his relation to his mother.

"This is going to get very messy, very quickly. We can't wait for the police. Pham, when I give you the signal, pull the circuit breakers for the basement. As soon as the lights go out, Mark and I are going to use some sleepy time gas grenades."

Mark and I quickly put on gas masks from our satchels and took out several gas grenades. I gave Pham the signal and the basement went dark. We tossed all our grenades and there was lot of shouting and screaming and some gunfire that lasted less than a minute.

We waited a minute longer then Pham reset the circuit breakers and the basement was flooded in light again.

We quickly removed the cuffs from the pastor and his wife and laid them gently on the floor. We took out our own zip tie cuffs and secured the three perps who'd been doing the questioning. Pham joined us and we went from each group of students and their teachers checking to make sure none were injured and cuffing each group's guard as we went, also confiscating their firearms. They were all brand new automatic weapons. Each guard had anywhere from six to ten full magazines. Where did they get such weapons?

Simone found some portable fans and opened up a few of the basement windows to help get rid of the gas. As people began waking, we helped them up the stairs. Mark helped Pastor Boa up the stairs with Sarge following closely behind. I helped Cam who was now muttering what I assumed were curses she hadn't had a chance to use on the perp that struck her husband.

We'd helped about half of the students when the police showed up.

CHAPTER 15

Questions, Questions and More Questions—Caleb

We used several large fans to clear the remains of the sleeping gas from the basement. All the children had been taken upstairs and each one was tended to by EMTs who arrived shortly after the police. Pastor Boa told the EMTs he was fine and didn't need any help but he was overruled by his wife who insisted he be examined. Even though she was a licensed nurse (in Vietnam) she wanted to get a second opinion.

Joshua called the Apostle and briefed him on what went down at the school and told him we and the local police would be investigating why this school was attacked. There were about 30 attackers who'd been taken to holding cells in Portland's city jail. Josh told him we would commence our investigation as soon as all the children were taken care of.

"Give me the address of the school and I will send food and counselors ASAP. Let the professionals handle that. I need you to get answers to a lot of questions. Make that your priority," ordered the Apostle. "I'm sure it's related to the Oregon Governor's mission."

Once we were sure Pastor Boa was okay, we met in a conference room on the first floor of the school. Besides Pastor Boa, his wife and our team, we were joined by two detectives from Portland PD, Joey Hong and his partner, Bill Cody. They'd arrived at the school along with a dozen or so police officers to help mop up the gang members and assist in helping the students and the faculty.

Joshua made the introductions, of course my name was never mentioned. Being a spirit has its limitations. I wondered if there would ever be a time when the rest of the world or at least Joshua's team and working associates, would ever be informed of me and the special talents I bring to the table. I hoped so. Finding the right time has been a real problem. I still wonder if the Apostle has some knowledge of me or if he's just guessing. He's one smart agent and if anyone would suspect I existed, I'd put my money on the Apostle.

Mark and Sarge had met with the two detectives during Joshua's second mission and it was like a reunion for them. I think Sarge was the most excited and jumped up on detective Cody, nearly knocking the man off his feet. He alternated barking and licking while Mark tried to calm him down. When Sarge finished greeting Cody he went over to detective Hong who gave him a casual pet on his furry head. Sarge barked once, gave his hand a courtesy lick, then returned to Mark. Hong looked at Sarge and said, "I guess it's obvious who the dog lover is," gesturing to his partner.

When the introductions were completed, Joshua attempted to contact the Apostle to include him in the meeting but he didn't pick up the call. I could tell that worried Joshua.

It's okay, Josh, I thought to him. *He's probably doing therapy or napping. We can record the meeting and brief him later when he's available.*

He nodded his head in response and asked Simone to record the meeting. "We have a lot of questions regarding this invasion and I think the first step is to put together a list of as many questions as we can think of before we begin answering them. Any comments on that approach?"

They all agreed. For the next half-hour, they brainstormed until they'd an extensive list which was put into a priority order. Pham took a few minutes on the computer compiling the list and handing out a hard copy to everyone, except for Sarge and me.

The prioritized list follows:

1. Who were the people who attacked the school?
2. What language were they speaking?
3. What were their objectives in invading the school?

4.   Who planned the attack?
5.   Who funded the attack?
6.   Who trained the attackers?
7.   How did they arrive at the school?
8.   Where did they get their firearms?
9.   Where were the students and faculty when the attack began?
10. How were the students and faculty treated by the attackers?

They cut off the questions and took a short break. Cam wanted to make sure her husband was still okay. There were several side discussions going on as they prepared to start answering the questions.

<u>Answers and More Questions—Pastor Boa</u>

My wife and I told everyone what we knew about the attackers, "The attackers arrived less than an hour before Joshua and his team arrived at the school. I didn't notice the attackers until I heard the front doors being chained shut and the barricades being drug in front of the doors.

"Cam and I ran to the windows to see what was happening. Several of the students who were between classes looked through the windows wondering what was going on. What we saw were about twenty-five to thirty men and women dressed in combat uniforms, each armed with several weapons.

"About five of the attackers circled around to the back of the school and found an unlocked door. They burst through the open door and began firing their machine guns. They weren't firing at anyone, mostly to the ceiling or floor. I think they were trying to create panic. At least that was the effect the gunfire had on me and everyone around me.

"The rest of the attackers came through the back door when the gunfire stopped and one of the men yelled at us in heavily accented English. I think it was English, it was very hard to understand what he was saying. I think he wanted all of us to lie down and not move. Within a few minutes all the students and staff were taken downstairs, including my wife and myself.

"It looked like the leader was going to give us orders, however before he could speak my smart phone began ringing. That seemed to catch them by surprise."

"Yes," said Cam. "They looked unsure of what they should do. They finally answered the call. Was Pham the one who called us?"

Pham answered, "Yes, Joshua asked me to see if we could visit you. We were very close to the school at the time, maybe ten to fifteen minutes away. When somebody answered the phone, I wasn't sure if I'd dialed in the right number. Whoever answered spoke in a language I'd never heard before."

"I think it was a Cambodian dialect," interjected Cam. "I'm not positive. Some of them spoke very broken Chinese. One of the women ended up speaking terrible English but good enough to be understood."

"What did the woman say?" asked detective Hong.

I answered, "I'm not exactly sure but something to the effect Pham had the wrong number, that they were the new owners and they would charge some ridiculous amount of money for anyone to visit."

Joshua interjected, "We recorded all of the conversation and we will supply everyone with transcripts. Hopefully we can use the recordings to determine their language."

The other detective, Bill Cody, asked me, "When they had you and your wife cuffed and sitting in chairs, what type of questions where they asking you?"

"They wanted to know where we kept our money. I think they searched all the classrooms, the rooms our boarding students lived in and our offices. They seemed to be under the impression we had a fortune in cash locked away somewhere in the school. When I told the leader we had very little cash, he became enraged and slapped me across the face. My wife began yelling at him to leave me alone using very nasty language."

My last comment made Joshua and a few of the others laugh. My wife seemed embarrassed and needed to justify her outbreak of profanity even if it was in a very obscure dialect, "I wanted to shock him, to distract him from my husband so he wouldn't keep hitting him," she commented.

Joshua said to Cam, "Didn't you realize your comments could have caused him to hit you instead of Pastor Boa?"

"It was worth the risk to protect him," Cam countered. "Besides, I saw you in the shadow of the stairs and knew you would save all of us."

A Summary of Our School Meeting—Caleb

The meeting ran less than an hour. Several of the questions were answered but there were just as many that led to more questions. Most of those would have to wait until the attackers were questioned. The bottom line that came out of our meeting was this attack made no sense. Joshua, along with my urging, suggested this was a diversion. Somebody took a group of illegals and told them the school had a fortune in cash just waiting for the taking. They were given very good weapons but only a few of the attackers knew how to use them. When the weapons were confiscated the safeties were still on. The guns that were fired when they came through the back door fired blanks. There were no bullet holes in the ceiling or floors. A random check of the magazines revealed none of them were loaded with live ammunition, only blanks.

Joshua summed it up, "This was a planned diversion, with the so-called attackers used as bait to keep us occupied while something else was going on. Whoever set this up knew we were coming to Portland and wanted us out of the way. They knew we would call in the local police and a large number of them were assigned to assist us. They probably expected us to come in with guns blazing, killing many of the attackers armed with unloaded weapons. In the process they expected some of the students and teachers would be killed as collateral damage."

He was right, of course. Just as the meeting was wrapping up, the two detectives received orders. Both of them and all of the uniformed officers were required downtown immediately. Seven of the city's largest banks were hit simultaneously. There were many reported deaths and two of the banks were still occupied by the bank robbers. Bank robbery is a federal offense and part of the FBI's jurisdiction. They were joined by the Portland PD and their SWAT group.

As the meeting broke up, Joshua suggested a divide-and-conquer approach. He along with Cam and one uniformed officer would go to the Portland jail and begin interrogation of the Cambodian Tong members, a name they called themselves. Detectives Hong and Cody called ahead to get permission from their boss to have Joshua lead this activity.

Hong and Cody, along with the uniformed officers who remained at the school would join the FBI and the Portland PD officers currently at the remaining bank robbery sites.

Pastor Boa, Simone, Mark and Sarge, along with Sniffer remained at the school to assist in any way they could. Sarge and Sniffier wore their therapy vests and became a God send. Sniffer was new to the role but he took to it naturally, letting all the children play with him. He really liked having the children throw a ball and let him fetch it. When he brought it back to the group he always gave it to a different child so everyone got to play. Sarge was great with the most traumatized children. He would find a child who was withdrawn and crying and would sit down next to him or her, lay his head gently on the knee or give a little lick on the hand and they would end up hugging him and the crying would stop.

Pham remained in the motorhome and became our news central. He would share all the information he could pick up from the news feeds that were pertinent to each group.

My job was to transport to the various groups as needed and keep Joshua informed of what was happening. When the Apostle replied to Joshua's voice message, Pham took the call. I was able to listen in and immediately pass on the information to my brother.

This was where I shined. As a spirit, I could do things human beings could never do. For example, I can pause time. No, actually that's not entirely correct. Time continues at its normal speed; however I can speed up my ability to evaluate a situation or in this case multiple situations, in what would seem like an instant.

From my perspective, it looks like time stands still. For instance, I transported to each of the banks where the robberies were still ongoing. Except they weren't ongoing the way the robbers intended. I popped into the first bank and spent what seemed to me to be about thirty minutes while everyone in the bank seemed to be frozen in place. I was able to identify each of the five bank robbers by accessing the FBI's data base and matching their mug shots with the people I was looking at. All of them had been previously arrested and one of them was on the FBI's most wanted list. I was able to determine what type of weapons they were carrying, how many people were being held hostage, how many had been shot and how many had died.

Best of all, I was able to access their escape plan by probing the mind of the leader. It was a brute force plan that called for the death of the hostages by blowing up the lobby area while they were planning to escape through a newly created hole in the wall of an adjacent building. I wandered through the hole and discovered another robber standing guard on the other side. It turns out the hole led to a lobby with a bank of elevators. One of them was an express to the roof and guess what was on the roof?

If you guessed a helicopter landing pad you'd win a kewpie doll. I strolled back into the bank and let time return to normal, Nobody can see a spirit so I didn't have to hide. I watched as one of the robbers finished setting the timer on a bag full of C-4 explosives. The other gang members picked up several large bags I assumed were full of cash stolen from the bank vault. When they were all safely through the hole in the wall and entered the express elevator, I waited until they were half way to the roof and then cut the power to entire building. I could hear the elevator stop its ascent to escape and returned to the lobby, freezing time again while I disarmed the explosives.

I contacted Joshua using telepathy and he in turn called Detective Hong and told him one of his CIs had informed him he'd been in the lobby of the building adjacent to the bank and saw a group of men in military gear get in the express elevator just before the power went out.

I need to add a side note for clarification. When I communicate with my brother, our telepathic conversations aren't like hearing words in sentences. When I gave Joshua the sitreps of the two banks, it was more like a burst of information that took less than a second for Joshua to receive and understand. Think of it as being instantaneous.

Detective Hong informed the FBI Special Agent in Charge, who sent his agents into the bank. Anticipating the possibility of explosives, two of his bomb squad agents were first in, found the satchel of C-4 and determined the bomb had been deactivated and was harmless. Other agents went through the hole in the adjacent building and flooded the elevator shaft with tear gas. After an appropriate amount of time for the tear gas to maximize its effect, power was restored and the elevator brought down to the lobby. All of the robbers were unconscious and easily restrained by agents wearing gas masks.

As soon as the FBI stormed the bank, I transported to the other bank with similar results, all in a day's work for Caleb the Just. I estimate it took me a couple of minutes in real time to take care of both banks. Then I transported to the jail just in time to listen in on the interrogation of the Cambodian Tong. I thought the tongs were a Chinese creation so I was anxious to hear about this mysterious Cambodian Tong.

CHAPTER 16

What the Heck is the Cambodian Tong?—Detective Hong

Once the two banks were secured, the FBI arrested the surviving robbers. To put it politely, they excused us from any further involvement with any of the seven bank robberies. I think they felt we were trying to infringe on their jurisdictions. My partner, Buffalo Bill Cody (Buffalo was just his nickname) thought he heard one of the FBI agents tell our boss, "Thank you for your help. We don't need you messing around in our case. Please take a hike!" Detective Cody isn't only my partner, he's also my best friend. However, he does have the habit of modifying the truth.

We returned to the station and met up with Joshua and Cam in one of the interrogation rooms. They both looked frustrated as one of our uniforms escorted a prisoner back to the holding cells.

"How's it going?" I asked.

"Not so well," answered Joshua. "We've gone through almost all of the them and most of them either don't understand any of the languages Cam and I know or they've been ordered to not speak to the police by whoever organized the attack on the school."

"Have any of them said anything?" asked Buffalo Bill (only I get to add 'Buffalo' to his name. He hates it but it's all in good fun).

Cam answered, "One of the women responded to me when I mentioned the name Cambodian Tong. Then she began speaking very fast in a dialect I didn't understand. When she saw we didn't understand her, she stopped and tried English."

"Were you able to understand her English?" I asked.

Joshua began laughing; Cam just looked frustrated. Joshua replied, "We could hardly understand her English. After several tries, we were able to understand what she said. Cam, you tell them."

Cam shook her head in disgust. "She said, Cambodian Tong. You pay five thousand dollar. I tell.'"

Bill and I both tried to stifle a chuckle. "I can't believe she hit you up for money," I said once I'd regained my voice.

Joshua asked me, "Do you know anything about a Cambodian Tong?"

"No," I answered, "However, I know somebody who might know."

"That would be your Uncle Chen, wouldn't it?" asked the Buffalo.

I smiled and said to them, "Bill and I are going on a little road trip."

Joshua and Cam finished up with the last few prisoners then headed back to the school. I called my uncle's restaurant to make sure he was available. Mei Mei, the restaurant's hostess for as long as I can remember, checked with my uncle. I could hear him shout back at Mei Mei in Chinese that I'd better bring my wife. "No wife, no meeting."

Bill and I made a quick stop at my apartment to pick up Lili, my wife of six months. Uncle Chen told me to never come visit him without my wife. I think he loved her almost as much as I did. He didn't care about Bill so much but Bill really liked my uncle's moo goo gai pan and it was near lunch time.

I called Lili to make sure she was available. When she found out we were having lunch with my uncle, she got so excited. I was worried she loved my uncle almost as much as me. Whenever she rode in my police cruiser she loved to sit in back. She said being behind the cruiser's security screen where the arrested people sat made her feel like a naughty girl. That got my juices flowing but not with Bill in the car.

She was waiting in the drive way to our house. Bill got out of the cruiser and opened the back door, pushing her head down gently, to keep her from hitting her head on the door frame, just like they do in police shows. I noticed she had a bag in her hand and I asked what was in the bag.

"It's a tin of double yolk moon cakes. You know how much your uncle loves moon cakes."

"You know your husband loves moon cakes too," I said in my best pouty voice.

"Of course I know," she answered. "That's why there's another tin waiting for you in our kitchen, you big baby."

We drove into Portland's China town district, passing under the China Gate on 4th Avenue, drove two blocks to Chen's Good Taste Restaurant and parked the cruiser in the side parking lot. I hadn't noticed Bill had a gift box until he opened the hatch and took what looked suspiciously like a box of donuts.

I grabbed a couple of umbrellas just in case it began to rain and followed them inside the restaurant. Mei Mei and Lili were chatting away in Cantonese as I came in. Bill didn't speak Chinese…oh wait, he does know a few words, like *nǐ hǎo* and *moo goo gai pan*. He stood smiling at Mei Mei, waiting for her to finish her conversation with Lili.

Mei Mei smiled back and gestured to the dining room. Of course it was empty, except for Uncle Chen who sat at his favorite table. When COVID-19 hit Portland, Uncle's restaurant was shut down, just like all the other restaurants in the city. Uncle Chen never reopened the dining room. He said he made more money focusing on takeout orders, however he opened the dining room for special occasions. This was one of those times.

Uncle Chen stood with his arms open wide as my wife ran to his embrace. He held her close for a moment then kissed her on the forehead and said, "My dearest daughter, it's so good to see you again. You're a ray of sunshine in a rainy day."

Lili stepped back and took the tin of moon cakes from her bag and with both hands and a slight bow, offered the tin of moon cakes to my uncle as she said, "Please accept this meager gift from my husband and me."

I swear, I noticed Uncle Chen's knees buckle ever so slightly. Regaining his balance quickly he reached out with both hands and took the tin box. I hadn't really looked at it but as my uncle inspected the box I could see it was beautifully painted with the image of a magnificent dragon. Neither he nor I missed the significance of the image; he was born during the year of the dragon.

The light in the dining area was dim but I thought I detected tears on my uncle's cheeks as he looked from Lili to me and said, "You've been blessed with a wife beyond measure. Cherish her forever."

He turned to compose himself and ended up facing my partner. He looked at the box in Bill's hand and asked, "Mr. Bill, is the box for me?"

"Uh, yes but it's nothing compared to the gift you received from your nephew and his wife. I'm embarrassed to give it to you," he answered.

"What's in the box, Mr. Bill?"

"A dozen donuts," Bill answered sheepishly.

"Are you sure the box contains a full dozen?"

Bill started to smile as he remembered the time I gave my uncle a box with only ten donuts. "I guarantee this box has twelve freshly baked, delicious donuts."

"Then I graciously accept your gift," Uncle Chen said as he turned his head and looked at me with a sour expression. "It's a complete gift. Let us all sit and enjoy our meal."

The meal was a feast, a traditional Chinese banquet, with plate after plate of delicacies to be sampled and enjoyed and a variety of teas from the homeland. As we ate we conversed about everything except business. That would come later as tradition demanded. It was truly a wonderful meal.

He opened the tin Lili gave him and shared the moon cakes with all of us, including Mei Mei. We ended the meal with a glass of Chinese wine.

When the food was gone and wine bottle empty, the preliminaries were complete as tradition demanded. Now was the time for questions. Lili excused herself and joined Mei Mei in the lobby while I asked the first question.

"Uncle, have you ever heard of the Cambodian Tong?"

"What an unusual question, my favorite nephew. Why do you ask?"

"We have a prisoner in custody. She may be the leader of a group of people who attacked a Vietnamese boarding school. She speaks an Asian dialect we cannot identify. In broken English, she said she was from the Cambodian Tong."

My uncle sat quietly for several minutes with his eyes closed. I began to wonder if he was trying to access old memories or had fallen asleep after the sumptuous meal. I was just about to say something to him when his eyes opened and began speaking to us in English.

"I haven't heard that name in many years, more like decades. Let me give you a brief history lesson regarding the Cambodian Tong.

"Around 1750 there was a Cambodian king named Ang Tong. A rival king from Vietnam attacked his kingdom and he was defeated. Tong managed to save his life by escaping into the hill country. A few years later he returned with an army and drove the Vietnamese out of Cambodia. He died about ten years later. As far as I know, that is the only Tong I've ever heard of from Cambodia."

He paused again, then added, "In the late 1800s many people left Asia and migrated to America in the hope of a better life. The vast majority of the Asians were Chinese; however I have been led to believe many of these people were from Southeast Asia, such as Vietnam, Laos and Cambodia. Many of them entered illegally into Washington and Oregon from Vancouver, Canada. These people were very poor and worked at the most menial jobs to survive. I've been told these people still exist on the fringes of China Town. I believe I've heard the term Cambodian Tong a few times in passing used to describe these people. Like our Chinese Tong, they group together, usually along ethnic lines. If I have heard correctly, the term Cambodian Tong refers to these people, even though they may not be from Cambodia."

Again he paused as he searched for English words, "There is a place under the ramp to the Burnside Bridge that is very dangerous. No self-respected Chinese ever go there. Even the police will not go there late at night. It has no name that I'm aware of. It is populated by scum, where people routinely kill each other for a little food. There are rumors of prostitution, slavery and murder for hire. Occasionally half eaten bodies have shown up downriver from the bridge."

He paused once more, shook his head of the images he described, "Please don't visit this place once the sun goes down. Even in daylight you should only go in groups. Protect yourselves at all times. Many of those people are no longer people, they're animals."

He stood up, signaling the meeting had come to an end. "Thank you for your gifts. I hope this information may help you. Goodnight Bill and to you, my favorite nephew. Say goodbye to your lovely wife. She will be a jewel in your life."

CHAPTER 17

Let the Games Begin—Joshua

When Cam and I returned to the boarding school, Pham joined us and said the Apostle called. While Cam and I were at the Portland jail, interrogating the people who attacked the school, Pham answered the Apostle's return call. He gave the Apostle a thorough briefing on what went down at the school. When he was done, the Apostle asked for the make of the automatic weapons the attackers were armed with. He also requested the serial numbers if they hadn't been filed down. Pham provided him with the requested information. He seemed pretty confident he could track the weapons to their source.

While we waited for the Apostle's next callback, the two Portland PD detectives also arrived and briefed us on what Hong's uncle disclosed. They recommended we release the Cambodian Tong woman and surveil her. If Uncle Chen is correct she might lead them to who put together the Cambodian Tong.

That sounds like a custom-made job for me, volunteered Caleb.

I replied, "I think that's a great idea. I know the perfect CI to conduct the surveillance. He's never let me down."

"Who is this perfect CI?" asked Bill.

"What does the C stand for in CI?" I asked

"It stands for Confidential," answered Bill as he shook his head. "We're the police, you can tell us."

"Not happening," I answered. "Case closed."

There was a moment of silence then my phone rang. It was the Apostle.

"Hello Joshua. Are you with your team?"

"Yes sir," I answered. "We also have Pastor Boa and his wife Cam. In addition, we have two of Portland's finest, detectives Hong and Cody, as well as my entire team: Simone, Pham, Mark and of course,

Sarge." Sarge barked once loudly and looked at Sniffer. "I almost forgot, also present is our newest member, Sniffer."

"Good afternoon to all of you," the Apostle said. I have some interesting information regarding the weapons the Cambodian Tong were carrying. We identified them as H-K automatic assault rifles. Someone had attempted to file off the serial numbers of the rifles, however upon further inspection it was determined they were part of a shipment that was delivered to the Oregon National Guard Armory in La Grande, Oregon less than a month ago. An investigation was initiated a little over a week ago to determine how the weapons were stolen."

That was a bit of a stunner. I said, "I wasn't expecting that."

Mark added, "I think that would make Colonel Pete Legleu a suspect or at least one of his subordinates."

"Where is Le Grande, Oregon?" asked Pham.

Detective Cody answered, "It's about a four-hour drive to the East of Portland on the I-84.

"Are there any results from the investigation so far?" I asked the Apostle.

"Yes, there are some preliminary findings. The shipment to La Grande consisted of a hundred cases with twenty-five rifles to each case. Five of the cases were sent to the Army National Guard Base in Portland. Supposedly none of the cases delivered to the Portland base were scheduled for immediate distribution. I requested an inventory of the cases and it was discovered one of the cases was missing. According to the inventory records, the rifles used in the attack on the school were from the missing case."

"Is there any surveillance video that shows someone walking off with the missing case?" asked Mark.

"Yes and no," replied the Apostle. "There's a recording of someone approaching the cases at 0300 hours two days ago, however there is a gap in the coverage after that. The surveillance video continues after about ten minutes. When the video resumes, one of the cases is gone and whoever was walking towards the cases is no longer visible.

"Aren't the magazines and ammunition packed in separate cases?" questioned Simone.

"Good point, Simone," answered the Apostle. "Each weapon is shipped with one empty magazine. Additional magazines were shipped separately as was the ammunition. They arrived the next day. It looks like someone requested thirty extra magazines and two hundred rounds of blanks."

"No live ammunition?" I asked.

"None," replied the Apostle. "You might be interested in who signed the order for the magazines and blanks. Does the name Colonel Peter Legleu mean anything to you?"

Tally ho! screamed Caleb into my brain. Of course it wasn't really a scream, it just felt like it. *We finally have something to hang the bastard with!*

I gave a wry smile and shook my head. "As much as I would like to nail that pompous ass, I'm sure he's going to deny he placed the order. To be honest, I think it's highly unlikely he would have signed off on something that would obviously make him a suspect.

Ah, damn it. You're probably right, bro. He paused then added, *I think it would be worthwhile to pull his chain and let him squeal for a while.*

"Based on the Colonel's arrogant attitude, I think we should pursue an investigation anyway just to take him down a notch," added the Apostle.

Let's hear it for the Apostle! Caleb thought to me.

Taking it to the Street—Caleb

"Why I go? Others?"

It was obvious to me she was very suspicious. Detective Hong was trying to calm her down. "Everybody go. You first," he said to the woman we called Ms. Tong.

"I clothes keep?" she said in her best English. "Clothes jail shit. Clothes Cambodian want."

Detective Hong turned to his partner. "Bill, get me the bag that has her uniform."

Detective Cody checked the tag on the bag to make sure it was the uniform Ms. Tong was wearing when she was arrested, then handed the bag to Hong.

Hong slowly reached out with the bag but the woman quickly stepped back and said, "No hit."

He dropped the bag on the floor, took three steps back and waited. The woman stared at him but didn't move. Hong gestured to the bag and said, "Your Cambodian clothes."

Both detectives stood in what they hoped were non-threatening stances and waited. Never taking her eyes off of Hong, the woman slid quickly forward, picked up the bag and clutched it to her chest as she backed away. She did a quick peak in the bag, then open it up and sniffed it. Apparently satisfied it was her clothes, she stepped farther back and began undressing. She stood their naked waiting to see what the detectives would do. Neither man moved but it was obvious she'd been badly abused. She was skin and bones with dark purple bruises over much of her body.

It was like looking at three statues. No one moved for several minutes. What was she waiting for? Finally, the woman said, "Sex want you? Sex hundred dollar." She pointed at Hong and said, "You sex hundred dollar." Then she pointed at Cody. "You sex hundred dollar."

When Hong spoke his voice was barely a whisper, he answered, "No sex. Cambodian clothes you wear."

She turned from Hong, looked at Bill, and said, "You sex?"

Bill looked away and answered, "No sex."

The woman began to tremble. She was angry. "Why sex no? No sex, no money. Need money."

She turned abruptly and put on her Cambodian uniform. When she was dressed she turned back and said in a trembling voice, "Now go."

Hong and Cody escorted her out of the interrogation room to an exit door. Before she left, both detectives gave her several twenty-dollar bills. Ms. Tong didn't say thank you, she didn't say anything at all, she just turned and walked out the door onto the street.

I didn't have the heart to let them know Ms. Tong spoke perfect English and a few other Asian languages as well. She had conned them both.

I was getting ready to begin my surveillance of Ms. Tong, when a man in an expensive suit walked up to the two detectives, "Do you still have the Cambodian woman in custody?" he asked. He was overweight and was panting from what for him was a long walk.

Detective Hong said, "No, she was just released a few minutes ago. She's no longer in the building. There's a CI tail…"

"Do realize what you've done?" he sounded exasperated.

"Yes, do you?" I could tell Hong was getting annoyed. "Who are you?"

The man replied, "I'm George Caldwell, assistant district attorney. Because you released that woman, we have to let all the others go too. The charges against them was for the entire group. I'm going to have to speak to your boss. I'm forced to request he issues reprimands for both of you."

The assistant DA turned on his heals and strode away.

The two detectives watched him walk away as Cody commented, "It looks like we're in trouble."

Hong nodded. "It won't be the first time."

Once outside the jail Ms. Tong turned towards the Willamette River and walked at a brisk pace. It was late afternoon and overcast, it looked like rain. Of course it always looks like rain in Portland. I followed her down the street as the raindrops started to fall. She turned into a CVS and I followed her inside. She palmed a few candy bars and slipped them into her uniform pocket when the kid working the counter wasn't looking. She found what she was looking for, a burner phone. She took the cheapest one from the rack and paid the kid at the counter with some of the money she had conned from Hong and Cody.

Back outside, she turned the corner and stopped abruptly. She peaked back around the corner to see if she was being followed. It was clear. She also looked across the street at the other corners and was satisfied she wasn't being tailed. The rain was coming down harder now and it was getting darker. By the time she got to her next stop she was drenched.

She walked into a Goodwill Store and went straight to the men's clothing rack. She ate one of the candy bars as she sorted through the clothes. She pulled a pair of jeans and a long sleeve wool shirt off the rack, then moved on to the shoes and slipped on a pair of boots. She took a black wool knit beanie cap off a shelf and headed to the end of the row to a deserted part of the store pulling off the tags from all the clothes as she walked. She ended up in a dead zone where the security cameras couldn't spot her. She took the phone and candy bars out of the uniform pockets and laid them on a shelf behind her then quickly stripped naked. Just as quickly, she put on the clothes, pocketed the candy, phone and cash and headed for the exit, leaving her wet uniform in a pile on the floor.

She picked up a large black umbrella and gave the clerk two one-dollar bills, declining the offer of a receipt and walked out the door into the rain. From the time she entered until the time she exited the store took not quite five minutes. This woman was a pro!

The street lights came on while she was in the Goodwill Store and she walked at a brisk rate towards the Burnside Bridge. She stopped at an empty bus stop with a roof over the bench. She took out her phone and punched in a number which of course I memorized immediately and waited for an answer.

On the third ring, a man answered. "Hello?" he said. That was the last thing he said.

Ms. Tong answered, "You set us up, you asshole! There was no money and no bullets. No thanks to you, none of my people were killed. I'm coming for you. You'll be dead before tomorrow morning, you miserable prick." She hung up and resumed walking towards the bridge.

I continued to follow her as I contacted Joshua and gave him the phone number she called and told him what she had said.

CHAPTER 18

I Fought the Law and the Law Won—Simone

Joshua wanted to know if I had any contacts within the FBI in the Portland area. He told me he would like to get two separate briefings. The first would be regarding the status of the ongoing investigations of the two banks where the men involved were captured. The second would be for the five banks where the robberies were successful and the robbers made their escape.

I checked the roster of FBI field agents assigned to the violent crimes task force at the Portland field office. I found two names of people I'd worked with when I was an agent with the DEA. It was a joint mission that involved federal alphabet agencies including the DEA and the FBI plus several others. Joshua and his team were the lead organization which led to the arrest of many of the world's drug cartel leaders, shutting down five of the largest of the cartels.

The first of the FBI agents I contacted was Larry Grimes. He was the lead agent who led the attack against a drug lord and five of his men. The gun battle took place at Gator Land near New Orleans. Larry was currently assigned as part of the team interrogating the five men who were arrested at the First Republic Bank on the West side of Portland in the downtown area. I arranged for Joshua and me to meet with him at the Field Office at 10:00 am the next day.

The second person I called was Priscilla Gomez. She was the group leader on the team assigned to capture one of the drug cartel bosses during our mission in New Orleans almost a year ago. She was now assigned to the FBI investigation of the successful robbery of the Heritage Bank on the east side of Portland. Heritage Bank was located in a residential area near the Lloyd Center, a huge shopping center which also had a heliport on one of the massive, elevated parking lots. She was very excited to meet with me and Joshua at the FBI command center bus located in the Lloyd Center parking lot near the heliport. The meeting was set for 2:30 pm the same day.

We made arrangements for a rental car and headed to the FBI field office early the next morning. We'd been staying in our motorhome parked in the boarding school parking lot since we arrived in the Portland area. The field office was located on the north east district, just east of Portland International Airport. It took us the better part of an hour to get to their facility. It took us another fifteen minutes to get signed in with all our creds while Larry was waiting for us in the lobby. We got our visitor badges and checked our weapons before entering. Larry escorted us to a conference room on the fourth floor. Waiting to meet us was Larry's boss, referred to as the SAC or more specifically, Special Agent in Charge.

The SAC introduced himself to us as George Palmer. He was a large man, well over six feet (but not even close to Joshua's six feet, seven inches). Like Joshua, he was well muscled and definitely in charge. Larry was barely five foot ten and the best way to describe him was wiry. However, I'd seen him in combat and he was a hell of a shooter and very energetic. Today both men were dressed in suits and ties, after all they were the FBI and with an image to uphold. Joshua and I were dressed in business casual.

After the introductions were made, the SAC bowed out. Before he left, he praised us for our mission in New Orleans. I believe he used the expression Outstanding! That gave me a warm feeling. For Joshua, every one of his missions were outstanding but he thanked the SAC anyway.

Larry closed the door to the conference room, took off his suit coat and loosened his tie. "Let's get down to business," he said.

"First of all, let me congratulate your CI for very timely information," he said. "Without you passing on his observations to us, the perps would have escaped and a lot more people would have died. Like my boss said, it was outstanding." He paused, then added, "Was he the same CI at the other bank?"

Joshua answered, "No, it was a second CI and it wasn't a he, it was a she. They're a team I use frequently."

Larry looked surprised. "Really? Are they married?"

Joshua smiled. "Don't know and don't care. All I know for sure is they're the best."

Larry nodded, then changed topics. "Let me tell you where we stand with the investigations on both of the banks where we captured the perps. I'm sure Simone told you I'm the lead agent for the investigation on the attempted heist of the First Republic Bank. Another agent has the lead on the Key Bank. We meet every evening to share updates and look for similarities and differences between the two failed bank jobs. Let me give you the details for my bank first then I'll cover the other bank. Please feel free to interrupt me to ask questions. Oh and just so you know, I have this room for two hours. If you need a bathroom break let me know and help yourself to the water bottles on the credenza.

"Okay, let me begin with the basics. We captured six men attempting to escape from First Republic. Actually, there were seven counting the chopper pilot on the heliport on the roof of the adjacent building. All of the men in the elevator were unconscious when we returned the elevator to the ground floor and opened the door.

"One of the perps was pronounced dead on the scene attributed to an overdose of the tear gas. Another one is still in critical condition and is currently located in a secure room at a nearby hospital. The doctors report he is unlikely to regain consciousness but we have an agent guarding his room twenty-four/seven.

"The pilot attempted to flee the scene when he saw agents with drawn weapons approaching his helicopter. He attempted to take off, however numerous rounds from our agent's assault rifles into the engine compartment aborted his attempt. He'd just made it to a hover before the engine conked out and he crashed back onto the pad from about ten feet. He had some minor injuries, none required extensive treatment."

"Was he part of the team that hit the bank?" asked Joshua.

"He claims he wasn't but we think he was aware of what was going down. We found several weapons in the copter. That was enough to hold him on accessory charges. He's currently in a separate holding cell with his request for bail denied."

"What's happening with the other four?" I asked.

"They are undergoing intensive interrogation even as we speak. All of them have extensive criminal records for various felonies and all of them have spent time in prison. Two of them were tried on murder one charges, both were acquitted on technicalities."

"Let me guess," said Joshua. "They were arrested in California?"

Larry smiled as he said, "Bingo. Good guess. Let's move on. These men are all pros. They've worked together as a team several times but this was their first federal crime. They are all being held in individual holding cells in this facility. They're all represented by a high class, read that as very expensive, team of lawyers. We believe they are an extension of one or more crime families."

"What do you mean by extension?" I asked.

"It means they aren't part of any of the organized crime families. One or more of the families contracts them to do a specific job for which the family receives a cut of the take. In return, they supply the gang with weapons, transportation, housing and a number of other things including lawyers if they're captured."

"Can we connect the lawyers to the crime families?" asked Joshua.

"Not yet," answered Larry. "We're working on it but nothing so far."

"I thought the crime families had their own lawyers, some of them are actually family members," I said.

"Yes, it's portrayed that way in the movies. It doesn't work that way in real life. The best lawyers have a number of clients, none of them are crime families. Occasionally they will handle a case where we think a crime family is paying the legal fees but it's never directly. The families give money to some organization or other who in turn give it to another company and so on. Each organization takes a small cut called a handling fee. By the time the lawyers see the money, it's been touched by five or six hands. It's very difficult to trace it back to a given crime family."

"Well that's disappointing," I replied.

"It sure is, Simone. That's life in the real world," said Larry.

"Speaking of disappointment, let me finish filling you in. All of the four prisoners are kept in individual cells with no communications allowed between them. The law forbids us from speaking to a prisoner without one of his lawyers being present. The lawyers quickly became a pain in our ass. When we offered a plea deal to each of the perps for them to roll on the other three, their lawyer jumped in for a private discussion. When we were allowed back in, the lawyer said his client declined to accept the lesser charges offered. When we threatened them with the death penalty, the lawyers countered with a civil suit against the FBI for using excessive force in subduing the perps which led to death for at least one of them, possibly two."

"Did you have their cells bugged?" asked Joshua.

"Yes all the cells were equipped for both audio and video," replied Larry. "However, when the lawyer wants to have a private conversation with his client, we're supposed to shut them off. We'd be breaking the law if we didn't shut it down. It wouldn't have mattered if we did or not. Each lawyer brought his own-high powered signal jammer just to be sure we didn't hear or see anything.

"Based on what's been happening the last few days, the best we can hope for is go to trial and pray they don't get to our eye witnesses of the murders. Just so you know, we're going to strongly recommend the death penalty for all of them."

"When do you plan to go to trial?" asked Joshua.

"The sooner the better," replied Larry. "The Oregon Governor is pushing hard to speed up the process. He's shooting for two weeks from now. The lawyers have been requesting a change of venue, claiming all the locals are biased against the perps. That would cause further delays. To counter, the Governor is calling for an executive order to eliminate a jury trial and let a tribunal of federal judges decide on a verdict. He went ballistic when he found out one of the people killed in the bank was a ten year old girl, along with her mother."

"What's the status of the other bank?" asked Simone.

Larry sighed and shook his head. "I'm sorry to say it's the same story. There was no escape helicopter involved, instead they were planning to fly out on a seaplane. They'd commandeered an armored truck as a way into the bank and were going to use it to drive the few blocks from the bank to the seaport on the Willamette River. They had a Turboporter on floats waiting for them to fly away.

"Their pilot was watching the news on his iPad and when he saw his crew was under siege in the Key Bank, he bolted. We found his plane abandoned about ten miles upriver. They're still searching for the pilot."

That wrapped up our meeting. We thanked Larry for his briefing and wished him luck with his case, then headed out to get some lunch before we met Priscilla Gomez at the Lloyd Center near the Heritage Bank.

CHAPTER 19

Under the Bridge—Caleb

I followed Ms. Tong in the drizzling rain as she headed towards the Burnside Bridge. I was mildly surprised at her spy skills which she displayed by continuing to cross streets, reverse directions, wait at a bus stop until the bus passed by, then back tracked to see who might be following her. She turned what would have been a twenty minute walk into almost an hour.

She finally made it to her destination well after the sun set; a very dark alley that led down to the Willamette River. The alley wound its way under the bridge. At one time there may have been lights along the alley. If there were, they'd long been taken out by the inhabitants. It was dark, very dark and very creepy as the alley turned into a gravel trail. It was a very scary place to go after dark and I thanked my lucky stars I was spirit and not human. I could see perfectly without eyes and no one could see me.

Apparently, Ms. Tong walked the path at night before. She was greeted by the residents who truly were the worst of the homeless. I counted at least a hundred of them living in what looked like garbage and I imagined smelled like a sewer. There seemed to be a collection of old rusted shopping carts from a variety of stores interspersed among the garbage piles.

As we walked I heard a woman wailing in grief. Ms. Tong stopped briefly to offer a few words of comfort. I gathered she knew the woman. I think it was a woman, it was hard to tell. They spoke in an obscure Cambodian dialect, an offshoot of Khmer. No wonder Cam didn't understand her. Fortunately, I understood them perfectly; spirits like myself aren't limited by speech. The woman was mourning the death of someone, perhaps a family member. Ms. Tong helped the woman pick up a bundle of rags and they walked down to the edge of the river and threw the small bundle into the water. Ms. Tong hugged the woman closely, speaking softly to her until she stopped crying. Just before she left, Ms. Tong reached into her jeans and gave her some money she'd conned from the two detectives, The woman thanked her profusely. She made little bowing motions as Ms. Tong continued down the path.

Listening to the two women, I found out Ms. Tong had a real name. It was Chanlina, which translates to Moonlight in English.

Chanlina continued to move down the path until she was directly under the middle of the bridge. It must have been considered prime real estate by the locals since the bridge formed a roof from the rain, though I'm sure it would've been noisy during rush hour traffic. She stopped in front of a cardboard, plywood and sheet metal lean-to which the residents of Bridge Town must have considered the Ritz in this environment.

She stood back from the opening and said in her Khmer dialect, "Hey, Fat Man, are you here?"

She waited, then added, "Hey Fat Man, I need your bike. Hurry up with the whore. I got money."

A large, mostly naked Asian man rolled out from under the flap of the lean-to and stood up. "How much money?" he asked in the same dialect.

Chanlina waved two twenty dollar bills under his nose. "This much," she answered.

"How long do you need it?" he asked as he reached for the bills with one hand and scratched his groin with the other.

"One, maybe two hours at most. You'll still be banging the slut when I get back. I got some business downtown. I need your knife too."

He reached under the flap and pulled out what I would have called a short sword, not a knife. "Who you going to kill downtown, a white man?" he asked.

"Yes," Chanlina replied. "Except this white man is black."

Fat Man smiled as he handed her the sword. "The bike is around back. Bring it back in good condition or it will be you in my tent working off the damages."

She smiled at him as she rolled the bike around to the front of the lean-to and put on the helmet. "We'll both have fun tonight. I'll bring you back a present."

Fat Man scowled. "I don't need another one of your victim's heads. Just bring me back more money so we can party in style."

She fired up the bike and waved goodbye, then headed back to civilization.

Of course I followed her. I sort of climbed onto the back of the motorcycle as she hit paved streets and began weaving in and out of traffic on her way to the kill zone.

The kill zone turned out to be in an office for a local vehicle rental business. I would consider the location as being on the outskirts of downtown. The motto for the business was written on a brightly lighted sign attached to the outside wall and clearly visible from the busy street. It read: Need a Bus, Rent From Us. I read it as Chanlina did a quick drive by. I gave it a three out of five on my motto scale.

She turned onto a side street which gave her a direct view of the company's parking lot. She shut the bike down, pulled out a pair of binoculars from a saddle bag and began scanning the lot.

I saw seven rental vehicles in the lot. There was one large Greyhound sized bus, two smaller buses, similar to school buses and four late model vans in various sizes. Using my secret spirit skills, I assumed one of the school buses was used to transport Chanlina and the rest of her gang to the boarding school.

She continued to scan the lot looking to determine how many employees were working and if they had any customers.

It must've been close to closing time. There weren't any customers and three men came out of the office. One of the men, a large black man, used a key to lock the office door as the other two men headed for two of the three cars parked in the lot near the office. As they drove off, Chanlina fired up the bike and headed back down the street. She waited until the two cars drove out of the lot then goosed the bike into the lot nearly knocking the black man off his feet.

He stumbled, regained his balance, pulled a large revolver from his waistband and began screaming at Chanlina as he attempted to shoot her, "You stupid chink bitch, you crazy ass…"

That was about all he could scream before Chanlina spun the bike around and went at him again. She pulled the sword from the sheath on her back and burned rubber accelerating the bike at the shooter. She leaned down pressing her chest against the bike's fuel tank but popped up just in time to swing the sword at his gun hand.

There was the distinctive sound of metal on metal as the gun flew from the man's hand along with several of his fingers. The bike came to a screeching stop and Chanlina jumped off the bike and kicked the revolver away from the man screaming in pain on the ground.

He was holding his bleeding hand with his other hand as Chanlina walked up to him and stomped on his groin several times until the man passed out. She grabbed him by the collar and drug him around to the back of the office, out of sight from the street.

"WAKE UP!" she screamed at him, slapping him on the face repeatedly.

When he finally regained consciousness, he was babbling as tears ran down his face "Don't kill me, Please don't kill me. I didn't know you didn't have any bullets. I thought it was just going to be a simple robbery. I swear I didn't know…"

"What is your boss' name. I need a name or I kill you here and now," she said in a menacing tone.

The man gave up the name immediately, even his address and phone number.

Chanlina thanked him for the information and turned as if to walk away, then turned back and said, "You're a stupid man. You think all Asians are chinks. Chinks are Chinese, japs are Japanese and people from southeast Asia are called gooks. I hate that name. I'm

Cambodian. Say it, you stupid black man. Or do you prefer I call you Negro? Or maybe you like nigger better?"

In a calm voice she said to him, "I want your boss to see what we gooks do to those who don't treat us with respect." She unbuckled his belt, pulled off his pant and underwear and used the sword to cut off his penis and testicles as he screamed in terror and pain. She waited for him to bleed out then opened the corpse's mouth and stuffed the bloody package into his mouth before she cut off his head and placed it into a plastic bag.

She placed the bag into the mini trunk on the bike's back fender, fired up the engine and headed towards Bridge City. I returned to tell Joshua all that I'd seen. I was thankful spirits didn't sleep. If I slept, I'm sure I would've had many, many nightmares. I will remember the man's screams for a long time.

CHAPTER 20

The Ones that Got Away—Joshua

It was lunch time when we left Larry at the FBI Field Office and headed towards the Lloyd Center. I hadn't spent much time in that area when I was involved in the human trafficking mission. I was glad the rental came equipped with a GPS system that guided us to our next stop. Simone was checking out restaurants in the shopping center while I was thinking about the burst signal Caleb unloaded on me last night.

In the late afternoon yesterday, when everything calmed down at the school, Pham and Mark decided to visit their old neighborhoods. Pham took an Uber to check on his office and get updates from the other attorneys who had offices in the same complex. Mark, Sarge and Sniffer rented a car and toured the Woodlawn District. He wanted to check out the memorial they built on the school grounds.

I used the drive time when Simone was checking lunch menus to reprocess everything Caleb and I discussed. When Caleb unloaded on me I was overwhelmed. I asked him to repeat what he communicated to me in his burst message but at the speed of a normal speaking conversation. It was still hard to believe but it seemed like the Cambodian woman (Caleb said her real name was Chanlina which meant moonbeam in English…no wait, moonlight, not moonbeam) fooled us all. It also looked like she couldn't take a joke and was ready to reap revenge on anybody and everybody she thought screwed her and her friends over. Caleb probed her mind and discovered she was the one who put together the team that hit the boarding school. Apparently, she felt responsible for them getting busted and now it was time for payback.

As soon as we finished up with the briefing from Priscilla Gomez, I needed to call everyone together on how we should move forward.

In the meantime, I'd asked Caleb to check out the boss who'd put together the attack on the boarding school.

The food court in the Lloyd Center was incredible. In addition, there were several stand-alone upscale restaurants that required a reservation and business casual attire wasn't acceptable. We decided on the food court. Simone found a place that served Cajun food and I opted for a double steak burger combo at (drum roll please) Steak and Shake! Who knew?!

After we finished our meals we strolled through the mall and almost got lost. We made it to our meeting five minutes early.

The command center bus was really an extra-large motorhome with three slide outs. It was crammed with all sorts of electronic gear, a large work area and two smaller offices for meetings.

Priscilla was standing outside talking with another agent when we arrived. It wasn't raining, however it looked like it might start to rain any minute. Of course it always looked like that. Welcome to Portland.

Pris introduced us to the other agent. We shook hands and he excused himself and headed to the helicopter landing pad. I heard the unmistakable sound of copter rotors getting louder as Agent Gomez ushered us inside the command bus.

"Watch your head!" she warned as I ducked down going through the entrance. "I forgot how big you are. The ceiling in the bus is seven feet high but the door is a little less than that. Have you had lunch?"

Simone answered as we followed Pris down a narrow hallway to the back of the bus, "Yes, thank you. We ate at the food court."

The two women exchanged pleasantries while we waited for another meeting to break up. I used the time to check out Agent Gomez. She was a little shorter than Simone but somewhat stockier, more muscular. She was wearing a long sleeve white shirt with her cred packed clipped to the breast pocket. Her jet black hair was pulled back into a pony tail which gave her the appearance of a no nonsense, in control person. When she spoke, her voice had a pleasant tone, however it was also an all business voice.

The office was a little tight, with a small table and four chairs. A window afforded a view of the parking lot and we paused as the chopper we'd heard approaching was now landing. The noise from the rotors was loud enough to drown out any conversation.

Agent Gomez checked her watch as the helicopter shut down and the noise level returned to normal. "Time for shift change but we're good here. No one will disturb us. Let's get to it, shall we?"

She opened a folder on the table and took out a few pages of briefing notes she used as reference.

"I'm most involved with the investigation of the robbery of Heritage Bank but I'll also cover what's going on at the other four banks that were robbed. There are numerous similarities."

She checked her notes one more time then put them down and began, "All of the banks were hit at the same time. So it was a coordinated effort, not just a coincidence. All of them used helicopters or conventional aircraft as a means of escape. There were customers in each bank at the time the robberies went down. At least some of the customers were murdered at each location. They all used explosives to generate chaos and additional murders as a cover for their escape. These were ruthless killers without any human compassion.

"It's estimated the total take for all five banks is over half a billion dollars. The banks are routinely restocked with cash each week or sooner if needed. The cash is delivered by a fleet of armored trucks. When the last car finished its delivery, the heists occurred.

"Surveillance cameras outside all the banks recorded a second round of armored trucks pulled up to the bank entrances within minutes of when the previous vehicles left. The trucks looked exactly the same. One witness across the street from Heritage Bank said she saw one vehicle leave and a few minutes later it returned. She said she thought it was the same truck who made a U-turn because they forgot something.

"The robbers entered through a side door into the bank. Apparently, everyone inside the bank, employees as well as customers, thought this was a routine follow up until two of the robbers shot the two security guards in the head from point blank range. There were smart phone videos of the shootings. Two of the customers began filming. They must have thought it was odd for the armored truck people to return so they began filming, just in case. We'll never know for sure. Both customers were killed during the heist. We recovered their phones under their bodies.

"We don't have much information what went down after that. After killing the security guards they destroyed all the internal surveillance equipment. The only thing we know for sure was they were in and out in fifteen minutes with millions of dollars of the bank's money. As a parting gesture, they detonated more than enough C-4 to sink an aircraft carrier which ensured the death of everyone left inside. Nobody escaped. It was worse than a war zone. We lost 37 people at Heritage bank, customers and employees from the branch manager on down to three children."

She stopped talking to gather her thoughts and I asked a question, "Do you have any intel on their escape?"

She nodded. "Yes, we had several eye witnesses across the street from the bank who heard the gun shots and the screaming of the victims. They began filming and captured pictures of six people leaving the bank and climbing into the armored truck. As it drove away, the bomb exploded. The blast injured pedestrians outside the bank and set off all kinds of car alarms. Not sure of the head count of injuries. I do know several people were killed.

"A few observers who weren't injured saw the armored truck heading up the ramp to the Lloyd Center's upper parking lot. A few minutes later a helicopter took off and flew north at what they thought was a very low altitude and very high speed. We were able to identify the helicopter. It'd been stolen earlier in the day from a flight school at Portland International Airport. They abandoned the armored truck when they left. It was wiped clean."

"Any leads on where the copter landed?" asked Simone.

"Not yet," answered Priscilla.

"How did the perps escape from the other four banks?" I asked.

"All four of them used their armored trucks to get away from the bank." Replied the agent. "Three of them abandoned their armored trucks for some type of aircraft. Two were at small local airports less than twenty five miles from their respective banks. We're still trying to determine what type of aircraft were used."

"What about the forth one?" asked Simone.

"Apparently, one of the escape aircraft crashed on takeoff. At least one of the robbers was killed on impact as well as the pilot. The other four managed to get back to the armored truck and drive away. The airport manager at the small private airport ID'd the armored truck. We issued a BOLO to the Portland PD and state police. So far, we haven't found them. We're not sure which bank they were from."

I heard Caleb in my mind, *Sounds like a job for the War Wagon, bro. What do you think?*

It could be time for a road trip. Let's go hunting!

CHAPTER 21

Follow the Yellow Brick Road—Caleb

As soon as Chanlina left the carnage at the bus rental place, I transported to Joshua and briefed him on what went down. He was as shocked as I had been. He kept thinking things like, *Really? No way! That's hard to believe,* and my personal favorite, *Oh my God, she did what?!!*

I let him know I'd accessed Chanlina's mind and 'borrowed' all the info on the man the bus rental guy reported to. His name was Harold Green and he was a big deal, a lawyer for the rich and famous in Portland, which made him rich and famous as well. He had a mansion in Portland's West Hills district. He also had an office downtown.

My brother suggested I go visit Mr. Green before Chanlina showed up with her sword. I agreed and transported to his home. Harold wasn't home but his wife, two children and three body guards were watching a Japanese movie on their huge TV screen with a terrific surround sound system. I think it was called *47 Ronin.* As much as I would have liked to have joined them, I moved on to his office complex and ended up outside the front door. I noticed two cars in the parking lot, both were high-end Mercedes. I didn't see any other cars so I assumed there were two people inside. Apparently, Mr. Green had a partner; the name on the door was Green and White, Attorneys at Law. It was a snappy name, very colorful.

I drifted through the ten-foot high front door and did a quick search of the offices. All the lights were out except in the lobby and one of the offices. I heard two voices coming from the lit office; a woman and a man were in the middle of a heated discussion. I positioned myself inside the office and listened to their conversation for about ten seconds. They were speaking in legalese which even with all my superior skills I couldn't understand.

The woman was dressed from head to toe in Saks Fifth Avenue and lots of gold and diamonds. It was hard to tell her age but I bet her plastic surgeon made a small fortune keeping her looking young. On second glance, it was probably a large fortune.

Mr. Green wore a suit worth a couple of thousand dollars and a green silk tie. I wondered if he felt obligated to wear a tie that matched his name. He was well tanned and wore a two-caret diamond ring on his pinky finger. I lost all respect for him after I noticed the ring.

While they argued, I snooped around looking for items of interest, downloaded all his client files to my extensive memory bank for further review. It looked like the discussion was going to last for a while so I decided to start going through his business records to see if I could find any evidence of his association with the seven teams of bank robbers or the raid on the boarding school. I found nothing of interest and then the doorbell chimed.

Harold excused himself from the client, walked through the lobby and stopped at the locked door. He checked his smart phone and saw a delivery person in a brown UPS uniform waiting to deliver a box. "I have a delivery for Harold Green, Attorney at Law."

"Please leave the box, I'll pick it up when I'm through with my meeting."

"I can't leave it. You have to sign for it."

He paused for a moment, then asked, "Who is it from?"

"Sorry, there's no return address."

Harold let out a frustrated sigh, unlocked the door and opened it. It was Chanlina. She walked in and set the box on the reception desk. She handed the clipboard to Harold and showed him where to sign. He scribbled his name and handed the clipboard and pen back to her. She handed Harold the box and said in perfect English, "You should refrigerate that as soon as you open it, I'm told it's perishable. You have a good night sir."

She turned and left abruptly. Harold turned and headed back to the office but stopped at the receptionist's desk. He checked the box but found nothing to indicate what was in the box or who'd sent it.

Apparently, his curiosity got the better of him and he opened the box. There was a black plastic bag inside which held something about the size of a basketball. When he pulled the bag off he dropped everything and began screaming. He stared at the severed head of a black man. It was covered in blood and its mouth was stuffed with something fleshy. Written on the forehead was a short message: $1,000,000 or this will be you tomorrow.

He continued to scream as he dropped the severed head at his feet. It bounced a couple of times before coming to rest face up with milky eyes staring directly at him. He stood frozen in place as Saks-Fifth Avenue came running out of the office to see what happened. She skidded to a stop, slipped on the blood and fell to the floor a foot away from the head. She joined Harold in screaming, "HAROLD!!! What have you done. Did you kill him?"

Harold managed to stop screaming terrible random sounds long enough to scream at her, "SHUT UP you insufferable bitch!!! Of course I didn't kill him. I don't kill people. I pay others to do my killing." He stopped screaming for a moment when he realized what he'd said. He turned to Saks and said in a very threatening voice, "Get the fuck out of here, you bitch. Don't you dare tell anybody about this or else."

As she turned and ran for the door, I noticed she'd slid into the pool of blood and brain matter. It was all over her expensive pants. What a pity.

Harold followed her out the door leaving everything untouched. The lights automatically shut off and the door locked as he ran across the parking lot and jumped into his Mercedes. I took the passenger seat next to him. It's a good thing I'm an invisible spirit. I get to listen to so many secrets undetected.

As Harold drove out of the parking lot into the street, he made two hand's-free phone calls. The first was to his home, "I need to speak to Hiroshi, right now!" he said to his wife.

A muffled sound came from the car's speaker before his wife answered, "He says to wait a moment. He's watching a very important scene in *47 Samurai.*"

He heard Hiroshi in the background, "It's *47 Ronin.*"

Harold exploded. "I don't give a shit what he's watching. Put him on right now or his Jap ass is fired!"

At least he got the correct racial slur, I thought to myself.

Hiroshi was on the phone in an instant and Harold ordered him and the other two security men to go to the office and clean the place up. "There's a severed head in the lobby you need to get rid of. Burn it or bury it. I never want it found, understood? The office has to be spotless by tomorrow morning, no excuses."

Hiroshi replied, "We'll take care of it, boss. No worries. Can I ask a favor?"

"What favor?" Harold asked in an exasperated tone.

"Can I watch the end of *47 Ronin* and then clean the office?"

Harold disconnected without answering. His next call was the important one. He scrolled the call directory on the Mercedes screen and came to the name Jimbo.

It rang once before someone picked up. Harold waited exactly five seconds and asked, "May I speak to James please?" His voice shifted. I could hear the fear.

Exactly five seconds later a woman's voice replied, "There is no John at this number."

Five more seconds, then Harold said, "Jimbo," and hung up.

This was getting really complicated. I needed to get back to Joshua.

CHAPTER 22

Which Way Do We Go?—Joshua

I called an all-hands meeting after we returned from getting our briefings from the FBI. All of our team members were busy with various assignments. On our return to the boarding school, I had Simone drive while Caleb and I exchanged information. Caleb waited patiently while we finished our FBI briefings, however now he was bursting at the seams to give me the entire story of Chanlina's escapades.

After she cut off the head of the rent-a-bus man, she took the head and went back to Bridge City. I thought she might be done for the night. I was wrong. She'd gotten the contact info for the next dude up on the hierarchy of creeps. She left immediately and I followed your recommendation and immediately transported to check him out before Chanlina could get to him.

It turns out the dude was a rich lawyer. I got all his client files including the ones that were encrypted. I was about to see if I could find out who the lawyer worked for when Chanlina showed up. She was dressed like a UPS driver and had a package for him.

At first, I thought she was going to cut his head off too but she gave him the box and left. When the lawyer opened the box it was the decapitated head of the rent-a-bus man. It was all gory and the lawyer freaked out. When he saw the note attached to the head, he really lost it. It said if he didn't pay her a million dollars, she was going to come back and take his head too.

The lawyer bolted and called somebody but it was all in code, some kind of James Bond stuff. I tried calling the number and got nothing. They didn't answer. I called three more times with thirty minute intervals between each call. Still no answer. When I made the last call, there was a recorded message saying the number was no longer in service.

I'm not sure what the next step should be. I guess the best thing would be to keep shadowing Chanlina. If the lawyer tries to buy her off, she'd take his money then kill him anyway but I'll bet she finds out who the lawyer's contact is. She is one ruthless woman, crafty but ruthless.

I agreed with Caleb's suggestion and asked him to continue following Chanlina. I also mentioned we would be taking the War Wagon out to track down the escaped bank robbers. I told him about the plane crash and how they were trying to make a getaway in an armored truck.

There was a pause, then Caleb thought to me, *Damn it, Josh. You screwed me again. Every time you break out the War Wagon, you've got me on some other assignment. I want to be where the action is!*

I replied back, *Isn't watching a castration and a beheading action enough?*

That wasn't action, it was disgusting, he countered.

Okay, I countered his counter and suggested, *How about I contact you when the action starts and you can transport to the War Wagon. There's going to be a lot of boring routine stuff going on before the action begins, assuming we can find the armored truck.*

Really? You'd do that for me? That sounds great! Okay then. I'm off to see what the Cambodian Assassin is up to.

Ten minutes later Simone drove the rental car into the boarding school parking lot.

Lawsuits, Lawsuits, Everywhere A Lawsuit—Pham

I took an Uber to visit some of my associates in the Law Clinic. I'd sublet my office to a close friend who'd been trying to get into the Law Clinic building for several months prior to me joining up with Joshua's team.

His name was Thanh Nguyen and we'd entered the United States on student visas. Both of us were fairly fluent in English and were awarded scholarships to the Oregon School of Law, part of the University of Oregon and located in the city of Eugene (Go Ducks!).

We met on a Viet Jet Air flight out of Tan Son Nhat International Airport in Ho Chi Minh City. We actually met waiting in line to board the flight and were able to make some seat changes allowing us to sit next to each other on the twelve hour flight over the Pacific Ocean.

We were in the same graduating class three years later. However, Thanh had to return to Vietnam shortly after graduation and passing his Oregon bar exams. He returned almost two years later but we kept in touch while we were separated. Unfortunately, the Law Clinic offices didn't have any vacancies when he returned.

I joined Joshua's team about six months after he arrived back in Oregon and was very excited about subleasing my office. He took over all of my cases, at least temporarily.

I called ahead to make sure he was available. He was and we arranged to meet in my (or his) office that afternoon.

We spent most the of the afternoon reminiscing and just hanging out. When I asked him how his case load was, his demeaner changed from light hearted to glum.

"What's up, Thanh?" I asked him in English, concerned there were problems with his work.

"So many lawsuits, Pham. Ever since Governor Johnson changed the Oregon gun control laws, I've been inundated with lawsuits filed against the state of Oregon as well as the Governor. With this recent crime wave of bank robberies, it's gotten even worse. My case load has increased by at least fifty percent since I took over your cases. It's insane, I routinely work twelve-hour days now. It's a good thing I'm not married…oh wait! I *am* married," he said with a grin. "It's an even better thing that she works in the office with me. She's been a big help."

"You didn't tell me you were married. How come?" I asked.

"I've been so busy, it slipped my mind…wait again. I didn't say that right. It didn't slip my mind that I've been married. We've been married for seven months now. I just forgot to mention it to you when we spoke on the phone. Let me introduce her to you. I think she's back from running an errand for me.

"Honey, are you here?" he yelled into the lobby.

"Coming, husband," she said in fairly heavy accented English, "Oh, company have you."

She was a very attractive Vietnamese woman, several years younger than Thanh, dressed in a modest, colorful dress and high heel shoes. She smiled at me as I stood up.

"Cais, this is my best friend, Pham. He was the one I told you about."

I smiled and extended my hand. She took it and shook once. "Hello, Cais," I said in Vietnamese. "It's a pleasure to meet you. Congratulations on your marriage."

Cais (her name translates to rejoicing person) gave a slight bow and smiled back. "Meet you my pleasure," she said in English. Then added, "Work now, must. Husband's slave."

She bowed again, turned and headed for the lobby.

"Her English is a work in progress," Thanh said sheepishly.

"So is she really your slave?" I teased.

"Some days, I feel like I'm the slave but she is the love of my life. We met when I made a trip to visit my parents in Vietnam, a little over a year ago. She was introduced to me by a mutual friend, my mother."

We continued our conversation until I received a phone call from Joshua requesting my return for an all-hands meeting. It was such a pleasure to visit with an old friend.

Visiting the Woodlawn District—Mark and Friends

I arrived back at the boarding school a little after Simone and Joshua returned from their briefings with the FBI. I'd taken Sarge and Sniffer along with me for the ride. They both rode in the back seat with their harnesses attached to the seat belts while we were on the interstate. When we turned onto Dekum Street, I slowed down to 25 mph and lowered the back windows. As I knew they would, both dogs stuck their heads out the windows and began sniffing the air.

As I pulled into a side street close to where Sarge and I lived for a couple of years, I wondered if he would remember our apartment. I kept both dogs on leash and let them jump out of the car. As we walked down the street towards where we used to live, Sarge stopped abruptly, turned his head to look at me for second, barked once, then almost yanked me off my feet. Sniffer had no idea why Sarge was running down the sidewalk but it must have looked like fun and he joined in. It was all I could do to keep up with them. Sarge stopped at the front door of our old unit and Sniffer joined him. Both dogs looked back at me and began barking.

Before I could get them calmed down, the front door opened and a young woman looked around the edge of the door and said, "What is all the barking about? Are these your dogs?"

I gave a hand sign and Sarge stopped barking. Since Sarge stopped, Sniffer stopped too. "I'm so sorry Miss," I said, hoping I sounded apologetic. "We used to live in this apartment. We were just taking a walk through the neighborhood to see if my dog remembered it."

"How did you get the dogs to stop barking so quickly?" she asked as she opened the door and stepped out onto the porch.

"There special therapy dogs," I lied, the truth was too long to explain and Sarge was truly a therapy dog, however he was so much more. Sniffer was a different story but he was learning.

"They're really therapy dogs?" she asked, then noticed the words Therapy Dog written on their vests. "Oh, I guess they are."

"Doggies!" said a young girl from inside the apartment. "Can I pet the doggies?"

"Would that be all right with you, mister…" she paused and I introduced myself as well as the dogs.

"Just call me Mark. The big dog is Sarge and the smaller one is Sniffer."

"My name is Maria and this is my daughter, Serena," said the young woman as the little girl stepped onto the porch and took her mother's hand. She looked longingly at both dogs, then up at her mother.

"Mark, could you do me a huge favor? Serena has been having nightmares. The counselors say they will pass with time. I feel so helpless. I don't know what to do." She paused for a moment, unsure of what to say next.

In a pleading voice the little girl whispered, "Please mommy."

She looked down at her daughter, then turned to look at me and the dogs. "Would you consider coming inside your old apartment and letting her be with your dogs for a few minutes? I think it would mean a lot to Serena."

"Of course," I answered. "We'd love to see what you've done to our old home. And both of the dogs really love children."

A few minutes became an hour. It turns out Serena was one of the survivors from the Woodlawn Elementary Massacre. Maria told me they closed the school and converted it into a memorial site for those who didn't survive. After a week of counseling, they began busing the survivors to James B. Faubion Elementary School located a couple of miles from Woodlawn. She thought it was too soon.

While Maria and I talked, Serena played with the dogs. She hugged and petted them both and they in turn, licked her cheek and made happy little sounds that seemed to please the girl immensely.

After about half an hour, Serena appeared to be running out of gas. Maria said she hadn't been sleeping well and was probably exhausted. The girl grabbed a small blanket and a pillow from her bedroom. When she returned to the living room, she said, "Nap time. Everybody lay down." They quickly laid down on the floor, covered herself with the blanket and laid her head on the pillow. Without being prompted, Sarge curled up next to her and Sniffer took the other side. Within minutes she was sound asleep with the two dogs sleeping beside her.

Maria and I talked for another half-hour. We talked quietly, checking on Serena every few minutes. The sleeping girl looked so comfortable with her two bodyguards.

I got a text from Joshua to return to the boarding school and get the War Wagon prepped for a search and destroy mission. I signaled the dogs to get up. They gently separated themselves from Serena who remained sound asleep on the floor.

"Do you want me to pick her up and put her in her bed?" I asked.

Maria shook her head. "No, please put her in my bed. She's been sleeping with me since the attack. By the way thank you for not asking me about a husband. I want you to know I'm a single parent. I also want you to know Serena and I can't thank you enough for what you and your dogs have done this afternoon. You're welcome to come visit whenever you want."

I placed the girl in her mother's bed, gathered Sarge and Sniffer who were operating in quiet mode, then headed for the door. Before I left she gave me a hug and kissed me on the cheek. There were tears in her eyes as she said, "You and your wonderful dogs have been a God send. Please come visit us again soon."

What Happened to Ms. Tong?—Detective Hong

Buffalo Bill and I were on our way to the Vietnamese boarding school to attend the meeting with…well I guess with everybody involved with the attack on the school as well as the attacks on the seven Portland banks. This could be a long meeting.

Our main interest was to find out what Joshua's CI had to report regarding the whereabouts of Ms. Tong. We also wanted to determine if she was involved with the grisly murder of a bus rental agency owner. The body was discovered early this morning by two employees. When Bill and I arrived at the scene, two patrol officers had secured the crime scene and a van from the CSI unit had already shown up.

Bill took one look at the body and turned away not looking well. When I took a quick glance, I had a similar reaction and was glad I hadn't eaten any donuts this morning. The ME gave us a short report, "This isn't your everyday murder, at least not in Portland, maybe in LA or New York but not here. The cause of death is he bled out from having all of his manhood removed by a very sharp blade. By the looks of it, it was probably a large knife or perhaps a sword. It took only one cut to remove everything."

"Where's the head?" Bill asked with his handkerchief covering his nose and mouth. The body was already beginning to putrefy and the stench was getting strong.

"Nowhere to be found. Perhaps the perp took it with him as a trophy. Probably has it displayed on his mantle by now, along with the other heads he's taken. Whoever separated the head from the body knew what he was doing. This wasn't the first time he'd beheaded someone. Again, it only took one cut, kind of like what you see in the samurai movies. That's not easy to do. It would take practice, lots of practice."

In addition to the beheading, we received a call late last night from a lady who swore she saw a decapitated head in the lobby of a law office. Since like the ME said earlier, we don't get a lot of beheadings, we think this had to be related to the murder of the bus rental owner. Again, we were interested in seeing if Joshua's CI can tie Ms. Tong to these events.

CHAPTER 23

All Hands On Deck—Joshua

It was late afternoon when our meeting began. We met in the boarding school cafeteria and pushed together a few lunch room tables to form a square large enough to seat all eight of us. Cam made sure there were snacks, water and other drinks available on another lunch table close to our square. I started it off, "The purpose of this meeting is to bring everyone up to speed on the progress being made on both the boarding school attack and the seven bank robberies. Let me begin by having Pastor Boa and his wife Cam fill us in on how the students are doing in the wake of the attack on his boarding school."

"Thank you, Joshua," relied the pastor. "We are doing quite well, thanks to Joshua and this team, that includes Sarge. While we were all frightened by the attack none of us were hurt physically, however many of the children and a few of our teachers and staff were pretty badly shaken. The counselors provided by the school board really helped most of the students overcome their fears. Unfortunately, a few of the parents have decided to remove their children from our school, at least for a little while. Those who board here have decided to stay. The older students have been so helpful in caring for the troubled younger students. I think in time, everything will return to normal."

Before he could sit down, Mark asked, "How are you feeling, Pastor? You're the only one who suffered any physical damage."

"Thank you for your concern but it was really nothing. Just a small cut on my lip and a little bruising."

Pham turned to Cam and asked, "Are you okay, Madam Cam? We were all very impressed at your verbal attack on the man who struck your husband. We had no previous knowledge of your assault vocabulary. It was very impressive to those of us who spoke Vietnamese, exceptionally colorful."

Cam blushed in embarrassment, then spoke in a firm voice, "I said what I needed to say to distract the animal who slapped my husband. I asked God for forgiveness of my vulgar language." She paused then added, "Only I am allowed to strike my husband."

That resulted in a somewhat shocked pause. Then Simone broke the silence, as she yelled "Right on, Cam!" and thrust her fist toward the ceiling. A round of applause followed as I called on the next speaker.

"Detective Hong, would you and your partner brief us on how things went with Ms. Tong last night?" I asked.

He and Bill did a quick description of how they went about releasing her. They left out the part where she stripped naked in front of them and offered them sex for money. However they did mention they gave her some cash as she left the police station.

Bill summed it up, "We released her to see where she would go and who she might contact. We were looking for a lead as to who set Ms. Tong and her people up. She was suspicious as to why we weren't keeping her in jail. We tried to convince her she was free to go because nobody got hurt. It was just a mistake, a misunderstanding."

Hong added, "Were not sure she understood what we told her but she left and we turned over her surveillance to Joshua's CI. So what have you got for us, boss?"

As Hong and Cody went to the snack table to pick up donuts and coffee, I took over.

"My CI followed Ms. Tong as she left the police station. It was late afternoon and the sky was overcast. He reported she was very suspicious she was being followed and did all types of tricks to evade surveillance. Fortunately for us, our CI is a pro and hung with her.

"She made her first stop at a CVS where she stole some candy bars and bought a burner phone. Apparently, someone in the police department gave her some money."

"What type of candy bars?" interrupted detective Cody, ignoring the comment about money.

I looked down at my notes then answered, "Two Almond Joys and a Snickers."

"Wow," replied Cody. "Your boy is really good. What happened next?"

"She walked down the block eating one of her Almond Joys. When she got to a bus stop she made a short call on the burner phone. The CI continued to walk by her and he was able to hear a few words."

"So what did she say?" asked Hong impatiently.

"He heard her say, '…to kill you.'"

"What happened next?" asked Hong.

"It started to drizzle and she walked several blocks and entered a Goodwill Store. She stole several items of clothes then walked to the back of the store where there wasn't any video coverage. She stripped naked leaving her rain soaked clothes on the floor then put on the stolen clothes. She transferred the remainder of her candy bars, her burner phone and the remaining money to the stolen clothes then headed out of the store. She bought a cheap umbrella on her way out.

"Once back on the street, she headed for the Burnside Bridge. When she got close to the bridge she turned down an unlit alley which turned into a gravel path. Our CI had a pair of night vision goggles and was able to continue following her in the near darkness.

"She stopped directly under the middle of the bridge where there was a lean-to. She yelled something in a dialect the CI didn't understand. Eventually a very large man came out of the lean-to and they carried on a conversation in the same dialect.

"The CI thinks he found out the Ms. Tong's real name. It's Chanlina. Does anybody know what that means in English?"

Cam spoke up, "Yes, I do. It's Khmer for moonlight. A common name for Cambodian woman."

I continued, "The CI said that Chanlina waved some money under the nose of the large man and he pointed behind the lean-to. She walked out of sight for a moment then reappeared pushing a motorcycle. She said a few more things and the man reached into the lean-to and brought out what looked like a short sword in a sling sheath.

"She slipped the sheath over her shoulder, fired up the motorcycle and drove off. The CI had no way to follow her so he contacted me and relayed what I just told you."

"That's it? He didn't follow her?" asked Cody.

I stared at him for a moment then said as if speaking to a child, "How could he follow her. He was on foot under a bridge, surrounded by homeless and potentially dangerous people. He was lucky he got out of there without being killed."

"Actually, that was great intel by your CI," said Hong as he tried to redirect the conversation away from his partner. "Let me tell you why.

"This intel makes Chanlina the prime suspect for a murder that occurred later that night. Now we have reason to believe she is trying to get back at the people who set her and her friends up as a diversion for the bank robberies. She wants vengeance and she also wants money, lots of money. I think she's going to continue killing people until they pay her off to the tune of a million dollars."

Cody joined in, "I think we should make a call tomorrow morning and see if she's with her friends under the bridge. I suggest we should hit the lean-to first. Maybe the big man is her boyfriend and she spent the night in his lean-to."

I nodded in agreement and added, "I don't mean to tell you how to run your operations but I suggest you come at the lean-to from both sides of the bridge as well as from the river."

"Excellent idea, Joshua," replied Bill. "I'm glad we thought of it a few minutes before you did. Even if she's not there we want to see if she brought the bike back. We'd love to see if she returned the sword. We'd probably have the murder weapon if she did."

He paused for a moment to look at his partner who nodded his consent. "If it's okay with you, we'd like to take our leave now. We have a raid to plan."

They said their goodbyes and each took a couple of donuts with them as they headed to their car.

The next order of business was to find the missing armored truck. We took a short break for snacks, drinks and trips to the bathroom. Before we resumed, Pastor Boa and Cam excused themselves saying they were needed to help with the children and they weren't really involved with finding the bank robbers.

Cam made a point of giving Simone a big hug for her support, Simone in turn mentioned something about the women sticking together. After they left we got back to business.

There were four of us seated around the table, well five if you included Caleb. Sarge was also there, as was Sniffer, also known as Sarge's shadow. I started it off with what we knew so far.

"The two FBI agents we visited today gave us good intel. Thanks go to Simone for setting those meetings up. Let me give you the short version of what we found out. First, the FBI has split their efforts into two camps. One is dealing with the captured robbers from the two heists gone bad. The other is trying to run down the five crews who successfully carried off their heists and were able to escape.

"At the present time I don't think we can offer any additional support to the FBI for the first category. Thanks to our CIs for providing the intel that permitted the FBI to make the arrests."

Yea for me! inserted Caleb.

I ignored him and continued on, "It looks like they're going to trial. The FBI is recommending the death penalty for all of the robbers. However, they're concerned that someone has provided the perps with some high powered lawyers.

"As for the second group, four out of the five teams were able to escape with hundreds of millions in cash. The FBI believes all five of the teams planned to escape using aircraft. Currently, four of the five are in the wind. The fifth team attempted to escape in an aircraft from the Troutdale Airport. Unfortunately for them, their aircraft crashed on takeoff killing the pilot and one of the robbers. The remaining four perps were able to get back to their armored truck and leave the crash scene. I believe our best plan of action is to use the War Wagon to run down the armored truck. Any questions so far?"

Mark asked, "Any chance all the escaped teams are planning to hook up somewhere?"

"Unknown at his time," I answered.

"Do we know if any of the perps who escaped the crash were injured?" asked Simone.

"Good question," I replied. "I don't know but I think we should follow up with the FBI and see if any witnesses to the crash are available."

"Do we know what type of armored truck they used for escape? I'd like to know what electronics they had on board as well as stuff like how much armor they have. I assume they have run flat tires but do they have any offensive weapons other than the assault rifles they used during the robbery."

"All good questions, Mark. I believe the banks in Portland use Loomis trucks to transport their cash. You're in charge of contacting Loomis and getting details on their trucks. We also need to find out how the perps got a hold of seven armored trucks that looked exactly like the Loomis versions. Were they stolen from Loomis or were they copy cats supplied by whoever was bankrolling the heists?"

I looked around at my team and could tell they were getting pumped up about having a specific mission. I was getting pumped myself.

I turned to Pham and said, "Pham you're responsible for getting the War Wagon up and ready for the search mission." I paused then added, "Lets upgrade that. Make her ready for a possible search and destroy mission. These perps have already killed a lot of innocent people. They won't hesitate to take us on."

In my head, I heard my brother, *What about me, Josh. What's my assignment?*

I want you to find out where the armored truck went. All the other trucks were abandoned so it should be easy for you.

Really? he thought back to me. *You think it's going to be easy to find one stinking armored truck in the whole state of Oregon?*

The FBI told me and Simone the truck left the crash scene heading east. The Troutdale airport is due east about twenty miles from Portland International Airport. It's right next to the Columbia River. There, that should give you a head start.

Oh thanks a lot, my bother. The airport is next to the Columbia River. How nice. That just means I have to include the state of Washington into my search along with all of eastern Oregon.

I have every confidence you will use your secret spirit powers and find our target truck in practically no time. As an incentive, I'm considering telling the rest of the team about my brother Caleb. It's getting harder to use the CI cover for you. And besides, I want the team to know how valuable you really are.

There was a long pause of silence before he responded. *Are you really sure you want to do that?*

I replied back to him, *Find me that truck and it's a done deal.*

CHAPTER 24

Under the Burnside Bridge—Detective Hong

Very early the next morning, Detective Cody and I along with a squad of uniforms raided the homeless shelter under the Burnside Bridge known as Bridge City. Assisting us were the Multnomah County Marine Patrol. They provided three boats with armed officers to ensure nobody escaped by boat or by floating down the Willamette.

The sun was barely above the horizon when we made our move. What a waste of time. There were still a lot of homeless people but none of them were Cambodian. We found the lean-to just where Joshua's CI said it would be. It was empty, no motorcycle, no sword, no people, no nothing. All thirty of her people gone over night. Chanlina played us again.

Since the raid turned out to be a bust, Bill and I decided to visit with Harold Green, Attorney at Law. Bill and I were curious why the decapitated head ended up in his office. The woman who gave us the tip refused to give us her name. She did happen to tell us Harold mentioned he paid to have people murdered. That got our attention.

We decided to arrive unannounced and had one of the CSI people join us. Bill had a hunch the head was no longer in the office lobby and the lawyer would deny there ever was.

We walked into the Green and White law office complex. We decided to play bad cop and really bad cop. To get into character, I thought about having a couple of donuts and find out the box was empty. That always pissed me off.

The three of us came through the really high front door and walked to the reception desk showing a lot of attitude. I let Buffalo Bill speak first, "We're with the Portland Police. We need to speak with Harold Green."

The receptionist didn't bother to look up, "Unfortunately, Mr. Green is with a client. Perhaps you can make an appointment for some time next week. He has a very busy sched…"

I walked passed Bill and slammed my hand down on the desk, causing the receptionist to jump back and finally look at us. I unloaded on her, "Your boss is a suspect in a murder case. His meeting with his client is over. Get him out here now!"

She pushed a button on her intercom and said in a trembling voice, "Mr. Green, there are policemen in the lobby demanding to see you immediately. They say you're a suspect in a murder case."

We could clearly hear the voice of a man shouting, "A murder case, that's ridiculous. This is some kind of joke. Did they show you their badges?"

While he was protesting so loudly, I walked to his office door, opened it wide with one hand and flashed my badge with the other. "Happy now?" I said.

I looked at the man who sat frozen in a comfortable looking chair across the desk from Harold. "Your meeting is over…get out of here…NOW!"

The man stumbled from this chair and nearly fell as he rushed to leave the office. Bill brushed by him and also flashed his badge. Bill turned to me, totaling ignoring Harold and said, "I've got our CSI guy checking the lobby floor for evidence."

I turned to Harold in time to see his knees buckling from the mention of CSI. Bill sat down and I took the chair beside him. I motion for Harold to also sit down but he seemed frozen in place. Bill ordered, "Sit down Mr. Green. Sit down now!"

Green fell back into his very expensive leather chair with polished mahogany inserts and brass fittings or maybe they were gold.

Bill and I sat silently staring at him as Randall, our CSI man, continued to check for evidence of a murder on the lobby floor. It took only a few minutes before Randall stuck his head in the door. "I found traces of blood and brain matter right in front of the reception desk."

I nodded and turned back to look at Harold. I said, "You're in big trouble, Harold. We have a witness who said she saw you standing over a decapitated head right where our CSI man discovered blood and brains. She also said you admitted to committing murders. It was obvious you tried to clean up the murder scene. We have all the evidence we need to charge you with suspicion of murder. Do you have anything to say?"

It was obvious Harold was completely freaked out. He tried to speak but nothing came out. He licked his lips, took a sip of water from a crystal tumbler on his desk, stared at both of us for a moment then said, "I want a lawyer."

We didn't move. After a moment, Bill said, "*You* are the lawyer, at least for now."

"Stand up and put your hands behind your back, You are under arrest on charges of suspicion of murder," I said as Bill cuffed him and read him his Miranda Rights. As we walked through the lobby, I said to the receptionist, "Your boss is being detained indefinitely. I suggest you cancel all his client appointments for the foreseeable future."

As we drove back to the station, I was feeling pretty good. It started out as a crappy day, however things were looking up. I couldn't wait to get him back to the station and begin his interrogation.

Troutdale Airport—Simone

I called my friend with the FBI to see if she could hook me up with any of the witnesses to the crash at the Troutdale Airport. Unfortunately, she was tied up in a series of meetings. I decided to contact the airport manager at Troutdale to see if he could give me any information regarding the crash. His assistant was very helpful and scheduled a meeting for me.

I took an Uber to the airport and arrived a little over an hour later. I showed the receptionist my government creds and he took me to a conference room. He told me the manager would join me shortly.

A few minutes later a tall man with a goatee walked into the conference room. He smiled warmly and said as he sat down, "Good morning. My name is Steve Nelson, I'm the senior manager for general aviation here at Troutdale Airport. How can I help you?"

"Thank you for seeing me on such short notice Mr. Nelson. I'm agent Simone Cantrell and I have some questions regarding the recent crash at your airport."

"Well, I'm your man. I happened to be outside and saw the crash and all the aftermath that followed."

That was encouraging and I followed up with, "Is it okay if I record our conversation? I want to make sure I remember what you tell me."

He nodded his assent and I placed my phone on the table and touched the record button. "Could you tell me what you saw? It would be best if you could be as detailed as possible."

"No problem," he answered, "Well, first of all, I went outside when the armored truck drove up. It usually comes in on Fridays and it was only Wednesday."

I was surprised by his comment, "Why would an armored truck come to the airport?"

"The Troutdale airport is a bank hub. Every Friday, commercial pilots flying light aircraft, pick up cash deposits and bank receipts from branch offices in the smaller cities and towns around the northern part of Oregon and fly them in here. They're referred to as 'bank runs.' Six aircraft land around 5:00 pm every Friday. The pilots take the lock box from their planes and turn them over to the guard on the armored truck. The guard signs for each delivery then takes the lock boxes to the main bank in downtown Portland"

"What happened last Wednesday?" I asked.

"I was standing in the lobby of the office when the armored truck drove by. It usually parks in a particular location close to where the bank run planes tie down. They have specific tie-down locations. This time the truck went right past their normal parking spot and continued down the ramp to where a visiting Turboporter was waiting."

"I'm sorry, what's a Turboporter?" I asked.

"Oh, sorry. A Turboporter is a certain type of airplane. It's a STOL aircraft, that stands for Short Take Off and Landing. It has a highly efficient propeller driven by a gas turbine engine. It can carry a lot of cargo or up to ten people. The plane landed about thirty minutes before the armored truck showed up."

"Was there anything out of the ordinary about the armored truck?"

"Not that I noticed," he answered. "It was the typical Loomis armored truck, same model, same color."

"Did anyone notice its license number or the Loomis ID number?"

"I didn't, however to get onto the airport ramp where the planes are hangered all vehicles have to drive through a security gate. There are video cameras which take pictures of each vehicle, both front and back, when they enter and when they leave. I'm sure we can get you those numbers."

"Okay, that would be great. What happened next?"

"I'd stepped outside to see where the truck was going and saw several people get out of the truck carrying several large, heavy looking bags. They threw them into the cargo area of the plane then climbed into the plane, leaving the truck's doors wide open. When I saw that, I knew something bad was happening. I turned to walk back to the office. I intended to call the police, when my assistant ran out shouting that several Portland banks had been robbed and a lot of people were killed. I told him to call the police and tell them what was going on here."

"What happened next?" I asked.

"The Turboporter started moving down the taxiway. I could hear sirens and see flashing lights. I guess the pilot saw them too. He didn't even try to get to the runway. I could hear the plane's engine go to full power and the pilot started his takeoff while still on the taxiway. He was going the wrong way and there was incoming traffic attempting to land. The Turboporter can take off at low speeds in a very short distance and it was off the ground in less than a hundred feet."

He got airborne but the oncoming traffic must have spooked him. He tried to bank away from the incoming plane but he didn't have enough altitude. His left wing tip hit the ground causing the plane to go through a number of gyrations trying to regain altitude but it was too late. The plane crashed onto the taxiway."

"The plane burst into flames and our onsite firetruck came out of its garage heading to the fire. I counted four men who made it out of the burning plane. They grabbed the large bags out of the cargo hold and ran to the open doors of their truck. I never saw the pilot or the other passenger. I found out later the pilot died on impact. I'm not sure what happened to the passenger."

"How did they get away?"

"Once inside their truck, they fired up the engine, it sounded like a diesel. Even before the doors were closed, the truck made a tight U-turn squealing the tires, then accelerated down the taxiway. The armored truck sideswiped the firetruck on its way to the fire and passed no more than ten feet from me as it turned onto runway 7 heading east."

"My God!" I said, "You're lucky to be alive." I paused trying to figure out how to word my next question, then said, "I know this is going to sound crazy, however I feel I need to ask. Did you notice anything different about the armored truck when it went by you?"

Steve closed his eyes and replayed that moment of near death. With his eyes closed he said, "The truck was a lot louder when it went by me, maybe it had a bigger diesel. Oh yeah, there were more gun ports, at least there were on the side next to me. Not only more but larger in diameter, maybe to accommodate weapons with larger barrels? I can't be sure, fear sometime distorts what you remember."

"Don't worry, I'm really surprised you would remember anything about that moment. You gave me great detail. Could you tell me where the truck went after it went by you?"

"Once it was on runway 7 it just kept accelerating. By the time it came to the end of the runway it had to be doing more than a hundred. I was shocked when it just kept on going off the end of the runway and onto grass and dirt. It went right through the retaining fence at the border of the airport property and disappeared into a thicket of trees on the other side. I lost sight of it after that.

"How long did it take the police to show up. Did they send any helicopters to search for the truck?"

"It took about ten minutes for the police to arrive but there weren't any helicopters; they were all out looking for the other aircraft the bank robbers used to escape."

Before I could ask any more questions, Steve's assistant rapped on the door. "Boss don't forget you have a meeting in five minutes with some of the aircraft owners."

"Tell them I'll be right there," he said as he stood up.

"Simone, I hope I helped in your investigation. If you have any questions, feel free to call or drop by any time. Don't forget to pick up the thumb drive at my assistant's desk on your way out. It includes the video of the armored truck coming through the security gate."

Loomis Armored Trucks—Mark

After I received the thumb drive from Simone that had the pictures of the armored truck from the bank robbery, I contacted the Loomis office in Portland and set up an appointment with one of their managers. His name was Russell Carter and he was responsible for truck maintenance.

I met him in the lobby of their offices. The first thing he did was to check my creds. He seemed satisfied.

"So you're an agent with Homeland Security. How long have you been with the agency?" he asked as we walked down a hallway to a conference room.

"A couple of years now," I answered.

"What did you do before you became a federal agent?" he asked

"I worked security for the Port of Portland, mostly at Terminal 6."

"Terminal B1is6? Were you involved with that human trafficking incident where they were smuggling in Vietnamese children on a container ship?"

"Yes sir, I was. My involvement on that crime led me to joining Homeland."

"Well good for you, Mr. Riley," he said as he closed the door and we sat down at the conference table. "How can I help you today?"

"I want to get some information regarding the armored trucks used in the recent bank robberies. Were any of your trucks stolen before the robbery?"

"No, none of our trucks were stolen. The first thing we did after we heard about the robberies was to take an inventory of all our trucks. I'm happy to say they were all accounted for."

I opened a folder I brought with me that had pictures of the robber's armored truck. They were excellent pictures showing the front and part of the driver's side. A second picture showed the rear and the left side. They were in color and to me they looked like all the other white Loomis armored trucks I'd seen when I drove through the company parking lot.

Mr. Carter took one look at the pictures and said, "It's definitely not one of ours. This model is bigger, more heavily armored and looks like it has a bigger turbodiesel engine than any of ours."

He continued to study the pictures, then said, "It has a lot more armor on it than any of our trucks. Are you familiar with the B rating system for truck armor?"

I shook my head, "Never heard of it."

"It's based on the ability to stop a bullet from penetrating the vehicle. B1 is the lowest level. That shielding would stop a .22 long rifle bullet. A B3 would stop a .44 Magnum round, a B7 should be able to stop a round from a military assault rifle."

He took another long look at the picture, "You know, I'd rate the armor on the truck in your pictures a B8. I just made that up. I think it's strong enough to stop a .50 caliber sniper rifle."

He laid the pictures down and shook his head. "I know this looks a lot like our armored CIT trucks but it's not."

"What's a CIT?" I asked.

"It stands for Cash In Transit. It's definitely not a CIT truck, it's more like an APC."

"Like a military Armed Personnel Carrier?!"

"Yeah, look here on the roof," he said as he picked up one of the pictures again. "Doesn't that look like a gun turret? See the barrels here?" he asked as he pointed to the picture.

"And look here on the front fender. Those look like rocket launch tubes to me.

He put the picture back down on top of the folder and shook his head, "If you're going after this vehicle you may need a M1A1 tank to win the battle."

Our meeting was over. I thanked Mr. Carter for his help and headed back to our motorhome at the boarding school. As I drove along on the interstate I kept thinking, *The War Wagon is going to be taking on a worthy opponent. Let the games begin.*

Where Did They Go?—Caleb

I'd been listening in on Simone's conversation with the airport manager from Troutdale Airport. The last anybody had seen of the armored truck was after it went off the end of runway 7 and through the fence that surrounded the airport property. From there, the truck drove into a forest of trees.

As Mr. Spock might say, "Logic dictates that a truck that big, going that fast is going to leave a hell of a debris trail." Therefore, I began my search at the edge of the forest.

Mr. Spock would have been correct. The truck had cut a swath through the forest ten feet wide. Surely the police had also seen the trail the truck left, however for the sake of completeness I followed it anyway. Sure enough, yellow crime scene tape extended down both sides of the path as far as the eye could see.

In addition to the damage to the trees the truck made, the large tires on the vehicle left substantial ruts in the terrain. I noticed the truck had four-wheel drive which helped it substantially as it meandered hither and yon through the forest.

I moved quickly until the trail exited the forest and the path intersected with an ancient, pot holed road that had seen much better days. It looked like the road hadn't been repaired during this century. The road ran primarily north and south and the mud that accumulated on the tires indicated the truck turned north towards the Columbia River, but it doubled back and headed south when it ran into a barricade with a large sign saying This Road Closed.

It appeared most of the mud on the tires wore off and it became more difficult to trail the truck, except I have special spirit powers. The exhaust of the enormous turbodiesel motor left a residue on the road wherever it went. The signature was very specific and very easy for me to track, even when it was days old. I could see that the truck left the road several times as if they were searching for something.

The third time they left the road they came to a stop. It was a prolonged stop with lots of cover. I guessed they decided to stop and wait it out until it got dark before moving on. Or maybe someone was injured and needed attention. Lots of reasons to choose from.

I sped up my time reference so several hours passed by in an instant. When I detected motion again, I began tracking them. I thought it was very gutsy of them to shut down when the police were so close to them.

Apparently, the police lacked my powers and the crime scene tape stopped rather abruptly. However, I was able to accelerate my search and raised my point of reference to about a hundred feet and added a visual scan to my repertoire. From my perspective it seemed like I was just strolling along but if anyone could see me (which they couldn't) it would have looked like I was moving at several hundreds of mile per hour.

As night fell they became more daring. They stayed away from the freeways opting for country roads. I was catching up to them but they had a substantial head start and I didn't want to lose them. Actually I felt very comfortable it was only a matter of time before I overtook them.

We were out in the countryside now and there wasn't much traffic. I could sense they were speeding up but I was still gaining on them, then all of a sudden, I lost their signal.

There were several options to consider. They could have a hybrid propulsion system and decided to shut down the diesel. Or, they could have stopped for the night to rest again. Perhaps they had a cloaking device which prevented me from any contact with them (that seemed pretty unlikely). Possibly they'd made it to their destination and were in some shielded garage or none of the above. It turns out the last option was the right one.

I'd been conducting my search for about an hour and their signal was getting stronger before I lost it. That indicated I was getting close, very close. I waited a few seconds (several hours in real time) for the sun to rise. All of a sudden, the diesel signal was back and I was right on top of them. Only, I wasn't. I did a visual scan of the entire area and there was nothing that looked familiar. There was no armored truck in sight. The armored truck was gone. Where had it gone to?

The signal began moving and I followed it. What I was now following looked like a really expensive motorhome. Then it dawned on me. Somehow, they'd morphed the image of the armored truck into something completely different.

I contacted Joshua telepathically and gave him a sitrep. His response was what I anticipated, *The armored truck morphed into a motorhome?!!! That's really sick. Did you see how they made the change?*

No, it was overcast that night, with no moon or stars and no lights coming from anything on the ground that I could see. When I lost the signal, I wasn't exactly sure where they were parked.

So you didn't see them transform from armored truck to motorhome? Joshua asked.

Something Joshua commented made me think, *What process did they use to morph? What was morphing? It was a method of transforming from one shape to something completely different…just like in the Transformer movies.*

That's it!!! I communicated to my brother. *The armored truck had the ability to mechanically transform into another shape. In our case they didn't become like the movies and transform into extremely big alien monsters, they changed into a different type of truck. Very cool! Sneaky but still, very cool.*

Very expensive too, Josh replied. *Whoever was backing the robberies must have some very deep pockets. I'm beginning to think there's more to these robberies than just the money.*

Any ideas what they might be? I asked

Not yet. I think this is kind of a test. Somebody wants to see how we'll react to the chaos and mayhem. Maybe they got some bigger plans. In the meantime, continue to follow the morphed motorhome and see where it ends up.

I agreed. *It looks like they're going to stay on the Oregon side of the Columbia River and continue east. I'll keep you informed.*

I was ready to sign off when I thought of a question to ask my brother. *Hey Joshua, have you heard anything about the other four bank heists?*

Not a word, he replied, *maybe they'll morph into a motorhome caravan and they'll all meet up somewhere soon.*

We should be so lucky. Bye bro.

I kept a close watch on the armored motorhome. For all I knew, it might change into something else when I wasn't looking.

One day later, Joshua's prophesy came true when the armored motorhome I was following drove into a trailer park on the outskirts of a small town in eastern Oregon. It parked next to four other motorhomes that looked almost identical.

I assumed they were from the other four bank robberies. However, I couldn't figure out how they got there. The best information I had said they dumped the armored trucks as soon as they could get to some sort of aircraft.

It occurred to me that all four of the motorhomes arrived at the same time and they would have very similar exhaust signatures. If they truly drove in a caravan the signals from the four exhausts would overlay and be very strong, even if it was a few days old. As best I could tell, it hadn't rained recently and there was very little traffic to contaminate the motorhome signatures.

What the hell! I decided to backtrack and see where they came from. I popped up high enough to avoid overpasses and tall trees and set off at a very high rate of speed. In less than a few minutes I was at the parking lot of a seaplane port on the Columbia River. I checked out the planes and there were several different seaplane models tied up at the dock. Some were under floating hangers and I did a quick inventory of all the planes. I found four Turboporter aircraft on floats with the same motto written across the cargo doors, 'River or Sea, Come Fly With Me.'

So this is what I put together and was ready to drop on my human brother: the crews from four of the bank robberies drove their armored trucks to somewhere close to either the Willamette or Columbia Rivers. A Turboporter from Come Fly With Me was waiting for each of them and they flew up to the seaport where the crews transferred to the motorhomes, then drove to the camp grounds close to some scraggly town in eastern Oregon. I'm not sure where the story goes from there but stay tuned.

When I shared with Joshua, he commented, "That's way too complicated and way too expensive. Were the second set of motorhomes also transformers?" Why wasn't there a fifth motorhome waiting at seaport? Was the Turboporter at Troutdale airport a rental from Come Fly With Me?" He went on and on completely deflating my party balloon.

<u>Getting the War Wagon Ready to Rumble—Pham</u>

I opened the back doors on the trailer, lowered the hydraulic ramp and slowly backed the War Wagon onto the boarding school parking lot. We kept the electric drive battery pack charged and I decided to go electric instead of firing up the diesel. Actually, it was a turbodiesel and it was really noisy. I didn't want to bring too much attention to our attack vehicle, especially in the residential neighborhood where the school was located. I knew it would also be a distraction to the students. I knew I would've been distracted to see a vehicle that looked like something out of a science fiction movie or a graphic novel.

While we were on our trip across the country, we made periodic stops to check on the War Wagon, which also involved keeping us sharp on our assignments. Joshua was our pilot and Simone the copilot. I had responsibility for the comms and all things electronic (Radar, GPS, Vehicle Security, Drone Operations, Sirius Sound System and things like that). Mark was our weapons guy. Our War Wagon was the best armed vehicle on the planet. We had twin turrets on the roof with both Gatlin machine guns and 50 caliber cannons that could punch through the toughest armor plating, armed Mach 2 drones for attack as well as for reconnaissance, a bunch of cheap expendable drones for additional reconnaissance, mortars that could deliver a variety of payloads including smoke, sleeping gas and explosives, also launch tubes for 2.75 inch diameter folded fin rockets to name just a few.

All the ammunition, explosives and other nasty things were removed from the weapons during our trip for safety. They were stored in separate cases inside the trailer.

Maintenance of all the War Wagon mechanical components and the electric drive system were Joshua's responsibility. However, he would call on us as needed to assist in maintaining our attack vehicle in top shape.

There was a limit as to what we could do in the parking lot. As an old pilot friend of ours was fond of saying, "You need to kick the tires, start the fires and stomp on the go petal." And that's what we did.

Oregon has a lot of open range land and sparsely populated areas that served our needs. Most of it was owned by the State of Oregon or the federal government's Department of the Interior. All it took to get us access was a short phone call from Joshua to the Apostle and the next day we had written permission to get on with it.

I drove the War Wagon back into the trailer and headed out in the Sweet Ride with the trailer in tow. I briefly considered leaving our motorhome at the boarding school and taking the War Wagon on the road but Joshua and I decided it would be better to keep it in the trailer. No point in taking the War Wagon out on the road naked for the whole world to see. There would be the chance some of the bad guys would spot us and we'd lose the element of surprise. All four of us climbed aboard Sweet Ride and headed out of Portland for a few days of prepping the War Wagon for action. Of course, Sarge and Sniffer joined us too.

The location of where we were to check out our War Wagon was about a three hour drive from Portland to Wasco county in north eastern Oregon. There was a small town within ten miles of our test area. A mile south of the town we saw what appeared to be an auxiliary runway site. I'd seen several of these abandoned runways as we drove through Arizona. Many of them had bone yards close by. Bone yards were where parts of old airplanes were dumped.

One of the Arizona auxiliary runways was next to the I-10, just south of Chandler, a suburb of Phoenix. It was located on what is now an Indian reservation. I remembered seeing a bone yard near that site. Just out of curiosity, I decided to do a Google search on these abandoned runways.

During World War II the Army Air Corp built a number of auxiliary runways used to train their pilots. Most of the runways were arranged in a triangle formation. They were always scattered near a centralized air base. These auxiliary runways had no control towers. Instead a Jeep from the central base was sent out to each of the auxiliary runway sites with two soldiers and a radio to act as tower operators.

There were no lights on these runways so they were only used during the day. At least one of the three runways at each site were paved. It wasn't unusual for the other runways to be dirt strips. When the war ended most of these sites were abandoned, at least by the Air Corp. Some of the auxiliary air strips were eventually converted into regional airports which were serviced by smaller commercial planes and general aviation aircraft. Others were used as refueling points for crop dusters.

I was curious to see how many auxiliary runways were built in Oregon. The closest one was located in Pendleton, a city in Umatilla county, over an hour away to the east from our test area. It was built by the US Army and became operational in July of 1941. It was named Pendleton Army Airfield. It was used for flight training during World War II and closed after the war in 1945. After the war, it became a civilian airport and is now called Eastern Oregon Regional Airport.

There were no other airports even close to where we would be getting the War Wagon operational, Something was wrong here. Joshua and I agreed. We needed to check it out.

Joshua pulled our motorhome to the side of the road and contacted the Apostle, "We may have a problem here. It could be related to the bank robberies."

"What's the problem?" asked the Apostle.

"There seems to be an airport where one isn't supposed to be," Joshua answered.

"Are you in Pendleton?" he asked after a short pause.

Joshua shook his head and rolled his eyes. "Of course not. We're on the road to the test area you assigned to us."

"Okay, good. What do you want me to do?" The Apostle asked.

Joshua was becoming annoyed. "This was a courtesy call to inform you of an abnormality we discovered that may or may not have anything to do with our mission. I'm asking if you want us to investigate or to ignore it and continue on to our test area."

"Ah, of course. I want you and your team to casually investigate the airport and report back to me. No guns blazing or any Krav Maga unless you're attacked. When you're done there, head back to the town and get in contact with one of my agents. He works at the only gas station in town. He's a small wiry man in his sixties with short white hair. When you see him your first words should be, 'How's it hanging, Bud.' His code name is Bud. His response to you should be 'Doing good Black Bond.' He will give you all the information you need."

Everybody in the motorhome sat stunned. Finally, Joshua said, "You set us up again! This is like when you messed with me when you were supposed to be teaching me spy craft."

"Apparently, you still have some learning to do," the Apostle replied. He paused for a moment, then said, "Sorry for offending you and your team. I get sort of squirrelly being cooped up in rehab all day. I really miss being on the streets."

He hung up before we could say anything in response. After a few moments, Joshua cleared his throat and said, "Let's turn the rig around and head back to the airport that never was."

We had to drive several miles in the wrong direction before we found a spot wide enough to make a U-turn.

CHAPTER 25

Questioning Lawyer Green—Detective Hong

Detective Cody and I entered the interrogation room to begin our questioning of Harold Green two hours after we brought him back to the station. It took that long to connect with his business partner and have him join us for the interrogation. His business partner was Benjamin White, who was acting as his lawyer. Both men were sitting across the table from us as we sat down. Bill touched a button on a remote and said to the two lawyers, "This meeting is being recorded. Mr. Green, you were read your Miranda rights when you were arrested. Is that correct?"

I studied the suspect's face. It looked like it was carved from stone. He didn't look at either of us. His eyes were focused on the wall behind us as he replied, "Yes."

Bill then asked him, "Do you understand the charges that were made against you?"

Another "Yes," was all he said again.

"And this man, Benjamin White will be representing you?" asked Bill.

A third "Yes."

I asked the first real question, "So why did you kill a man in the lobby of your law office?"

His eyes moved quickly for a brief glance at his lawyer then back to the wall as he answered, "I didn't kill anyone."

"We have an eye witness who swears she saw you holding a severed head in your hands. The witness went on to say you admitted being a killer. Isn't that correct?"

His lawyer answered for him, "My client categorically denies ever killing anyone. Your witness came on the scene after a box containing the head was delivered to his office. He opened the box and discovered the severed head. He was shocked and appalled at the grotesque murder. Someone else must have committed the murder and attempted to blame him for the crime."

"Is that right counselor? Then why did he hide the evidence instead of calling the police?" I asked. "The head was nowhere to be found and it was obvious he'd tried to clean up the crime scene. That seems pretty incriminating to me."

"Not at all," his lawyer rebutted. "My client was so distraught, he left the building immediately. It must have been the night cleaning crew who got rid of the head and attempted to clean the floor. My client was so upset he failed to leave any instructions for the cleaning crew."

"That is an implausibly weak response, counselor. Don't you think the cleaning crew would have called the police to report the murder? Just to be sure, we will contact the cleaning crew to question them."

A quick glance at the perp revealed he was beginning to sweat. I asked the next question, "So you left your office all distraught and drove directly home, except on the way you stopped to make a phone call. It was a coded conversation. Would you care to explain that?"

Green turned his head quickly to look at his lawyer. There was the tiniest of head shakes, almost like a spasm as his stony expression turned to a look of fear. His attorney answered for him, "I think we're done for the day, detectives. I need a private moment with my client, please turn off your recorder."

Bill pressed the off button on the remote, shutting down the recorder as we walked out of the interrogation room and closed the door behind us. We waited in the hall for them to finish their private conversation.

As we waited, Bill said, "I think you really got his attention with your last question. Did you just make that up to see how he'd react or did one of Joshua's CIs give you a tip."

"The latter, Joshua told me what he said but he refused to tell me how his CI was able to listen in on the phone call. It was obvious Green had no idea we were onto him. He had an answer to all our questions except the last one. He looked like he'd seen a ghost."

Bill nodded. "I think maybe he's going to join the headless horseman. Then he'll become the ghost."

Who's Next to Die?—Chanlina

As I drove away from the front of the lawyer's office on Fat Man's motorcycle, I could hear the lawyer screaming. I knew it was very unlikely the lawyer would come up with the money by the next day. If he did, that would be a bonus. What I really wanted to know was who he reported to. When I delivered the package to him, I was able to clone his phone. He was too busy signing for the package and never noticed me touching my phone to his when he laid it down for a moment on the reception desk.

I parked in a dark spot in the parking lot and waited for him to leave the office. I knew he was going to call someone and I wanted to be close enough to listen in. When he drove away I followed him closely. When he made the call, I heard it all on my phone too and I recorded both sides of the conversation. I heard them exchange codes which was a little frustrating but not unexpected. The good news was I got the location of the person he was talking to.

I let the lawyer finish his trip home while I stopped the bike and immediately checked the address of the next person up the chain of command. I needed to get there before they had the chance to leave. For all I knew the code was a warning to get out of town. I couldn't have that. Fat Man's knife was thirsty for more blood.

When I searched for details of my target's residence, I was amused to find it was the home of one of the governor's bodyguard. The address for the residence was in Salem, Oregon, the state's capitol. I didn't want to go alone to Salem on the bike, so I made alternate plans.

I drove the bike back to the bus rental office. All the crime scene tape was missing and the office was closed for hours. I managed to shut off the security system, break into the office and stole the key for the largest bus on the lot. I stored Fat Man's bike in one of the bus's luggage bays then headed back to Bridge City.

It was late when I arrived at the alley that led under the bridge. I told Fat Man my plan, gave him my last twenty dollar bill and evacuated my 26 team members in fifteen minutes. When you don't have much, it doesn't take long to leave. By midnight we were on the freeway, heading to Salem.

Fat Man recovered his bike and his knife and was going to remain in town to see how much money he could get out of Mr. Green. If he had any problems, I suggested he use his knife on him. Either way, he was to join up with the bus in Salem.

Revisiting Harold Green—Fat Man

It felt good to finally be on a mission again. It had been a long time. Chanlina wouldn't let me go to the boarding school, she said she wanted to keep me as a backup in case things went sideways. At the time, it really pissed me off. I tried to convince her I would be more valuable if I joined her. She just kept shaking her head. Since she was the boss, I finally gave in.

It was the middle of the night and the sky was clear with pinpoints of light on black velvet. The wind on my face was cool as I headed to the lawyer's house. I stashed the bike a block away from the house. As I quietly made my way to his residence, an old saying came to mind: "Kill all Lawyers." I had no idea who said it but it seemed like the right thing to say tonight. I waited outside the fence which surrounded the backyard to see if he had any bodyguards or dogs patrolling the grounds. I waited for about fifteen minutes and saw no movement at all. I jumped the fence and headed for the circuit breaker box on the side of the house. I remembered to turn on the signal jammer Chanlina gave me to take care of any external security devices.

When I got to the box I saw a really cheap padlock on the front panel and smiled. I pulled my multi-tool from the holster on my belt. It was a present Chanlina had given me many years ago. She told me it would be the best tool I would ever have and she was right. I used the bolt cutter feature and quickly removed the lock, then shut off all the power. Unless the lawyer had sprung for a very expensive security system that had its own power source there wouldn't be any alarms going off. I quietly closed the panel, then using another blade on my multi-tool, I jimmied the lock on a patio door and slipped inside.

It was pitch black. I couldn't see anything until I put on the cheap pair of NVGs I'd stolen a couple of years ago. I could see everything clearly in bright green and discovered the patio was next to the master bedroom. There were two people sleeping in a very plush king-size bed, a naked woman and an almost naked man.

I moved silently around the bed until I was standing next to the man. He was snoring and making very funny sounds, I guessed he was having a nightmare. I smiled quietly, I was going to become his worst nightmare. I noticed there was a .357 magnum on his nightstand and I picked it up put it in the waistband of my pants.

I pulled my knife, I liked to call it my pruning knife and put the sharp edge of the blade against his throat as I bent down and whispered in his ear, "Wakey wakey."

His eyes opened wide in fear and confusion. He wanted to scream but I pushed the knife blade harder against his throat with one hand and put a finger of my other hand against my lips. He got the message. I made a gesture for him to get out of the bed and stand up. He slid from the bed and stood up as I slipped behind him with my knife never leaving contact with his throat. I pushed him toward the closed bedroom door. He quietly opened it and tried to look back at the naked woman. I began to pull the blade across his neck and he froze. He was trembling now as I shoved him through the opened door and into a hallway. It was a long hallway with several doors. I assumed they led to other bedrooms or perhaps a bathroom or two.

At the end of the hall, we walked into a large family room with an adjacent dining room table big enough to seat ten or twelve people. As I guided him to one of the chairs I thought to myself, *What a nice house this is. It's a mansion compared to my lean-to but nothing like the real mansion I lived in for so many years in Cambodia. How quickly things change.*

When he was seated, I took my knife from his throat and took a seat across from him. With my NVG I was able to see there was some blood on his neck from where my knife nicked him. There would be more blood later, lots more blood.

Speaking in almost perfect English, I asked in a whisper, "Where is the money?"

He said nothing, he just sat there in his ridiculously tiny underwear and began to cry.

I asked again, "Where is my money?" This time a little louder, then added, "Where is the million dollars my boss said I should collect for her." There was a large, expensive grandfather clock against the wall behind the table. "I will give you ten minutes to give me the money or I will start killing your family one by one. I will start with the naked woman in your bed, perhaps your wife. Then I will kill your children, from the oldest to the youngest. Guess who I will kill last?"

In a pleading whisper, the lawyer said, "I don't have a million dollars here. I can get it tomorrow…"

I waved him off and asked with best threatening voice I could manage in a whisper, "How much money do you have, here in this house, tonight?"

He shrugged his shoulders, then answered, "I'm not sure. At least a hundred thousand, maybe two."

"Show me," I ordered.

He stood up and I followed him to the other side of the house to his office. He tried to turn on the office lights but nothing worked. He moved to a large window and opened the curtains letting in some light from the street light behind his house. It was enough for him to see a large painting of flowers on the wall behind his desk. When he moved the painting aside I saw the safe. It was an old fashion type with mechanical tumblers and he quickly dialed in the combination. Before he could open the door to the safe, I reached over him and pushed him aside as I opened the safe and looked in. The first thing I saw was a large revolver. It was a match for the one I'd taken from his night stand.

I turned on him and said in a normal voice, "You were going to shoot me, weren't you? Nice try. Take everything out of the safe and lay it on your desk."

He protested as he began removing the contents of the safe, "I wasn't going to shoot you. I hadn't opened this safe in a long time. I forgot I had the gun in there."

I slapped him hard across the face, knocking him back and onto the floor. "If you lie to me again. I will cut out your tongue. Count the money."

The cash was in bundles of crisp new hundred dollar bills. He counted all the bundles and said, "Two hundred eighty thousand. That's all I have."

Without looking at the cash, I took my knife and slashed him across the face, from under his eye down to his chin. He let out a muffled scream and grabbed a handful of tissues from his desk to stop the bleeding.

"So where is the other safe, the one not in your office, probably in another room or your garage. You have one minute to tell me or I will give you a matching scar on the other side of your face."

Five minutes later, I had another three hundred thousand dollars from a safe in the family room, inside the grandfather clock.

I put all the money into my backpack and was getting ready to leave. I had only one more task to complete.

"I've done everything you asked, Please don't kill me and my family," he whined.

"No you haven't," I replied. "You gave me a little less than six hundred thousand. You were supposed to give me a million."

"Are you going to kill us?" he asked, his face a mask of terror and fear.

"Yes and no," I answered.

"What does that mean?" he asked in a trembling voice. Of course he knew what was coming.

"Your family will live but you must die."

"Why? Why must I die?" His voice was garbled, almost unintelligible.

"Because you were part of the organization that set us up to be slaughtered at the boarding school. We could have all been killed."

"Please, I beg you don't do this. Have mercy."

I shook my head and asked him a question, "Do you know who Pol Pot was?"

He looked puzzled by my question. He nodded his head and whispered, "He was the Cambodian leader who kill hundreds of thousands of Cambodians."

"No! He killed almost two million. Pol Pot was my grandfather, I was a young man when the cleansing took place. I was required to participate in the removal of the undesirables. Much to my surprise, I discovered I liked killing. It made me feel powerful to remove the heads of the old regime. I miss those days," I said as I swung my blade through the lawyer's neck.

It was a clean cut, one stroke and the head was lying on the table, a look of surprise on its face. I took a sterling silver platter from the China closet and placed the head so it was facing the bedroom. I cleaned my blade on the expensive table cloth and sheathed my knife. I left through another patio door, jumped the fence and strolled to my bike. I fired up the bike and headed out to Salem.

I really missed the killings. I hoped I would have more to come.

CHAPTER 26

Another Head Bites the Dust—Detective Hong

It was early the next morning after our interview with Harold Green the previous day. I was still sound asleep when my phone began ringing. Lili nudged me and said in a sleepy voice, "Answer the phone, honey. I'm still sleeping."

It was Bill. Why on earth would he be calling me before I had my coffee? I became fully alert as soon as he said, "Wake up, lazy bones. We got another case of a man losing his head. It belongs to your favorite lawyer."

The sun was trying to peak over the horizon as I met Bill at Harold Green's residence thirty minutes later. He was waiting for me, leaning against the front of his car with a cup of coffee for me along with a box of donuts resting on the car's hood.

He began to say something but I waved him off. I never spoke to anyone before I had my coffee. That included my partner and my wife. After a long sip of a Brazilian roast with hazelnut creamer and a touch of sugar, I gestured to Bill to give me a sitrep. I took a donut out of the box and began eating as Bill told me the gory story.

"The lawyers wife called it in about five am. She said she got up to use the bathroom and noticed her husband wasn't in bed. After she finished in the bathroom she went looking for him. The lights didn't work so she took a flashlight. She checked all the bedrooms and the family room and when she got to the dining area she found her husband's head sitting on her favorite sterling silver platter staring at her. She saw his body lying on the floor in a pool of his blood.

"She began screaming, which woke the children who came running from their bedrooms. When they saw their father's head, they began screaming too."

I'd just finished my first donut (I always have at least two) and asked Bill, "Who called it in, the wife?"

Bill took a sip of his coffee and a bite of his donut, then managed to say, "No," as he finished chewing. "It was a neighbor who heard all the screaming and called it in. When the uniforms arrived, they found the head, the body and a naked woman lying on the floor with the children huddled in a corner of the room. It took them a while to sort things out. Our crime scene people showed up about thirty minutes later."

I took my second donut from the box and asked, "What's the status now?"

"They got the power back on. They discovered the master circuit breaker had been tripped, they found some boot prints in the backyard, leading from the fence to the house and back to the fence. A door from one of the patios was opened and unlocked. It led to the master bedroom suite. They got a few boot prints on the carpet in the bedroom, hallway, family room and an office on the other side of the house. There was an open safe in the office with the lawyers prints on the combination lock. The safe was empty; there were some papers on the desk."

"How's the wife?" I asked as I finished my donut and drained my coffee cup.

Bill finished his breakfast and said, "An EMT arrived just after the crime scene people. One of the children said they'd gotten her bathrobe from the bedroom and covered her up after she passed out. The oldest one told the EMT woman it was the first time they'd seen their mother naked. The EMT said the kids seemed more traumatized by their naked mother than seeing their father's decapitated head. The mother checked out okay physically. She apparently fainted from the shock of seeing her husband's head."

We headed inside the house through the front door and put paper booties over our shoes to keep from contaminating the crime scene. We also placed paper plugs in our nostrils to minimize the odor of death. The CSI people had just finished taking pictures of the head and body when we arrived and cleared us to take a look.

We checked the head first without comment, then moved to the body. Even with the nose plugs, the smell was over powering. The corpse had emptied his bowls and bladder as his head was being removed from his neck.

After we'd seen enough, we moved to a less odorous portion of the house to compare notes.

"Does any of this look familiar to you?" asked Bill.

I nodded. "Absolutely, the head was removed with a single cut, just like the head of the bus rental owner. I think the killer is working his way up the chain of command and Chanlina or one of her subordinates are murdering the people she feels did her wrong. I don't think it will stop with Harold. Did you notice anything different with this killing?"

"I sure did!" answered Bill. "The killer let Harold keep his cock and balls. I would consider that a small mercy."

I nodded and said, "Praise the Lord for favors big and small."

Then Bill added, "I think we should tell Joshua about what happened here."

Checking Out the Ghost Airport—Joshua

We drove back the way we came, then stopped Sweet Ride about a mile from what looked to us to be one of the old auxiliary airports. Pham had seen what he called a bone yard next to the perimeter fence. However, no airport of any kind showed up on any maps or aeronautical charts that Pham checked after our brief conversation with the Apostle.

On our first pass of the airport, we passed a paved road that led to a security fence. I estimated the road was almost a mile from the highway. With a lot of wild underbrush and scrub trees it was hard to see much detail. There must have been a gate of some kind at the end of the road. Before we drove and knocked on the door, I wanted to get an idea of what was inside the fence.

I looked back at Pham and said, "Launch four of our small drones and take a better look."

"Roger, that, boss," replied Pham.

If we'd been in the War Wagon launching a drone was a simple task, all four recon drones would have been on their way in less than a minute. However, we were ordered to stay undercover, at least in the beginning.

As Pham got up to step out of the motorhome, I received a call from Detective Hong. He informed me there was another beheading. This time it was the lawyer who was killed. He believed it was either Chanlina or one of her troops who was the killer. She was working her way up the chain of command to get her vengeance on those who set up her and her people at the failed boarding school attack. He didn't think she was going to stop; however he'd no idea who her next target would be. He was hoping I could put one of my CIs on the case. I told him I would see if they were available. After he hung up, I contacted Caleb and gave him his next assignment.

Pham exited our motorhome and opened the hatch on one of our low-level storage bins. A case of our small recon drones slid out on a support rack. Pham opened the case while Simone provided cover just in case someone came snooping. She was wearing her body cam and packing a Beretta as she walked to the front of our ride and did a quick visual. Then she turned around and did the same check from the back. She used the comm-all feature as she headed back to Pham. "All clear," she said to us all and Pham pushed a button on the small control box inside the case to launch the drones. One after another, the drones launched vertically and climbed to about five hundred feet and hovered as Pham closed the lid and slid the case back into the storage bin.

Once inside, he sat at the computer station and quickly programed the drone's missions. The large monitor on the desk provided us with real time images of what each drone saw. Everything was recorded for future reference. We were very surprised at what we saw. Shocked may have been a better way to describe it.

The drone transmissions provided us with a view of three runways arranged in a triangle. Each runway was about five to six thousand feet long. All of that was similar to the ancient auxiliary runways built years before there was a US Air Force.

That was where the similarity ended. Each of these runways were estimated to be at least a hundred feet wide with all the bells and whistles you'd expect to see at a new international airport.

The old auxiliary airstrips had only a wind sock in the middle of the triangle. This airport had a two story control tower with a bunch of antennas on top. We counted fifteen state of the art hangars, five next to the inside of each runway. We could also make out runway lights. They had something Mark called a Visual Approach Slope Indicator or VASI to assist the pilots in landing their aircraft if the electronic equipment malfunctions. It turns out Mark has his private pilot's license. Who knew?!!

There was a large square on the tarmac, just in front of the tower. None of us could figure out its function. Perhaps the most surprising thing about this phantom airport was the lack of people. The drones were up for over an hour providing us with high resolution images; none of those images revealed any life forms. In addition there were no aircraft either, none of the fifteen hangars had anything in them. No planes, no people, no work benches, nothing. I've heard of ghost towns, seen a few in movies but this was the first ghost airport I'd ever seen. Who would build an advanced state of the art airport then abandon it?

I decided we needed to get a closer look.

We disconnected the trailer with the War Wagon still inside and then drove the motorhome onto the road which headed to the fence surrounding the GAP (That's short for 'Ghost AirPort. Simone made it up). Mark and the dogs remained with the trailer and the dogs immediately went looking for varmints to chase.

It took us only a few minutes to drive up the road to the fence. A wide, sturdy looking gate blocked our entrance to the GAP. Like the GAP, the fence looked brand new as did the gate.

There was a control box a car length from the gate. A red blinking light in the upper right corner of the box gave us the first sign of possible life inside. I opened the driver side door, slid out to stand next to the box. There was a dark screen the size of a laptop with a keypad below. Below the key pad was a bright blue button with a short sentenced embossed on it. PLEASE PUSH ME.

I pushed. Nothing happened. I pushed again, still nothing. I pushed several more times in rapid succession and the screen lit up with a message, **Please enter your nine digit code.**

I typed in nine numbers chosen at random. The monitor showed **That code is incorrect. You are not permitted to enter. Please leave the premises immediately. Have a good day.**

I considered ramming the gate. I hate it when a computer gives me instructions I don't like. Instead of crashing through the gate, I backed the motorhome all the way to the highway and headed back to the trailer, where we met up with the Mark and the dogs who looked well exercised.

I contacted the Apostle, debriefed him, and suggested we pursue a night investigation. He cleared us to make the recon mission, then closed with, "Please try to avoid killing anyone unless they attack you."

I answered with, "We'll do our best to avoid any deaths, especially ours."

CHAPTER 27

Who's Next?—Chanlina

It took us a little over an hour to drive from Bridge City to Salem. I was careful to keep the bus under the speed limit to avoid any highway patrol attention. I shut off all of the cabin lights when we started our journey down south. A few minutes after I pulled onto the I-5, I heard the sounds of many people snoring. It was still late at night as I pulled the bus into a Walmart parking lot and shut the it down. I found one of my lieutenants awake and asked him to take charge of the bus until I returned.

Outside the bus, I turned on my phone, went to the Map Quest app, and entered the Salem address for my next victim wondering, how many people I would have to kill to get the leader. I sighed and thought to myself, *I will kill as many as it takes to satisfy my vengeance. Then and only then will the killings stop.*

I waited outside the bus for Fat Man to appear. I knew it wouldn't take long for him to catch up with us. He always drove as fast as his bike could go. A few minutes later, he joined me in the lot.

"You made good time. Did you have to kill any highway patrolmen on the way?"

Fat Man gave me a warm smile and said, "It was difficult but I managed to control myself." He paused and then bowed his head and added, "Thank you for allowing me the honor of the kill. I look forward to many more."

I nodded and replied, "I think there is a very good chance you will soon have the opportunity to add more notches to your killing knife."

He handed me a back pack and I asked, "What's this?"

"He gave up almost six hundred thousand dollars. Sorry I didn't get the million he owed you," he replied.

"You keep it," I said. "We will use that money to fund our escape after we have completed the necessary killings."

He straightened, made a slight bow and said, "I will be happy to oblige."

"Would you like to join me on a recon ride?" I asked, "This would be only a drive-by to familiarize myself with the target residence. I need to know the lay of the land. If it looks promising you could put another notch on your knife tonight."

I climbed on the back of his bike and he accelerated to cruise speed as I held the map in front of him to show him the route to the kill zone. Ten minutes later we were only a few blocks away from our target, when I got this very strange feeling.

"Stop the bike. Stop right now!" I yelled in his ear.

He brought the bike to a rapid stop and I jumped off the rear seat. I almost fell as I stumbled to the curb; Fat Man grabbed me to keep me from falling. I sat down on the curb and was holding my head.

"Are you all right? What happened?" he asked and I could hear the concern in his voice.

I was rocking back and forth, holding my head in both hands. "I've never felt like this before. I feel like someone's inside my head, poking around."

I stopped rocking, sat up straight and put my hands down beside me. "I'm being probed…who are you?...get the hell out of my head!"

Well That Never Happened Before—Caleb

As my brother requested, I attached myself to Chanlina and discovered she was riding on the back of a motorcycle in the middle of the night. A large man was driving and I couldn't help notice he had a small sword or a very big knife hanging from his belt. I did a quick Google check and the knife was most likely a Cambodian machete. It had a gentle curving blade about two feet long with the end of the blade squared off. I also noticed several notches cut into the handle of the machete. I was pretty sure I knew what that represented.

I gently slipped into Chanlina's mind to find out where she was headed. I'd done this before and was able to easily access her memory. This time it was different. The best way to describe it was some of her memory was fuzzy. At least it was to me. The bottom line was I couldn't read who the next target was going to be.

As stealthily as I could, I began to see if I could reduce some of the fuzziness without her being aware of my intrusion. I was making some progress and felt I was just on the verge of identifying the next kill candidate, when she realized I was probing her. And she was very unhappy about it.

She yelled at the driver to stop the bike. As she got off the bike she was experiencing both fear and rage simultaneously. She stumbled and almost fell. Fortunately for her, the driver managed to keep from falling. He was larger than I thought, however still substantially smaller than Joshua.

I needed to back off and see if she would think I was gone. Better yet, I decided to withdraw completely from her mind and hope she and Fat Man would continue their trip to the target residence.

It took her a while to get over my probing of her mind, at least I thought she had until she told Fat Man, "I know he's still here. I can sense his presence. Even though he stopped trying to gain information by probing me. He's still here waiting to attack again."

Fat Man looked confused, "Who is this person? I see no one."

"Of course you don't because he isn't a person. He's a spirit. He was once a man and then he died. Now he is a spirit." Chanlina paused and looked at the confusion on Fat Man's face. "Think of him as a ghost of the dead."

Fat Man's entire demeanor changed when he heard the word 'ghost.' So did mine. The man began quickly looking around him as he put his hand on the handle of his machete and said, "Ghosts are evil. They work for the Devil. We should leave this place."

"All in good time, my friend, all in good time. First, I will see the house of our next target. Then we will return to the bus and wake our comrades to plan our attack. This will be much more difficult than the first two."

Fat Man climbed onto the bike and Chanlina joined him on the back. He started the motor and revved the engine. Before they drove away, Chanlina looked around as if searching for someone and said, "You're welcome to join us, my ghostly friend. However, don't ever try to probe me again or you will suffer something far worse than death, much worse."

As they drove off, I followed at a respectable distance and made no attempt to probe her mind. This woman really spooked me. I never thought of myself as a ghost. I always thought of ghosts as evil beings. I'm not an evil being, I'm a good spirit. Just thinking about ghosts would send chills down my spine (if I had a spine).

Recon of the Unreal Airport—Joshua

We left the motorhome at 0200 hours. It was pitch black except for the stars and the sliver of a moon. I wasn't sure if it was waxing or waning. I think we could see more stars than ever before. Eastern Oregon is on a high plateau and where we began our recon mission there were no visible lights at the airfield or anywhere else for at least ten miles. Without light pollution, we could see the dimmest of stars.

Pham stayed in the War Wagon and coordinated our approach to the perimeter fence. He would let us know if the drones we'd just launched detected any activity at the airport.

Sniffer remained in the motorhome with Pham. The dog was learning fast but he wasn't ready for stealthy operations. We headed out in two teams. Sarge and Mark were team one and Simone and I were team two. We were all dressed in black combat gear, body armor with NVGs. Even Sarge had his armored vest and special NVGs designed by Mark.

Weapon wise, the three humans carried the very small close-in-combat machine gun and a side arm along with flash-bang grenades, Tasers, batons and our Ka-bar knives. Sarge didn't carry any weapons; he was his own weapon, perhaps the most lethal of us all.

As quietly as we could, we made our way through the forest to the perimeter without any difficulties. Mark tested the fence to make sure it wasn't electrified or outfitted with any sensors, then he gave us the all clear sign.

We breached the fence and spread out as we headed toward the airport tower. Each of us had sensors that would sniff out any booby traps. Sarge was his own sensor; he would sniff out any explosives way before our sensors would warn us.

It took us the better part of an hour as we cautiously approached the tarmac and then on to the side of the tower building.

Pham was giving us routine updates on any potential problems that might arise as well as to confirm our comms weren't being jammed.

We split up with Mark and Sarge going around one side of the tower and Simone and I around the other. We were looking for an entrance to the tower; none were discovered as we met at the front of the building. We were facing outward toward the large secret square about a hundred yards from us when several things happened at once.

First, Pham comm'd us with, "Incoming, multiple bogies, at least five maybe more. Advise you seek shelter immediately." We took Pham's advice and moved into the shadows of the control tower.

Second, the lights came on. Lots and lots of lights: runway lights, taxiway lights, runway threshold lights, flashing lights imbedded in the tarmac showing the way from the active runway to the secret square and lights on the tower.

Third, there were sounds of generators spooling up and equipment coming on line.

The only thing that was missing were people.

Pham came back online, "We have a convoy of motor vehicles approaching the gate." There was a pause, then he added, "Apparently they know the nine digit code. They are driving through the gate. All five of them have passed through the gate, however they are holding short of the tarmac."

There was another pause, then Pham comm'd again, "First bogey on approach."

We saw the…not sure what to call it, I guess flight vehicle will have to do. We actually saw it before we heard it. It was the size of a medium commercial airplane. Instead of large swept-back wings with turbofan engines slung under each wings, there were four very quiet ducted fan pods; one at each corner of the blocky vehicle.

The DFP plane (that's my simplification of Ducted Fan Pod) slowly approached the secret square at about fifty feet above ground level

(AGL). As it reached the square, the pods rotated to vertical and the plane hovered motionless.

As the plane hovered, the square began to sink below ground level and then slid sideways until it was completely out of sight. The DFP plane began a slow descent through the open square and disappeared out of sight.

As soon as the first one disappeared, the second DFP plane followed. It took very little time before all six of the DFP craft disappeared through the square.

After a short pause, five almost identical motorhome vehicles drove onto the tarmac and down a ramp I'd never noticed. When all five joined the DFPs below the ground, the ramp retracted, the square closed over the opening, all the lights went out and the airport returned to silence without ever seeing any human beings anywhere.

"What the hell just happened?" asked Mark.

"Beats me," I answered. "I don't have a clue. However I truly believe they must have a huge underground parking garage."

"I bet there's more than just a garage down there, a lot more," said Simone.

Mark asked, "What's next, boss?"

"Back to the motorhome to brief the Apostle," I replied as we headed for the fence. "Oh, by the way, Mark, you had your body cam turned on, didn't you?"

There was a long pause, before Mark said in a small voice, "You didn't say anything about a body cam."

Simone joined him. "That's right, Mark. Joshua never reminded me either. I hope yours was turned on, Josh. You're going to need to send a copy to the Apostle."

I stopped walking abruptly. "If this is a joke I'm not laughing. If it's not a joke and you didn't have your body cams on, you're going to walk back to Portland, both of you and Sarge too."

"Ah come on, boss. It was just a little joke. Don't be so uptight," said Mark.

We walked in silence until we got to the fence, then I said, "All right, no penalties. I'm glad you both had your body cams on."

Sarge barked and I said to him, "Good dog, Sarge. Your cam was turned on too."

As we started to go over the fence, Simone asked, "You forgot to turn your body cam on, didn't you, Joshua?"

I waited a beat, then answered, "Maybe." Simone slugged me in the arm. She can really throw a punch. Mark just laughed along with Pham, who'd been listening. Even Sarge laughed, I could tell by the way he barked.

CHAPTER 28

Back and Forth, Back and Forth—Caleb

Chanlina and Fat Man made a slow drive-by of an apartment complex adjacent to the Oregon government buildings. Most of the people living in the apartments were upper level government employees or those who had the ear of the governor and his staff. Judging from the exterior of the complex, these weren't two bedroom walkups. I estimated the rent was running between five to ten thousand a month.

I also noticed there was security everywhere, both private and government funded. Every front door I could see (only the cheaper units) had signs advertising which agency was protecting them with the latest and greatest electronic surveillance equipment. There were security people in cars, golf carts and on foot patrol (always in pairs) cruising the streets and pathways of the entire complex.

Only a few of the security people carried guns, some only pepper spray, batons, stun guns, tasers or a combination of them all. I quickly accessed Google and found out the crime rate in this part of Salem was almost non-existent. There hadn't been a death-by-gun ever since the governor came up with his new gun laws.

I was surprised, maybe shocked would be a better word, when Chanlina turned and looked in my general direction and said to me, "So what do you think, Demon? Do you think I can beat this security, execute my victim and escape unharmed? What would you recommend?"

She paused and looked like she was listening to someone. I was sure it wasn't me, however it got me wondering if some other spirit was communicating with her. Then she smiled and said, "You know, I was thinking the same thing. I need a diversion. A very significant diversion, maybe more than one, to draw the security people away from my victim. I'm so glad we agree."

She turned back around and said to Fat Man, "I've seen enough. It's almost dawn. Let's head back to the bus and plan our attack for tomorrow evening."

Fat Man made a U-turn, getting prepared to head back to the Walmart parking lot when Chanlina asked to stop next to the curb. She turned her head and looked directly at me and said in an almost sweet voice, "It was so good to see you again. I look forward to more visits. Good night, Caleb."

She slapped Fat Man on the shoulder and they headed back down the street.

I was frozen. I couldn't move. My non-existent mouth was open in shock. She called me Caleb?!!! How could she possibly know my name? Is this going to become another battle between spirits like our last mission? I needed help. I transported to Joshua and told him what happened.

What's Next?—Joshua

Simone and I were asleep in our bed in the motorhome suite. The whole team was pretty tired after spending most of the night on our recon of the GAP. It was too late to call the Apostle after we returned. Everyone agreed we needed to sleep first and call him tomorrow morning. We found a wide spot in the road and pulled off. We set our security alarm for the Sweet Ride and the trailer, removed our combat gear and fell into our respective beds. We were instantly asleep.

I would have slept longer if Caleb hadn't transported to us at dawn. *Bro, wake up. I need to fill you in on some really weird stuff. Please Joshua, wake up!*

I managed to open one eye, then a minute later, the other one. He started in but I held up a restraining hand. *Let me use the head first.*

He followed me as I left the bedroom and headed for the two captain's chairs at the front of Sweet Ride. I reclined the seat so it would appear I had fallen back to sleep.

Okay, Caleb, Let me have it.

He ran through what happened as he 'accompanied' Chanlina and Fat Man. When he got to the punchline, he had my full attention. *She called you by name? How could she possibly know your name? How did she communicate with you?*

She spoke to me as if I were human.

Did you try to use telepathy on her?

No, in fact when I was trying to probe her to get the address of her next victim, she told me to never probe her again or she'd kill me.

She can't kill you. You already died.

You think I don't know that? When she looked straight at me and said she would kill me, she was very convincing. I will not assume she was just saying that to scare me off.

I changed topics, *Did you find out who she plans to kill next?*

No, just the general neighborhood. She and Fat Man are the leaders, they were going to get all of her troops together and figure out what type of diversion they were going to create. I'm sure she wants to carry this off very soon. Maybe you should contact Hong and Cody and get them involved.

I thought for a moment, then replied, *Salem would be out of their jurisdiction. Maybe they have contacts in Salem PD they could inform. It would be worthwhile to keep them informed. I'll call them after we finish up.*

I changed topics again. *How would you like to have a different assignment, get away from Chanlina and Fat Man for a while?*

What did you have in mind?

I replayed our body cams to show him what happened on our recon mission then asked, *Would you be able to descend through the square and give us feedback on what you see down there?*

In my mind I could feel his smile, like a load was lifted off his shoulders, at least for a while. *Why don't you go back to sleep while I check out the underground facilities. When you wake up I promise to give you a thorough briefing.*

He was gone the next instant and I staggered back to the bedroom and fell into bed. I didn't get up until our alarm went off. Us twins just got the shock of our lives (perhaps existence would be a better word). I owed it to all of us to see who it was.

<u>Planning the Diversion—Chanlina</u>

I already had an idea for the diversion, however I wanted Fat Man and my five lieutenants to hear my plan then give me feedback on how to improve it. All my officers have considerable experience in these types of missions and I wanted their opinions. I have three female lieutenants and two male. Fat Man is my major and my sixth officer. Next to me, he has the most experience in these types of the missions. All of the other five have been bloodied at least twice.

They're also skilled actors; they played their roles as poor homeless people exceptionally well, especially Bopha who acted the part of the grieving mother who lost her baby. I'm sure Caleb was impressed.

Speaking of Caleb, he was so easily manipulated. Of course, the spirit of my deceased father made that possible. I let Caleb observe everything right up to the point where I scared him away without revealing our next victim. We are getting close to reaching our goal and we can't tolerate any interference until that goal is attained.

To summarize our plan of attack, we will have two diversions separated by 15 minutes. The first will be a series of violent explosions staged in the three side-by-side dumpsters which contain the garbage of the many rich and famous. They will be located on the west side of the complex. With the explosions, there will also be fire as the result of the gasoline poured on the garbage before the explosives. To ensure the fire spreads to the nearby cars, several of the vehicles will also be blown up over a period of a few minutes. Fifteen minutes later there will be similar series of explosions and fires on the east side of the complex.

A minute after the second set of explosions, Fat Man and I will attack our victim. Before I let him separate the head from the body, they will tell me the name of possibly the last person responsible for using us as cannon fodder. We will have our revenge, whatever it takes.

On Our Way to Salem—Detective Hong

After Joshua told me Chanlina's next hit was going to be in Salem, I reminded him Salem was out of our jurisdiction. He suggested I might want to contact the Salem police and 'suggest' Bill and I be allowed to join them since I was providing them with information about a possible attack on a high up government official. He also suggested that I let them know we are working with Team Joshua on this case. He said it wouldn't hurt to mention Team Joshua is part of the governor's task force.

I asked him why he didn't just become our spokesperson and speak to Salem PD on our behalf, since he had all that clout with the governor. He wasn't amused, so I called Salem PD and told them what Joshua said and dropped names like Governor Johnson and Team Joshua.

My contact at Salem PD wasn't too impressed. However, he spoke with his boss and Bill and I were approved to 'assist' in the case. Thirty minutes later, we were in our cruiser on our way to the state capitol.

Spying on the Underground Airport—Caleb

I transported from Sweet Ride to the underground airport. I know the rest of Joshua's team calls it the ghost airport, however since my run in with Chanlina, I'm trying to stay away from the word *ghost*.

I did a quick tour of the above ground facilities, then transported underground to begin my recon. I dropped straight down through the square's sliding door to floor level. I was shocked at the size of it. Joshua and I had been briefly aboard the world's largest aircraft carrier just before our deployment to Afghanistan. The Gerald R. Ford was longer than three football fields. Below the square was like being on the hangar deck of the aircraft carrier. It was over a 1,000 feet long and 200 feet wide.

I did a quick inventory of the models of aircraft being hangered underground. There were a wide variety, fighters, transports, helicopters and unmanned drones for observation as well as attack. How in the hell did they get all these aircraft underground without being noticed? You can't just misplace multi-million dollar planes without somebody noticing.

As I moved north down the hangar bay, I discovered there were other types of war vehicles. I saw tanks, armored personnel carriers, howitzers and rocket launchers. Then I finally saw some people, lots of people, lots and lots of people, at least a thousand men and women and the barracks that housed them and base exchanges and commissaries. It looked like the underground city extended all the way to the small town we passed through.

At first, I thought this was a fortress, later I discovered it was a full scale city with multiple levels, all underground. How is this even possible?! Perhaps an even better question is why does it exist?

I traveled through the entire city, recording everything in my spirit-brain. I accomplished everything in ten minutes by speeding up my time reference, then transported back to Joshua and briefed him on all that I saw.

He was more freaked out than I was. It was time to meet up with Bud, the Apostle's secret agent in Antelope. That was the name of the very small town we passed through on our way to the War Wagon's check runs. Hopefully, Bud could shed some light on what the hell was going on.

CHAPTER 29

The Town of Antelope Welcomes You—Joshua

I decided we needed to get started on checking out the War Wagon. We drove Sweet Ride pulling the trailer with the War Wagon inside to the area where we were authorized to do our testing. We disconnected the trailer and left Mark and Pham to begin going through the check list of evaluations while Simone and I drove the motorhome to Antelope to meet up with special agent Bud. Of course, Caleb was with us. I knew he wanted to hear the story first hand.

It was about a 20 minute drive with no traffic on the narrow road, except for a very slow moving tractor pulling a hay wagon. We pulled into the town's only gas station and Simone began pumping gas while I went looking for Bud.

I found a man who seemed to fit the Apostle's description. He was sitting in a rocking chair near the door to the small convenience store. The man looked to be in his sixties with a full head of grey hair. He stood and I could tell he had a wiry build. There was nobody else around. This had to be him.

"How's it hanging, Bud?" I asked just as the Apostle ordered.

He looked me over, from top to bottom and answered, "Doing good, Black Bond." Then he added, "Our friend didn't tell me you're a giant. When your partner gets done pumping gas, why don't you two join me inside the store?"

While Simone finished up we chatted for a bit. "Are you a native of Antelope?" I asked.

"Oh hell no! I was sent out here in the eighties when the Rajneesh came to town. I was a resident of Cleveland, Ohio when I got reassigned." He noticed the puzzled look on my face and he said, "You don't have any idea who the Rajneesh was, do you?"

"None," I answered.

Me either, thought Caleb.

"Well, I see your friend is done filling up your tanks, why don't we all go inside and rest a bit. This is going to take a while."

"Is it okay to leave the motorhome at the pump?" asked Simone as she joined us.

"Lady," said Bud. "I've got four pumps and on a good day, I can get maybe three or four customers. Leaving your ride next to a pump isn't going to be a problem."

We walked inside and we took seats at a small round table with four unmatched chairs. He brought us both bottles of Dr. Pepper from a cooler and popped the caps. "Dr. Pepper is all I have," he said apologetically as he handed us the bottles and sat down at the table. "The Coke truck isn't due for a few days."

He took a sip from his bottle and said, "Let me tell you about the Rajneesh." He reached into his pocket and pulled out a jammer, set it in the middle of the table and turned it on.

For the next couple of hours, Bud told us an unbelievable story. Well, with what I heard from Caleb's debriefing this morning, I guess it wasn't unbelievable at all.

"In the early 1980s, an Indian *Guru* named Bagwan Rajneesh set up a commune near the town of Antelope. His followers purchased sixty four thousand acres and built a fortress complex which accommodated 2,000 residents. The total number of people living in Antelope at that time was around 50 people. The population today is only 35. Antelope was a ghost town then and remains a ghost town to this day.

I wish he'd stop mentioning ghosts, thought Caleb.

Easy, bro. It just means the town is practically deserted, I thought back.

Then why didn't he just call it a deserted town?

Simone asked Bud, "Why does the Apostle keep you here if it's a ghost town?"

Damn it. There's that word again.

"There are a few farm families here. However, I'm here to find out what's happening underground. He knows something is hinky and he wants someone onsite to find out what it is. Let me finish my story about Rajneesh then I'll fill you in on what I think is going down.

"The people who lived in the commune and those who visited frequently weren't your typical religious freaks. Most of them were professionals, many of them very well to do, like lawyers and high level government people. It's estimated that the members of the commune generated 120 million dollars from business interests. Just an example of how rich these people were, it was reported 93 Rolls Royce cars were donated to Rajneesh."

That's a ton of money!

I ignored Caleb and asked, "What happened to the commune?"

"A couple of things turned bad. The commune leaders were arrested for attempted murder of the U.S. Attorney, Charles H. Turner. In 1984 commune teams were engaged in bio-terror attacks, poisoning salad products with salmonella at restaurants and shops throughout the county. It was reported 750 people were poisoned in The Dalles, the largest city in Wasco county. The motivation for the attack was to fix a local election to gain political power in the city and county.

"Lastly, Ma Anand Sheela, Rajneesh's longtime girlfriend and second in command, was arrested on attempted murder charges. She tried to poison Rajneesh for losing interest in her and having regular sex with several of the younger commune women.

"Shortly after these occurrences, Rajneesh was deported and the commune collapsed, however the fortress still remains.

"I suspected the fortress might still be viable and kept searching the building for clues. About a year ago, I discovered a large vault door on the south side of the basement wall. It was hidden from view by some debris. I wasn't able to open it. However, I began checking it frequently. A few weeks later, I detected sounds of construction coming from the other side of the vault. In addition, I'm pretty sure I saw construction on the surface about a mile from town. I knew something was happening so I contacted the Apostle.

"Now you know everything I know. However I speculate that someone is refurbishing whatever is behind the vault door. I know for a fact the commune had an arsenal of weapons and I believe whoever is doing the construction is resupplying the cave perhaps with new weapons in addition to the ones left by the commune. Someone is getting ready to launch an attack on some major target, something a lot bigger than the recent bank robberies."

Wakeup, Time to Die—Chanlina

It was 2:00 am the next evening. The sky was overcast and there was drizzling rain. Everything was ready. My two diversion teams were in place. The explosive devices had been planted at both sites and Fat Man and I plus two additional soldiers were in position. It would be a stealth approach into the apartment with the soldiers guarding the stairs leading up to the victim's residence.

The first charge to detonate would be the one farthest away from the apartment, but close enough to draw any of the security people close to the vic's apartment to the site of the explosion and fire.

We waited in the shadows as the two man security team made their pass of the target building and headed to the next cluster of apartments. We were dressed in black and covered from head to toe, including our faces. They never saw us.

Five more minutes.

Then, three, two, one, now.

There was a deafening explosion and the sky was bright with flames. The second explosion followed and then the third. The whole parking lot a hundred yards from here was ablaze with yellow-orange fire.

Fat Man bounded up the stairs two at a time with me right behind him. The door to the apartment began to open and he slammed into it, knocking the person on the other side of the door off his feet and onto his back in the entry way. He stood over the man, his machete drawn and the blade touching the man's throat.

I pulled out my Maglite and shined it in the man's face. It wasn't my target. "Who are you?" I asked, turning the light on a picture of the victim. "Where is this man?"

"That's my father. He's out of town and won't be back for a few days."

I reached for my com and said in Khmer, "Mission aborted. Abort second explosion. Recover explosives if possible. Return to bus. Acknowledge."

There were a series of clicks on my phone indicating they received my orders.

Fat Man gestured to the young man on the floor. "What about him?" he asked.

"Are you right or left handed?" I asked in English.

"Right," he answered, looking somewhat confused.

I turned to Fat Man and said, "Take the left."

In one quick motion, the man's left hand was severed from his arm.

The man began screaming and I shoved a rag in his mouth. "You need to cauterize the stump as quickly as you can or you will bleed out and die."

We left, closing the door behind us and hurried down the steps. As we walked quickly to the bike I asked, "Did you take his hand as a trophy?"

He shook his head as he climbed on the bike and I climbed on back. "I don't keep hands, only heads."

We sped down the road to the bus. I had to figure out where the target went as soon as possible.

That Got Our Attention—Detective Hong

Bill and I arrived in Salem in the early evening and checked in with the Salem PD. We met up with Detective Granger, a former Portland PD officer who sold out to become a detective. We were invited into a room full of Salem officers to share what information we had on Chanlina and her soldiers, especially her second in command, a big man called Fat Man.

They projected a map of the apartment complex near the government offices which was identified by Joshua's CI as the likely location of the attack. Detective Granger asked me to brief them on where the diversions were most likely to be.

"Joshua's CI told us they will most likely be looking to find one particular target. He couldn't tell us the exact address for the target but he felt confident it would be one of the eight apartments in building E, located here," I said and pointed to the location of a square on the projected map. "The building has two floors, each with four apartments. The most likely place for the two diversions are here and here," I said and pointed to two different locations.

"There's no guarantee these are the exact locations, however the CI was pretty confident. My recommendation is to wait for the first diversion then quickly surround the E building and see which unit comes under attack."

One of the Salem officers frowned and asked, "So we're using the victim as bait?"

"You're right," answered Bill. "These people have already killed two people by beheading them. However, the people they killed are no angels; they're the planners who set up a boarding school attack in Portland risking the lives of 200 children, teachers and staff. This could have resulted in another Woodlawn Elementary massacre."

"Any other questions?" I asked. There were none.

One of the Salem detectives briefed everyone on the show time and location for each squad. Bill and I left for dinner with Detective Granger then agreed to meet at the assembly point at 10 pm.

We parked our unmarked car in the complex parking lot close (not *too* close) to the E building, turned off the engine and opened a box of donuts. They would be our dessert for the night. No one knew for sure what time it would go down, so after dessert, Bill took a two hour nap while I listened to an audiobook, a crime novel by Barry Eisler. At midnight, I woke up Bill and it was my turn to nap.

A little after 2:00 am I was jarred awake by an incredible loud series of explosions followed by several smaller explosions, massive fire and a lot of screaming and yelling.

Bill was out of the car in a flash and I joined him as we hooked up with several Salem police collapsing on the E building. We heard screaming coming from one of the second floor units and saw two people streaking down the stairs and away from the building. They were out of sight for a few seconds then a motorcycle with two people dressed in black onboard, burst across the yard, dodging the running police and streaked away before anyone could detain them.

The second diversion, if there was ever one planned, never happened. The screamer turned out to be the son of the intended victim. Fat Man must have gotten frustrated that the real target wasn't home and took out his frustration by cutting off the young man's left hand. The good news was, he didn't bleed out. Even better news was they identified the intended victim, it was Lt. Colonel Brian Clark, Colonel Legleu's executive officer for the Army National Guard.

The follow-on questions were, where was he and why wasn't he at home?

CHAPTER 30

A Meeting of the Minds—Lt. Colonel Brian Clark

The Antelope Airport was finally open. I was looking forward to visiting the new facility. I was surprised I was selected to attend the first meeting of the Ruling Council. Beside the Five Leaders, there would be five from the Second Tier and then an additional five from The Organization who would be attending.

I'd seen videos of the construction of the underground hangar and the upgrade to the commune fortress. It took the better part of a year to finish and that included the delays caused by Governor Johnson's new gun control laws. It was unfortunate the assassination attempts weren't successful. The General Council was all set to replace the governor and cancel his executive orders. You could blame that on Colonel Legleu's security people. I hope to get a chance to take him out. He's been a real pain in the ass not only for his job as the leader of the governor's security team but also for him being in charge of Oregon's Army National Guard. I should've been the one to get the promotion to colonel, not Legleu. Once he's eliminated, I will automatically become the National Guard commander.

Speaking of pains in the ass, the presence of Team Joshua added to our delays. If he hadn't shown up at that cursed Vietnamese boarding school, I'm sure many of those Asian children would've been killed and we would be rid of those heathen devils. That goes for the pastor and his wife as well. It really pisses me off that Boa pretends to be a Christian. It would've been a small step in our ethnic cleansing program if those Cambodians finished their job. Now they're blaming us for their screw up.

I kept telling the Ruling Council we needed Christian soldiers to get the job done right. They told me to stand down. Apparently one of Pol Pot's descendants was on the Ruling Counsel. That was a bitter pill to swallow until a federal senator took me aside and made me aware it was all part of the plan to get rid of both Cambodian assassins as well as the Vietnamese children. He told me there was a blood feud between the Pol Pot council member and the assassins. It was going to be two for the price of one. Unfortunately, Joshua and his people along with the Portland police prevented that from happening.

I was looking forward to the meeting and sat back and relaxed in one of the new transport aircraft. The propulsion system was new state of the art using ducted fans instead of fan jets. They made for a very quiet ride. My only regret was that I wasn't allowed to tell my son anything about my visit to Antelope. In fact, he knew nothing about my membership in The Organization. If he only knew, I was sure he would have been very proud.

<u>The Spirit of Caleb Must be Destroyed—Chanlina</u>

I was unpleasantly surprised twice, once when I found out my target, Lt. Colonel Brian Clark wasn't home and second, when we were almost captured by the police as we made our escape. There was nothing I could do about the first one; my people were watching the house and they never saw him leave. The second surprise was because of Caleb. I thought my threats would have been sufficient to scare him off. Instead, he must have told the police where we would be.

I underestimated him. I thought the spirit of my dead father would have made sure he didn't intervene. I was wrong about that as well. For some reason I don't understand, the spirit of my father is no longer available to me. That is a major concern; without his assistance I feel blind.

I must focus on what I can control; I believe destroying Caleb will not only be possible, it will be my delight. Of course, I can't kill him directly, however, if…no, not if. When I kill Joshua, Caleb dies a second time and I will be free of him forever.

When Fat Man and I returned to the bus, I took a head count of my people and found out two of the soldiers were captured by the police. One lost her life. It was Bopha, one of my lieutenants and a close friend.

I had to leave. My heart was filled with grief and my mind was filled with anger. I took the bike and drove as fast as I could as if my life didn't matter anymore. For the first time in my life, I failed in my mission. Losing Bopha wasn't the first loss of a soldier but this one was a dear friend.

I drove to a deserted campground, then around a chained entrance with a sign that read, **Do Not Enter**. I shut down the bike in the pitch dark parking lot and found a bench. I began to cry. For the first time in a long time, I cried. I permitted myself ten minutes of grieving. Then pushed it to the back of my mind, replacing it with anger. I had people to kill.

As I returned to the bike, my latest burner phone rang. I didn't recognize the number but answered it anyway. "Yes?"

"Ms. Tong, please."

"You have wrong number. No Tong here, Song?"

"Chanlina, you're ordered by the Ruling Council to attend the first meeting of The Organization…"

They gave me instructions on how I was to get to the meeting. When I returned to the bus, I placed Fat Man in charge and told him to get to the forest park I just left.

He drove me to a private airport and I boarded a strange looking aircraft with four large pods on the corners of the vehicle. I took a seat in the rear and attached my seat belt. Apparently, I was the last one to board. The engine pods began to spool up. As we flew to the meeting location, I wondered what was in-store for me as well as my troops.

Priming the War Wagon for Battle—Joshua

After Simone and I wrapped up things with Bud in Antelope, we returned to the trailer and saw a plume of dust moving across the high grassland at a very high rate of speed. The plume made a sharp turn and headed towards the paved road next to where we parked Sweet Ride.

As the plume hit the road, we could see the War Wagon just in front of the plume. We noticed the dust disappeared to be replaced by black smoke from the wagon's four tires as the vehicle made a high-speed turn and accelerated towards us.

The smoke vanished as Mark slowed down and brought the War Wagon to a stop next to us. Pham opened the rear passenger side door and stepped out with a wide grin on his face. Mark joined him as he exited the driver side door.

"Is she ready to rumble?" I asked.

"Too soon to tell," answered Pham. "Mechanically, she's as tight as ever."

Mark interrupted, "We were clocking over a hundred in the tall weeds with hardly a shudder. On the pavement, we hit 150 before I shut her down. She would've done close to 200 if we'd a longer stretch of road."

"That's terrific!" Simone said excitedly just as we saw two fast moving creatures barreling through the grass. Sarge exploded out of the weeds and jumped into Mark's arms, barking his delight at getting to run full speed. A few minutes later Sniffer joined in the celebrational barking and licking hands to show he was just as pleased. There was plenty of petting, barking and licking before we could get back to the results of War Wagon's test runs.

"We haven't started evaluating the weapon systems," commented Pham as he continued to pet Sniffer. "If all goes well tomorrow, we could be ready for real combat the next day."

"What can we do to help?" asked Simone.

Joshua added, "Why don't you put the War Wagon to bed for now and meet us in the motorhome. I want to brief you on what we found out in Antilope. Bright and early tomorrow we will begin checkout of the weapons. We need to be on call for action very soon."

Simone and I told them about what Rajneesh had done to Antelope almost 40 years ago and both Mark and Pham were amazed. "I never heard anything about this. I guess it's ancient history," commented Mark.

Pham added, "I'm in the same boat. It's really hard to believe somebody could take over a town like that."

"Can you imagine people donating 93 Rolls Royce cars to that crackpot? I can't even picture that," replied Mark.

We continued our meeting through dinner and went over how we were going to do the weapons checkout. As we were wrapping up, I got a call from the Apostle.

"Good evening, Black Bond. Please put this call on speaker. I want your entire team to hear this message." His voice sounded weak, as if he were in a lot of pain.

"Yes sir, you're on speaker," I said as I pressed the speaker button on my encrypted phone. "Are you all right, sir?"

He ignored my question. "I'm placing you on high alert status as of now. Things are going to get intense very soon. It looks like the ghost airport has gone active. They are preparing to take over the entire government of the state of Oregon. Bud said to tell you the vault is open and there is a lot of traffic. I told him to get out of Antelope as soon as he could. Unfortunately, he hasn't confirmed my order.

"Behind this coup is an international group who call themselves, The Organization. They have stepped up their timing due to Governor Johnson's new gun laws. Apparently, they are expanding on the Rajneesh plan from the 1980s, except this time they have more money and power behind them.

"Their underground bunker is considered to be impenetrable and they are currently refurbishing the old Rajneesh fortress. We estimate they will be able to put 2,000 troops into action within the week."

There was a prolonged pause and the sound of muffled coughing before he came back on line. His voice sounded even weaker, "You and your team will receive specific mission parameters later today. In the meantime, I need to speak to Joshua and Simone in private. But first I want to say goodbye to both Mark and Pham. You have been special team members and I want to let you know the missions you served on were successful because you preformed above and beyond any expectations we had. I just wanted to acknowledge your contributions." He paused again then added, "Now get out of here so I can deal with Joshua and Simone."

The two men looked at each other, then turned to me with expressions of concern. I gestured toward the door and they left immediately, taking Sarge and Sniffer with them.

"We're alone, boss," I said, trying to keep my voice neutral.

"I was never your boss, Joshua, just your advisor. I'm sure everyone is aware…my health is declining. I'd like to advise you just once more before I leave this…this life." He began coughing again, when he spoke again his voice was barely a whisper, "It's time you tell Simone about Caleb and Carlos. I would recommend you tell Mark and Pham as well. You will be a stronger team if you tell them. Good luck on your mission Marine, Semper Fi." The line went dead.

Oh my God! I can't believe he's gone, thought my brother.

Simone looked totally surprised. "Who was talking in my head?" she asked. "Was that Caleb?"

CHAPTER 31

Let's Start a Revolution—Matt Justice, 1 of 5 Leaders

I stood on the elevated stage and watched as members of The Organization entered the courtyard of The Fortress. The other four of the Five Leaders joined me on the stage and were also taking in the moment. A moment that we all waited decades to accomplish.

I felt honored the other four had chosen me to be the first speaker. I would've been crushed if they hadn't selected me. After all, as the great grandchild of the founders of the Antelope Commune I was entitled to that honor.

I remember when they began the construction of the Fortress we're now standing in, watching it rise from a set of drawings, to excavating the multi-basements and tunnels, the laying of a strong foundation and finally seeing the completed fortress of strength and power. I was thrilled as a child to hold the hands of my great grandparents and walk through the magnificent structure. I loved the courtyard that we now stand in. The sight of it now is just as overwhelming as it was then.

I was very young then, almost six decades ago and my memories aren't as good as they used to be, however my memories of that walk through the Fortress are still vivid. Thinking back to that day, I remember how proud my great grandparents were. It was so unfortunate things didn't work out the way they planned.

I continued to watch as the courtyard filled with The Organization's one thousand invitees. The remainder would be able to watch this momentous event on closed circuit TVs throughout the Fortress and in the underground facilities. We expect nearly three thousand will join us.

The sound of a gong signaled it was almost time to begin and the crowd hurried to find their assigned seats. The next time the gong sounded, the courtyard doors would be closed and locked and the security guards would take their place at the doors and around the stage.

I turned and looked as the other four Leaders took their seats. I noticed the enormous monitor behind their seats, I think it was called a Jumbotron. As I watched the screen came to life in vivid clarity and color. I turned back as the last of the invitees took their seats, the gong sounded and the doors were closed and sealed.

I approached the rostrum and looked out over the crowd as the lights dimmed and a spotlight brightened above my head. The courtyard became silent and I began my introduction.

"Ladies and gentlemen, my name is Matt Justice. I am one of the Ruling Five and a descendent of, Bagwan Rajneesh and Ma Anand Sheela, the founders of the Antelope Commune and the builders of The Fortress. Recently, there have been numerous upgrades to this building and the creation of a state-of-the-art underground airport and complex.

"My relatives had a dream and they were well on their way to turning the dream into reality. Unfortunately, the dream wasn't allowed to come true. Shortsighted people were in power at that time. They couldn't understand the vision, the vision of a utopian society for everyone. They were the naysayers, the people in charge. A small percentage of the population controlled the lives of the many. They were wealthy, powerful people who wanted to keep the wealth and power for themselves.

"The descendants of those shortsighted people are still in power today. Our goal, our very reason for existence, is to get rid of those shortsighted, selfish people so that all of us can live the lives we are entitled to. No one should be able to tell you what you can or cannot do."

The crowd was getting into it. They were starting to feel it. I wanted to leave them with something to cheer about, something simple to remember.

"Let me close with a mantra. In 2011, the Isley Brothers came out with a song that sums it up. *It's your thing, do what you wanna do. No one can tell you what you gotta do.*"

A video of the Isley Brothers singing that song was displayed on the Jumbotron. By the time it ended, everybody was singing along. When it was over and the audience calmed down, I began to chant.

"Do what you wanna do…Do what you wanna do…Do what you wanna do." The audience joined in. For several minutes the chanting continued as I sat down and the next speaker approached the rostrum. She stood quietly listening to the chant and smiled. As the chant began to die down she turned to me and gestured for me to stand, then turned back to the audience and said, "Let's hear it for Matt Justice."

The entire audience stood, applauding and cheering. It sent chills down my spine. They were ready to sign up for whatever we told them. I had done my part. Now it was time for the others to tell them how it would get done.

How Do We Get Free—Senator Brenda Blankenship— 1 of 5 Leaders

I looked out at the audience, they were eager to hear our plans for being truly free.

"Ladies and gentlemen, what I'm about to tell you may surprise many of you. I want to tell you all up front what we need to do, then tell you how we will accomplish it. Are you ready?"

I looked out at the sea of nodding heads and said, "To be completely free of the tyranny that dominates us, the state of Oregon needs to secede from the United States of America."

I could hear the gasps of many of the people in the audience; I waited for everyone to compose themselves before continuing, "It's the only way for us to be truly free of Washington DC's control. I've been a senator in the US Congress for two terms and before that, a member of the House of Representatives for one term. I can honestly say none of my associates gives a damn about Oregon. Almost none of them have ever been to our state and we're considered the bastard child of America's family by most of them. They don't understand our way of life and have no interest in finding out. If they come to the west coast at all it's always to California or occasionally to our cousin to the north in Washington.

"Don't get the wrong idea, just because they don't think of us as worth a second thought, they would never consent to us leaving. They think of us as property, poor undeveloped property but still property. They will resist us from divorcing them unless we show them the costs would be unacceptably high.

"Some of you might be curious of what 'unacceptably high' means. It means if we're met with armed resistance, we will counter that resistance. That will most likely be the Oregon National Guard, SWAT teams and local police. The FBI might be used at the onset but once they see the death and destruction we will rein down on them, they will most likely pull their agents out of Oregon. The same goes for all other federal agencies.

"Governor Johnson's new laws on gun control has delayed our initial attacks but he will be first on our list to be eliminated. It turned out we were too subtle in our first two attempts. That will be rectified in the next few days. Prior to his elimination we will remove the head of the National Guard who is also in charge of the Governor's security.

"We plan to attack Oregon's capital following the Governor's death. It will be a blitzkrieg attack, fast and furious. If you haven't checked out our underground hangar area you should do so before we go active. We have more advanced weapons than most middle sized countries. We also have the men and women who are experts at handling them.

"Once we have captured the capital, we will begin negotiations with the federal government for Oregon's freedom.

"The longer they delay the more areas we will attack. The last target will be the city of Portland. We plan to wall off the city and lay siege to the entire population and starve them out until they see the light and surrender to us.

"That concludes my presentation. Let me introduce you to our next speaker. His name is Gerald Bright and he is the former CEO of several defense related corporations, such as weapons manufacturing and contracted paramilitary companies. He's the one who will make sure we have the right number of highly trained soldiers and the necessary weapons and ammunition required to meet our needs."

I'm Not 1 of the 5 Leaders—Caleb (the Spy)

I arrived at the Fortress early. When Joshua found out from the Apostle things were going to get dicey, he assigned me to monitor everything that was going on at the Fortress and the underground hangar.

Nothing of importance was happening the first day I was on the scene. I kept bouncing around from site to site and still had time to sit in on the War Wagon weapons calibrating sessions. What a blast! It was like watching something from a sci-fi movie but this was the real deal.

All the time I was moving from site to site I was concerned about Simone, actually not only Simone, Chanlina too. It seemed like they could sense my presence and even detect my thoughts when I conversed with Joshua. How could this be happening? As soon as I had that thought, I was transported to wonderland for another short, very short meeting with my spirit guide.

I felt silly with my avatar dressed for a tennis match. I discovered I was holding a tennis racket in my right hand and a yellow tennis ball in the left. My spirit guide and former commanding officer stood on the other side of the court similarly dressed.

"Why do they dress us like Barbie and Ken dolls?" I asked.

"More like Ken 1 and Ken 2. I have no answer for your question. It's irrelevant, you asked a question and I'm here to answer it."

"You mean the question of why we are dressed in tennis attire?"

"No, doofus," he answered. "The question about why Simone and Chanlina are beginning to 'hear' you when you converse with Joshua. Both of these women have had contact with spirits of relatives, both with their fathers. Simone had Carlos and Chanlina had her father whose Cambodian name I can't pronounce and don't have the interest to find out. By the way, do you realize the Apostle could also 'listen in' on conversations between you and your brother?"

"Yes, he intimated he'd contact with me just before he passed away."

"Wrong, he listened in on every conversation you had with Joshua from the moment you were bonded to your brother."

"What?!! Why didn't you tell me?"

"Need to know, Caleb. Neither you nor Joshua were aware of it. However, that was the main reason he chose Joshua for these missions. He knew Joshua would need your help. He made sure you got it for him."

"So he's been listening in on all our conversations? How could he do that? Was he a spirit?"

He ignored my question, glanced at an illusionary watch, and said, "Time to go. Good luck saving Oregon from the assholes."

He was gone and I was back at the Fortress. I heard one of the guards standing next to the courtyard door speaking to one of the other guards, "Who left the tennis racket on the floor?"

"I don't know but I found a yellow tennis ball," he said, then added, "I didn't know we had tennis courts."

Spirits have a weird sense of humor. Time to return to my spy sleuthing.

Rather than give you a blow by blow narration, I'm going to summarize what the next three of the Five Leaders had to say.

The third presenter (I'm not going to call them the Five Leaders. It sounds too pretentious) was already introduced by the senator. His major claim to fame was he provided all kinds of weapons and ammunition for the insurrection and very well trained soldiers of fortune with a lot of combat experience. I did a quick check of his list of soldiers and found out the vast majority were dishonorably discharged from their respective services for brutality against not only their enemies but also their battle brothers. Most of these men were already at the Fortress and chomping at the bit to see more action. I was tempted to see if any of these combatants contracted COVID and their brains transformed from human to Neanderthal.

However, I thought it would be a long shot and I should spend my time on more critical endeavors.

The bottom line for Gerald Bright was the guns, ammunition and well-trained fighting men and women were all ready to begin a war.

Next up was a Marine two-star general who declined to give his name or show his face. His strength was mission planning and he'd everything laid out for the conquest of Oregon. It all began with the death of two people, just as the senator mentioned during her brief presentation. Colonel Legleu was to go first followed by Governor Johnson. If possible, it could be a double elimination. That would be possible only if they could be taken when they were together by one assassin or if they were separated, by two assassins. The two assassins were identified as our friend Chanlina and her archenemy, Lt. Colonel Brian Clark.

Obviously, the general had no idea of the hatred they had for each other. When Brian found out Chanlina was trying to kill him and cut off the hand of his son, he had to be restrained when they met up for this meeting. It should prove interesting to see how things turn out.

Last but not least was a descendant of the Cambodian leader Pol Pot. He was the dictator of the Khmer Rouge from 1976 to 1979. During his reign as dictator, 1.7 million Cambodians lost their lives due to starvation, execution, disease or worked to death. In January 1979, Vietnamese troops seized the Cambodian capital of Phnom Penh, toppling the regime of Pol Pot and his Khmer Rouge. In 1979 he was captured by a splinter group of the Khmer Rouge and placed under house arrest until he died of natural causes in 1998.

The descendant of Pol Pot was in his middle 50s and a distant relative. He professed to be a huge fan of Pol Pot and embraced the only way to win a war was to annihilate not only your enemy but all of their relatives as well. He was in charge of the trained assassins he brought to the state of Oregon. They were the ones who would eliminate the leaders in Oregon's government. Not only the governor but all of his staff as well. At least that was the original plan but when things had gone sideways with their first mission, the mission at the boarding school, things changed for Chanlina and her people. She wouldn't have minded taking out the governor, all of his staff and all other government workers who happened to be in range. However, their priorities changed. Getting rid of the incompetent Americans who failed to support their mission was prime. So far, they'd taken the heads of two of them and were close to number three. In fact, she discovered number three was sitting two rows in front of her during their flight to Antelope and the underground airport. Unfortunately, she didn't find that out until they entered the courtyard meeting and were introduced.

I was reading her thoughts when the outburst occurred. She'd been composed, there was no point in killing him in front of everyone. She would wait until the time was right. *Unfortunately, the idiot American must have had a testosterone attack,* she thought to me. *He went berserk and tried to attack me. He should have been thanking me for sparing the life of his son and took only his left hand as a token of my anger. Instead, he shouted stupid profanities at me as if I was bothered by his insults. Are you getting all this, Caleb?*

Every thought, I replied. *When the time comes I hope you're successful in your vendetta.*

She smiled in my direction or the direction she thought my words were coming from. *You're a worthy adversary, Caleb. I hope it will not be necessary to end your existence.*

Me too. I also hope you and your people get out of this alive.

You're a fool…but a gracious fool.

The conference ended, the doors were unlocked and opened wide. Some decided to go down to the Fortress's basement, through the vault and into the hangar bay. They toured the tools of war and everyone agreed they were invincible. What fools, I felt sorry for the lives that would be lost.

Before I returned to Joshua and the rest of the team, I stopped by the Fortress IT control room and downloaded a complete copy of the meeting to what I call my spirit memory bank. When I returned to Sweet Ride I transferred my copy to a thumb drive. Joshua told the crew he received a copy of a meeting just held in the Fortress by one of his CIs. All of them watched the entire Fortress meeting. When we were done watching, Joshua had Pham send an encrypted copy of the meeting to the governor and his so-called head of security. We all knew the war was only a few days away, maybe sooner.

CHAPTER 32

Prepping for Armageddon—Joshua

While Mark and Pham took the War Wagon through her weapon's drills, I felt it was an opportune time to explain to Simone about Caleb. I was mildly surprised when she totally accepted the story of my dead brother's spirit with very little hesitation. When I explained how her father, Carlos, attempted to bond with her during our mission in New Orleans, her first comment was, "So I wasn't going crazy after all. What a relief! I understand why you couldn't tell me during the mission. That clears up a lot of unanswered questions for me." She paused then added, "I don't understand why all of a sudden, I can hear Caleb in my head when he's communicating with you. We're not related. I thought you said I can only connect with a close relative."

"You're right," I replied. "Unfortunately, I don't have an answer to your question. Maybe he can explain it to both of us when he gets back from his recon at the Fortress."

I'm back. What question?

"How come I can hear you in my head when you're communicating with Joshua?" asked Simone.

Oh, that question. I don't have a good answer. I was recently told by my spirit trainer, it was an added ability that was bestowed on me. You and I are not bonded like Joshua and I. He and I can communicate with each other over long distances, like half a world away. You and I can communicate only when we are line-of-sight. Before you ask, I have no idea why it works that way, I'm just happy I can now share info with you directly.

"What about the rest of the team? Will you be able to communicate with Pham and Mark?" she asked.

Yes but not yet, Caleb answered. *I know Joshua has to decide when that will happen.*

"Probably after this mission is over," I replied. "It could happen sooner. It really depends on Caleb's spirit guide, not me or Caleb."

"How about Sarge and Sniffer?" asked Simone.

I thought she was joking but Caleb took her seriously, *I never thought about it but I remember a few times when Sarge seemed to know what I wanted him to do. I'll have to pay more attention.*

Pham and Mark spent several hours that day checking out every weapons system installed on the War Wagon. That goes for the fire control computers as well. We had two of those, one online and the other a backup. We also replenished all the ammunition that was spent during the checkout and recharged or replaced the surveillance drones used to spy on the airport facilities.

The day before we checked and tested the run-flat tires, the break system, all facets of the turbodiesel engine, the two electric motors used in the hybrid propulsion system and the two auxiliary power units (APUs) which supplied the electricity for everything except the electric motors; they had their own dedicated battery packs. Pham had done a very thorough check of the armor plating and found out one plate was cracked. That plate was replaced. He also checked the drop-down shields when it was necessary to keep our windshield and side windows covered during an attacked

There were probably a hundred other things on the checklist, however by midafternoon we were ready for action. Oh, yeah. We also filled the fuel tanks with diesel fuel and made sure the electric motors battery pack were completely charged. Now we were truly ready.

<u>Mission Planning 101—Joshua</u>

We were back in the motorhome with the trailer attached and the War Wagon inside. We'd driven back though Antelope and pulled into the trailer park where Caleb saw the transformer armored truck-to-motorhome almost a week ago. There were only a few trailers, a couple of fifth-wheelers and three motorhomes of various sizes and paint jobs pretty evenly spread out around the camp grounds. We took up two parking spots to accommodate the trailer far away from the rest of the renters. There were three fairly tall trees near our ride with a good sized yard with real green grass. Sarge and Sniffer were pleased to roll around on the grass making little grunting and snorting sounds.

The four of us sat around the dinner table and I started it off. I sensed Caleb was present as well. "I see this as a two pronged attack. The first order of business needs to be shutting down any assassination attempts. We need to inform Lt Colonel Lopez he is a prime target for assassination and the next is Governor Johnson. This is so important, we need to make that phone call right now. Simone, would you make two calls to the emergency numbers they gave us when we had the sit-down with the Governor? Tell them we know the names of the assassins. Be sure to tell the Colonel his second in command will be gunning for him. He could also be going after the Governor if they're both together. Chanlina is the most dangerous of the two. She may have added the Lieutenant Colonel to her kill list as well as the Colonel and the Governor. They should have pictures of both of the assassins."

"On it, boss," she said as she left the table and walked to the computer desk to make the calls.

I turned back to Pham and Mark. "We need to keep the zealots from getting loose. We have two targets to deal with and we have to do it simultaneously. The first should be the underground facility, where all their aircraft and heavy weapons are located. I think our team can handle that ourselves. I have a contact inside who I think could open the square. Once the square is open and the ramps are in place, we take the War Wagon inside and do so much damage none of their aircraft, other vehicles and large weapons can be used."

I bet I'm the inside person who gets to figure out how to open the square then close the square and sabotage the controls after the War Wagon escapes. Am I right?

Yes, I replied quickly. *No more comments, please.*

"Once the mayhem is finished, the War Wagon exits up the ramp, the square is closed and the controls trashed never to be used again.

"While all that is taking place we need to close and lock the vault to prevent the escape of their troops housed in the underground barracks."

Let me guess, that's on me as well? thought Caleb sarcastically.

I glanced at Simone who was smiling at Caleb's comments. Her expression changed abruptly to all business as she continued her conversation. I assumed it was with the colonel.

I didn't reply to Caleb and continued my briefing, "As far as we know, those are the only exits available. We estimate there could be as many as a thousand troops housed in the underground barracks. With all the exits blocked we could use sleepy-time gas to put most of the combatants out of action. The others who avoided the gas would be another problem, probably fire fights unless we can get them to surrender. That would require the National Guard to come into play and probably state police. I need to contact Colonel Legleu when Simone finishes her calls and brief him about the situation. My hope is he can get enough of the guard here in time to be effective. Are there any questions or suggestions?"

Mark smiled and asked, "Who gets to drive the War Wagon?"

I smiled back. "Who do you think?"

"You, of course," he replied answering his own question. "With Simone as co-pilot and Pham on weapons. I suppose Sarge and I will handle locking the vault and anyone who happens to be in the Fortress basement at the time."

"Sounds like a good plan to me," I said.

Wait a minute! I thought that was going to be my job. I can handle both assignments, whined Caleb…again.

Simone interrupted, "Joshua, I've got Colonel Legleu and Governor Johnson waiting to speak to you. They say it's urgent. They want it to be on encrypted video."

I frowned and moved to the computer desk as Simone activated the system. Both looked unhappy. The colonel was angry unhappy, the governor looked sad.

"What kind of horse shit are you slinging now, Sergeant Brown? What's all this about assassins and Oregon trying to secede from America?"

I countered with, "Nice to see you gentlemen," in a calm voice. "Colonel, have you neglected to keep Governor Johnson updated on the briefing I sent to both of you?"

"Oh, like the fiasco here in Salem a few days ago when some college kids blew up a few garbage dumpsters. I heard Brian's son lost his hand in the ruckus. Don't you think calling in all the police was a bit of overkill?"

"Did you happen to examine the wound on Brian's arm. His hand was cut off by a machete. By the way, do you know where your second in command is this moment?"

"He's on leave," the colonel replied smugly.

"I meant do you know his physical location because I do. He's in Antelope right now, planning your assassination. He and about 2000 mercenaries are about to start a major war. Killing you is the first step, with you out of the picture, the Governor is next. Would you like to see the videos my CI managed to smuggled out of their mission briefing? It's going to be just like old times when Bagwan Rajneesh and his cronies captured the town, except this is going to be on a whole order of magnitude worse."

The colonel started to say something but looked over at the governor as the man collapsed into his chair. The governor looked up, his voice a whisper, "Yes, we'd very much like to see the video. Please send it to us ASAP."

"It was delivered to your head of security two days ago. We have his signed receipt. Please get back to me after you find time to watch it." I hung up and waited.

I went back to the table and continued my plan for the Fortress as I waited for the call.

Prepping for the Sneak Attack—Caleb

I left the motorhome and dropped in uninvited onto the underground airport hangar deck. When the governor called back, Joshua would contact me and I would transport back to Sweet Ride. In the meantime, I needed to determine where the controls for the square were located. It turns out the controls were nowhere to be found and trust me, I'm a terrific searcher. Then it occurred to me, maybe the controls were in the two story tower and not under the square. I looked for a way to the tower. That turned out to be a dead end, so I transported myself onto the second floor where I expected to find the flight controllers' stations. Guess what? They didn't have any flight controllers, not human ones at least. Instead they had a very sophisticated AI system that controlled pretty much everything. This was going to make things a lot more interesting.

As you would expect, there were all kinds of security doodads I had to figure out. I was very careful not to trip any alarms. I know this will come as a shock to the reader; I was unable to find a way around the trip falls. I fell back on the old saying, When uncertain, when in doubt, run in circles, scream and shout.

"What do you want this time?" asked my spirit guide. He seemed annoyed. "If this is related to humans, I can't help you."

"No human's involved," I answered meekly as I notice wonderland had changed seasons. It was mid-fall and a little chilly. We were both wearing wool coats and caps. The leaves on the trees changed to yellows, oranges and reds. A nice change.

"Okay," he replied gruffly. "What's the spirit's name?"

"Well, it isn't exactly a spirit," I answered tentatively, "but it definitely isn't human."

"Well, what is it? A seagull? A horse? Maybe a tortoise?"

"None of those, sir," I replied sheepishly. "It not alive, not really. It's an artificial intelligence computer."

"An AI?" He paused then said, "Stand by one."

He was gone for an instance and materialized almost immediately, however he was now wearing a heavy sweater and a different hat indicating he had been busy checking on things. I wasn't sure it that was a good sign or bad.

"You're referring to the AI at the underground airport near Antelope, Oregon?"

"Yes sir, that's the one," I answered hopefully.

"What are your objectives?"

"I want to be able to take control of the square over the underground hangar. I want to be able to open it and close and lock it down when I need to," I answered firmly.

"Okay, your request is approved. Anything else?" he asked.

I was shocked at his response and wasn't sure if I'd heard him correctly. "How do I do that? I mean, do I need to say abracadabra or some code?"

"Really? You think this is a magic trick? You just think the square is open and it opens. If you want it shut, it shuts. If you want to lock it, say abracadabra, maybe that will lock it."

He looked at his wristwatch and said, "Time to go, bye."

I didn't even have time to say thank you.

Suddenly, I was inside the tower. I had to test it. It couldn't be that simple. I felt like I had to say something. So I said, "Open sesame!"

I'll be damned; the square began sliding open. Before it moved too far, I quickly said, "Close." Instantly the door reversed direction and closed.

Before I could do anything else, Joshua contacted me. *Return immediately.*

I was back in Sweet Ride immediately. Being a spirit has some interesting perks.

More Planning—Joshua

I pushed the speaker button so everyone could hear our conversation, "This is Joshua," I said in my most in-charge voice.

"This is Colonel Legleu, Joshua. The Governor is with me in his office. We just finished watching your video of the Fortress meeting," he paused a beat, then continued, "I owe you an apology. We definitely have a situation at Antelope. I have to admit, the tour through the hangar bay was beyond belief. I can't imagine how they acquired all that fire power. I assume you have put together plans on how to stop this insurrection before it begins."

"Yes Colonel, we have." I quickly briefed them on our plans to handle the underground hangar and barracks, then moved on to how the colonel needed to be involved.

"The Fortress houses as many as a thousand troops. Based on what was revealed during their recent meeting, these men and women are well trained, well-armed mercenaries. My question to you is, can you get enough guard troops to keep the mercs contained within the Fortress?"

His response was immediate, "I don't have enough guard members to handle that assignment." He paused for a moment then continued, "I think I can activate enough Army reserve people to assist the guard. Let me make sure I understand what you're asking. You want my people to contain the mercs inside the Fortress. You aren't requiring an all-out assault on the building? Is that correct?"

"Yes," I answered. "It could possibly limit casualties on both sides. We would give them the opportunity to surrender. If they refuse and want to fight their way out, we level the Fortress before they break out. Do you have tanks, and artillery available?"

"Yes we do. We'd have to bring it in from Portland and other bases in the western part of the state. When do you expect all this will begin?"

"It could be as soon as tomorrow. I recommend you bring as many troops and heavy equipment as soon as possible. It all depends when they send out the two assassins to get rid of you and the Governor. We have twenty-four-hour surveillance watching for them. I would recommend when we see them head to Salem, we begin our assault."

"Roger that," said the colonel. "Governor, do you want to add anything?"

"May God be with us," he replied.

"We'll keep you informed, Joshua. Good hunting," the colonel said and disconnected the call.

I turned to my crew and asked, "Any questions or comments?"

"I do," replied Mark. "How do I and Sarge get inside the Fortress to secure the vault?"

Without thinking, I answered, "Caleb will show you the way."

Everyone stopped and turned to stare at me in disbelief.

Caleb screamed at me, *Joshua, what are you doing! Only Simone knows about me. Now's not the time…*

"Sorry, I was lost in thought for a moment," I said sheepishly. "I'll show you the way tonight."

Simone asked, "Would you like me to accompany you? Remember, I went with you and Bud to check out the vault."

"I'll be okay, Simone. I'm just a little tired. I think I'll take a short nap. Pham let me know if anything happens."

"Me too," said Simone and followed me to the bedroom.

Me three, added Caleb.

CHAPTER 33

Are We Ready to Rumble?—Joshua

Later that night, I took Mark and Sarge through the labyrinth of passage ways that led to the vault. Of course, Caleb joined us.

When we arrived, the vault was wide opened and we hid in the shadows to see how much traffic was coming and going. It was about 0200 hours and hardly anyone passed through.

I'll stand guard while you and Mark check out the door and how to lock it. If anyone shows up I'll give you plenty of time to hide out, volunteered Caleb.

Sarge seemed to be looking at where Caleb was located. When Caleb moved into the vault opening, Sarge followed him, making little whining sounds. I wasn't ready for another reveal and asked Mark to call him to a heel position. Sarge reluctantly obeyed and sat down next to Mark as we went over the vault controls.

When Mark was confident he could handle locking the door down, all of us left. We walked out through the gas station office and drove back to the trailer park. I wondered if Bud had escaped from the crazy people residing in the Fortress. I said a short prayer he made it out safely.

From that time on, I assigned Caleb to lookout duty. It was most likely, Brian and Chanlina would take one of the ducted fan pod vehicles to transport them from the underground hangar to a site in Salem close to the government buildings. They would probably leave late at night. We weren't sure if they would attempt the assassinations in the government buildings or their residences. Caleb would track them and keep me informed of their locations at all times. All we had to do was be prepare for anything.

The next night, Caleb woke me from a really cool dream.

It's on, Josh. I'm in the hangar and the two of them just boarded the DFP vehicle. They were accompanied by four security guards. They fired up the pods and the square is opening. I'll keep you briefed.

I woke up Mark and drove him and Sarge to the gas station in Antelope. I told him to wait out of sight until I contacted him.

Then I called the colonel and told him to prepare for company. He told me he would wake up the governor and take him to a secure bunker under his office. He said his troops were ready and could be at the Fortress in less than an hour. I told him to wait for my order. He agreed.

Simone, Pham and I opened the trailer and backed the War Wagon out. We left Sniffer in Sweet Ride to act as security. He wasn't amused and barked his disapproval.

As I drove the War Wagon to the gas station in Antelope, Simone told Mark it was time to lock up the vault. We'd used the electric motors to propel us. The turbodiesels were just too noisy. We parked near the gas station's office and waited. Ten minutes later, Mark and Sarge burst out of the office and jumped through the War Wagon's passenger side rear door. "The vault is secure. I've got company coming. Four or five bogies shooting at us. I returned fire. Not sure I hit any of them Sarge took one of them out. Here they come!"

Pham rotated the top mounted mini-machineguns and fired a short burst at the pursuers. Three seconds later they were all toast.

We remained in place to see if there were any further attacks. None came.

As we waited, Caleb contacted me. I sat there appearing I was lost in thought.

They just landed in a park across from the government building. Two of the security guards got out first and are making a sweep of the area... It's all clear, the two guards got back in and the aircraft just lifted off. I assume it's returning to Antelope... Chanlina and Brian are having an argument...what potty mouths they both have…wait…somebody just pulled up on a bike close to them…Brian just pulled his gun…Chanlina broke his arm with a baton…I think the biker is Fat Man…Yes, I'm sure it's him… he just pulled his machete…Brian's running, trying to escape…Chanlina tackled him…Fat Man handed the machete to Chanlina…Brian's screaming…Oh my God…she just cut off his head…There's blood everywhere…They're walking towards me. She gave the machete back to Fat Man and he's walking back to his bike. She's right in front of me.

"Good evening Caleb. I can sense you're near me. There will be no more killings tonight. My revenge is complete. Before I left the Fortress, I also killed the man who claimed he was a distant descendant of Pol Pot and one of the Ruling Five. He was lying but was gaining power in Cambodia. He was the man Brian reported to. Once I'd killed them both, my vendetta, my revenge was completed.

"I will not kill the Colonel nor the Governor. No one will. We will take the money we received from the pig of a lawyer and return to Cambodia. I don't like Americans, they can't be trusted…all except for you. Good night my friend. Go stop the evil people in the Fortress."

Did you get all that? She just blew me a kiss…she got on the back of the bike and they drove away. What should I do now, Joshua?

Transport back to the War Wagon, I replied silently. *We still have to deal with the evil people.*

CHAPTER 34

Let's Dance—Joshua

It was 0300 hours when we arrived back at the underground airport. I got a report from the colonel informing me they were moving into position surrounding the Fortress. Caleb had accessed the nine digit code and was able to open the gate in the perimeter fence. He told me he had a 'working relationship' with the airport's AI and was sure no one would be alerted to a new visitor.

Once inside the fence, Caleb opened the square and made sure the ramp leading to the underground hangar floor was in place. He warned us there were a few of the enemy servicing one of the aircraft, an F-35, very close to the ramp.

We were running the electric propulsion system as I silently drove down the ramp and into the enemy's lair. I spotted two techs checking out the F-35, wondering how a multimillion dollar fighter could have ended up in the underground hangar. You'd think someone would have noticed it was gone.

I stopped at the bottom of the ramp, lights off and as quiet as a mouse. Pham and Mark were working as a team with our weapons preparing for the assault.

Pham gave us a sitrep on the attack, "All weapons successfully transitioned from standby to active. Targeting computer selecting target sequence. Ready to commence firing in…five, four, three, two, one, ready to fire on your command, boss."

I moved us quietly toward the back of the hangar and into the area of tanks and artillery. My plan was to work our way back as we destroyed everything in sight, ending up at the exit ramp.

I did a quick survey to make sure I was satisfied with the layout then ordered, "Light it up."

The night turned from a sleepy slumber to a screaming thunder and lightning. I backed the War Wagon up as each of the individual weapons was destroyed. Some of them were apparently armed and our attack ignited secondary explosions throwing shards of metal into other weapons making them unusable.

Josh, we got a problem, one of the F-35s is powering up.

Roger that, I answered back.

"Take out the F-35! He's trying to escape."

Mark said something into his microphone and the roof mounted turret swiveled around until the cannon was pointing at the F-35. In spite of the cacophony of explosions, we could hear the whine of the jet engine spooling up. However the sound of the War Wagon's rapid-fire cannon drowned out the whine.

Mark tattooed large explosive holes directly into the engine section and tongues of fire began shooting out of the aircraft's aft section. This was followed by the shrieking scream of the engine coming apart and engulfing the entire vehicle.

I had to swerve to avoid the debris and backed into a helicopter in the process. I slammed the shifter into drive and fired up the turbodiesel at the same time. There was no point in trying to run silent on the dual electric motors any longer and the diesels gave me more power, a lot more power. I was in four-wheel drive as I gunned the War Wagon towards the ramp, all four tires squealing. We'd created enough havoc for one day.

Just as we approached the ramp, a large motorhome almost T-boned us. I veered to the left and screeched to a halt as the other vehicle dodged us and headed up the ramp. I got a brief glance as it ripped by us and thought it might be one of the motorhomes/armored trucks from a bank heist.

Caleb!!! I screamed in my mind. *Is that one of the transformer motorhomes?*

It looks like it to me. There's another one coming from the bay on your right.

"Mark!" I yelled.

"On it, boss," he replied and quickly acquired the target and pulverized it with multiple cannon rounds. It burst into flames and crashed into the other F-35, completely blocking any of the other transformers.

I maneuvered around all of the debris and headed up the ramp as quickly as I could. There was no way I was letting the first vehicle get away.

"Close the square," I yelled as the War Wagon roared up the ramp and on the tarmac. "Lock it up. Where did that first transformer go?"

Joshua, you can't be giving me orders out loud!

I'll deal with that later, Where is the damned truck.

He's heading toward the gate.

Got him, I thought back to him.

"Pham, new target. The transformer is heading for the gate. Take it out with the rockets into the rear engine compartment. Take that bastard out."

I locked the gate, Caleb thought to me, *He'll have to ram it to get out.*

Before I could reply. The motorhome transformed quickly into a tricked out version of the armored truck. The gun turret on the top of the truck rotated until its guns were pointing at our windshield. "Shields now!" I yelled and the armor plated shields slid to cover the windshields.

We were rocked by a salvo of cannon fire. However, we were still intact and quickly maneuvered and returned fire from our own cannons. We could see the target clearly on our monitors. We couldn't see any damage to our target yet but we were persistent.

The enemy vehicle began to back away from the gate at a high rate of speed and turned to attack us. As it turned, Mark attacked the run-flat tires with the mini machine guns, firing 600 rounds per minute. The run-flat tires were designed to survive punctures but no way could they withstand the withering attack which turned all the tires on the right side of the vehicle into shredded rubber within ten seconds rendering the vehicle unmovable.

That didn't keep it from continuing its attack on us. We could hardly communicate with each other from the sound of its bullets pinging off our own armor.

I'd had enough. "Attack with the rockets," I yelled

"Roger that," yelled back Pham. "Six rockets ready to launch."

"Fire!" I ordered.

Three 2.75 inch rockets were fired simultaneously from the tubes on each side of the War Wagon. They covered the 200 yards in less than a second or two to reach the immobile truck. All six rockets slammed into the rear of vehicle, exploding on contact and penetrating the armor plating like a hot knife through butter.

The force of the explosions lifted the rear end of the truck and flipped it over onto its back. The entire truck burst into flames. The armored truck that escaped us once was no longer a threat.

The War Wagon sat still on the tarmac. The square was closed and locked. All of the millions of dollars of war vehicles were trashed. I knew it wasn't over. I needed to call the colonel to see how the attack on the Fortress was going.

As I reached for my comm, Simone moaned, "No way! No fucking way!!!"

I turned to see where she was looking and was shocked to see four F-15 Eagles, each one parked in one of the hangers next to the runways. How did we miss that?

I comm'd the colonel. When he answered I could hear the sound of heavy artillery fire in the background. "Colonel Legleu speaking," he said in a no nonsense voice. "I'm very busy right now. Call back later."

"Was that a recording?" asked Simone.

"No," replied Pham. "He was live. I guess he didn't want to speak with the man in charge…That would be you, Joshua, I'll call him again."

This time Pham called. When the colonel began speaking, Pham said in a loud voice, "Please hold for Agent Joshua Brown, the Special Agent in Charge of this mission."

Pham nodded at me and I began speaking, not giving the colonel a chance to interrupt, "Colonel, do you know anything about the four F-15 aircraft in hangars at the airport?"

"Of course I do," he answered in an annoyed voice. "They're from the Air National Guard Squadron based in Portland. I ordered them to be on alert for Close Air Support of my mission at the Fortress. In fact, I just ordered two of them to make bombing runs on the Fortress courtyard."

Simone nodded to me and said, "There are two F-15s taxiing to the end of one of the runways."

"Colonel, did you offer the people in the Fortress the opportunity to surrender?" I asked.

"That must have slipped my mind, Special Agent Brown. We've been pretty busy returning fire to the enemy. I need to supervise my troops, any other questions? I need to finish moving my troops from the blast zone."

I hung up on him and we all watched as the F-15 lined up on the runway. The runway was pretty short for an F-15 and both planes locked their brakes and went to full afterburner. As soon as the engines went to full thrust, they released brakes, screamed down the short runway, and used every inch of it before they lifted off.

Once airborne both aircraft separated far enough apart to permit separate bombing runs. The lead aircraft approached the target from about 5,000 feet and began descending rapidly to less than a 1,000 feet.

It was apparent the Fortress mercs didn't have much in the way of antiaircraft weapons although Mark claimed he spotted a couple of shoulder-launched-missiles, he thought they were both Stingers. He said neither one hit the aircraft, it was just too fast for the Stingers to lock on to the target.

When Caleb and I were in Afghanistan, we'd called in CAS aircraft several times and it was scary amazing to see how much damage one 1,000 pound bomb could do. These F-15s had two computer guided,1,000 bombs attached to their bellies.

I estimated the first plane approached the target at between 300 and 400 knots. Both bombs were released simultaneously. Both bombs hit the center of the courtyard and their detonations were decimating. It was shock and awe all over again. Not only did they obliterate the courtyard, every window in the entire Fortress was blown out, along with hundreds of bodies hurtling to their death on the ground below.

The second aircraft was only a minute behind and finished the job with its two bombs. The Fortress structure was weakened by the first bombing run, the second run finished the job. The entire building collapsed to the ground into a pile of rubble. It reminded me of the terrorist attack on the twin towers, although on a much smaller scale. Many civilians were killed on 9/11; I was sure everyone inside the Fortress had died.

Our overall mission was a success but it could've been a success without the loss of so many lives. On the other hand, for the most part almost everyone who died in the Fortress was a mercenary paid to kill civilians. If they'd succeeded, millions of Oregonians would have suffered and many innocent people would've died if they opposed the new regime.

I sighed and thought, *another 'War on Crime' mission successfully completed. When I began these assignments, I thought Caleb and I could make a difference, make America a safer place to live. Maybe we did but I don't feel it's enough. The world is full of evil people, how can we possibly make even a small improvement in reducing crime.*

Then I heard a voice. The voice inside my head sounded familiar. It wasn't Caleb and it wasn't Simone, who was it?

Joshua, do you remember when I told you you'd be the first of many who would join in the war against crime. You were the test case and you succeeded well beyond our expectations. Because of your success, others will follow, many others.

There will always be evil in this world but you and those like you will make a difference. Not only in America, everywhere in the world good people will benefit. Keep your head up. I will always be with you.

Apostle, is that you? Are you a spirit now or are you still alive and can communicate with me like Simone does? Apostle?

No one answered. However the feeling of melancholy had left me. The words I heard gave me hope and I and my team will continue in the War on Crime and look forward to those who join our cause. I can't wait to speak with the Apostle again.

EPILOGUE

Joshua

The mission was over and Oregon still remained part of the United States of America. Most of the money from the bank heists was recovered from a fireproof safe discovered in the ruins of the transformer armored truck. An official document declined to disclose the exact amount of money recovered but rumors suggested it was over half a billion dollars.

The governor held a big hoop-de-do celebration. He said many nice things about how our team was key in discovering the attempted coup and our part in shutting down the planned attack. He personally awarded each of us with medals and certificates of valor. I found it embarrassing, however Sarge was eating it up, literally. They gave him and Sniffer the largest bag of dog treats I'd ever seen.

Of course, they didn't forget the roll the Army National Guard, the Air National Guard and the Army Reserve played in the complete destruction of the Fortress at Antelope. All kinds of awards and citations were given out to those involved.

The last award was given to Peter Legleu, the governor's head of security and commander of the Army National Guard. For his role in leading the joint effort of the various military organizations he was promoted from colonel to brigadier general. Governor Johnson removed the silver eagles from his shoulder boards and replaced them with the single star on each board. In closing, the governor mentioned that General Legleu was the first Oregon national guard commander ever to attain the rank of brigadier general.

Following the award celebration, there was a huge party in a Salem ballroom. Our team stayed through the dinner and a few dances, however none of us were fully recovered from the combat and left early. Simone mentioned she felt sick to her stomach and blamed it on Legleu's promotion to brigadier.

We parked Sweet Ride and the trailer with a refurbished War Wagon inside at the secure underground parking garage in the government complex. We decided to stay in a suite at the best hotel Salem had to offer.

We stayed for a week. Pham spent a few days with his lawyer partner and his wife. Mark and Sarge visited with a lady and her child who lived in his old apartment in the Woodlawn District. They took Sniffer too. The little girl squealed with delight at two dogs she could play with.

The last day of our R&R, we all got together at the hotel to discuss the future. I started it off by making the big reveal.

"You all know I have a couple of CIs working for me undercover. I made a point of keeping them confidential and told you it was for their protection." I paused for a moment then added. "That was a lie. I don't have any CIs and never did."

Pham and Mark looked confused, "If you didn't have any CIs how did you come up with all that information we acted on?" asked Pham.

"I have a source that is much better at providing me with critical information than any CI could begin to provide."

"So tell us about this super source," said Mark. He looked at Simone and asked, "Do you know who this is?"

"Yes," she replied, "but I just found out a few days ago. Joshua wanted to tell you the same time he told me. I suggested it might be better to tell you after the mission was over."

"This is getting kind of creepy," said Pham.

Simone giggled and said, "It's going to get a lot creepier."

"I'm going to tell you a story that may be hard to believe," I began. "Please let me get through this first then you can ask all the questions you want and I'll do my best to answer them."

They looked at me and over at Simone, then back at me again. "Okay," said Mark. "We all love creepy stories. Let's hear yours."

For the next hour I told them everything I could remember about Caleb after he died. Actually, it was about the both of us and what we went through. All during that time, Caleb never communicated with anyone but me.

When I was finished, Simone took over and told her story. She began with her experience with the spirit of her dead father that almost caused her to take her own life. She then explained what happened a short time ago when Caleb began communicating with her.

When we were both done, Pham and Mark sat quietly for a few minutes processing what they'd been told. Finally, Mark asked the question they'd both wanted to ask, "Those were very interesting stories, only mildly creepy. We want to believe you but we'd like some kind of verification what you told us is true."

I smiled at them and said, "I'd be disappointed if you didn't ask. Caleb, why don't you say hello?"

I shut my mouth so they would know I wasn't a ventriloquist and waited for a few seconds. When Caleb began, it felt like he was choked with emotion. *I have waited for so long to be able to communicate with all of the team. Everything that Joshua and Simone told you is true. At last I feel like I'm truly a member of Team Joshua.*

He stopped and waited for a response. Mark's mouth dropped open in astonishment and he'd temporarily forgotten how to speak so Pham asked, "Can you hear me…I mean us?"

Loud and clear. As Simone said, as long as I can 'see' you we can carry on a normal conversation. Well, maybe not a normal conversation but you know what I mean. You speak and I will answer using telepathy.

Mark finally found his voice and asked, "Will we ever be able to converse with you without speaking?"

Probably, it took Joshua several days before he could do that. Keep trying and it should become second nature. It would allow us to communicate without speaking which could come in handy in certain situations. As an example, Joshua could eat and communicate telepathically. He didn't have to stop chewing his food, which was very important when eating a steak burger from Stake and Shake.

We continued to talk about a lot about everything and nothing. The last question was obvious: where do we go from here?

Before I could respond a different voice appeared in all our heads. *You are truly a team now and you will become more effective in a very short period of time. I am planning your next mission and will get back to all of you soon. In the meantime, power down, take a fun vacation or two, your uncle will cover all your expenses. Consider a sea cruise but don't forget Sarge and Sniffer. That's all for now, this is the Apostle signing off.*

ABOUT THE AUTHOR

I've been a fan of science fiction ever since I was in grade school (a very long time ago). In those day's there were three outstanding science fiction authors: Isaac Asimov, Arthur C. Clark, and Robert A. Heinlein.

My favorite author was Heinlein. He began writing his science fiction stories for young people. His stories were so believable to me and I couldn't wait to get to his latest book. As I matured, so did his books. I have read every book Heinlein published and still have most of them in my personal library. I think my all-time favorite Heinlein story is *Stranger in a Strange Land.*

My current favorite author is Orson Scott Card. Again, like Heinlein's stories, I find myself 'living' the story as it unfolds. *Enders Game* and *Prentice Alvin* are two of my favorite Card novels.

I've always had an interest in writing science fiction novels. I would read books by new authors and say to myself, "I could write a better story." However, when I tried, publishers didn't agree. When Covid-19 broke out, I had a lot of spare time on my hands and decided to give it another shot.

During the last three years I have published a total of ten novels. The War on Crime series currently consists of four titles. A fifth book will be added in late 2023 or early 2024.

**If you enjoyed reading *Team Joshua*
you'll love the first 3 books in the War on Crime series.**

Book 1 in the War on Crime series. This book introduced the terrible accident in Afghanistan of one of the twin brothers and then moves forward to the crack team doing God's work against some very bad players in the world.

Book 2: *Joshua* recounts the three trial missions he is required to conduct without the aid of Caleb. As he moves from one mission to the next, they become more complicated and deadly.

Book 3: The spirit of Caleb teams with his brother in *Caleb and Joshua* in a much more complicated mission; shutting down five major drug cartels. This year's Mardi Gras in New Orleans becomes deadly, very deadly.

Coming in December 2023:
Book 5: The New War Wagon

www.ingramcontent.com/pod-product-compliance
Lightning Source LLC
Chambersburg PA
CBHW061229210726
48293CB00003B/715